RIGHT UNDER YOUR NOSE

Fifty-one-year-old **R. Giridharan** churns out murder mysteries both in the form of books and screenplays. A multifaceted personality, he is currently a general manager with the Reserve Bank of India. In the last two and a half decades, he has worked in Goa, Mumbai, Pune, Nagpur, Chandigarh, Delhi and Jaipur. He is also an international sports commentator with All India Radio and has covered many test matches and one-day internationals, including World Cup matches. He is also an expert panellist on Doordarshan. He has anchored many panel discussions and compèred shows. He presently lives in Mumbai.

RIGHT UNDER YOUR NOSE

R. GIRIDHARAN

Published by
Rupa Publications India Pvt. Ltd 2020
7/16, Ansari Road, Daryaganj
New Delhi 110002

Sales centres:
Allahabad Bengaluru Chennai
Hyderabad Jaipur Kathmandu
Kolkata Mumbai

Copyright © R. Giridharan 2020

All rights reserved.

No part of this publication may be reproduced, transmitted, or stored in a retrieval system, in any form or by any means, electronic, mechanical, photocopying, recording or otherwise, without the prior permission of the publisher.

This is a work of fiction. Names, characters, places and incidents are either the product of the author's imagination or are used fictitiously and any resemblance to any actual person, living or dead, events or locales is entirely coincidental.

ISBN: 978-93-89967-93-7

First impression 2020

10 9 8 7 6 5 4 3 2 1

The moral right of the author has been asserted.

Printed at HT Media Ltd, Gr. Noida

This book is sold subject to the condition that it shall not, by way of trade or otherwise, be lent, resold, hired out, or otherwise circulated, without the publisher's prior consent, in any form of binding or cover other than that in which it is published.

I dedicate this book to my family:

Mr N. Ramaswamy, my late father. He is watching from above
Mrs Mythili, my mother, who always blesses me
Suchitra, my wife and the architect of my life
Avanti, my daughter and the light of my life
Meena, the elder sister in whose footsteps I learnt to walk
Srikanthan, my brother-in-law and mentor
Siddhartha and Prahlad, my lovable nephews
Mrs Malathi and Mr Padmanabhan, my caring parents-in-law
Srivats, my brother-in-law, who is a pillar of support

Prologue

Kumudini's brown hair fitted her small head almost like a cap. She had a petite figure that matched perfectly with her narrow face, small nose, little lips and pouting mouth. She was pretty, and men fell for her in hordes.

An outstretched hand held a prepaid card and a paper with perforation. The hand came closer.

She snatched the prepaid card of a well-known multi-retail brand, with childlike impatience. She turned it over in her hand. Then she kissed the card, a symbol of her new-found wealth. She beamed with gratitude written all over her face. 'A stored value of two hundred thousand rupees in Reliance Digital.'

She ripped the perforation. 'The PIN is two thousand,' she shrieked.

Kumudini watched as a pencil-shaped recording device along with a written script was placed on the table. A button on the device was pressed, a signal for her to read from a script.

She read, 'Leave your motorcycle at the foothills and climb up. Take left from the giant teak tree, where the number "100" is inscribed.'

She stopped. 'Are these directions to reach a place?'

'Shut up and do as you are told or return the card.' The whispered voice was glacial. The record was deleted, and the recording button was pressed again.

She raised her right palm as a gesture of conciliation. With the device switched on again, she rattled off the written speech.

'Let us celebrate!' The whispered voice was once again warm and smooth. 'Your performance was swell!'

She took the proffered glass of whiskey mixed with beer. She took a small sip, savouring the expensive foreign liquor. For a fleeting moment, doubts assailed her mind. Was she too one of those people that her brother described as 'the lowest form of human life'? Her brother often said that one who does anything for a quick buck is like a stray dog that wags its tail at anyone who offered it a breadcrumb. Pawns, to be used in a gambit, are the worst form of humans.

More whisky, mixed with beer, was poured into her glass.

'Enough…' She sounded groggy. 'I feel faint.'

'Just this much?'

'I cannot,' she protested.

'If you cannot do even this,' the voice said, taunting her, 'how do you expect to earn millions?'

She took a swig. Then she reclined on the sofa, her eyes almost drooping.

'Try, try.'

She faintly heard the exhortation. With supreme effort, she gulped down half the contents of the mug. 'I feel nauseated,' she complained.

'Splash your face with water and go home,' the voice advised sternly.

'Can't I spend the night here?' she begged. 'I do not feel like driving.'

'No way!'

'My brother will kill me if he finds out that I was boozing.'

She was handed a bottle with a strong-smelling liquid. 'Rinse your mouth with this mouthwash.'

She dutifully gargled.

A strong arm held her and led her to her scooter.

She shook her head, climbed on to her scooter, and gingerly pressed the self-start button. It spluttered to life, and she drove away unsteadily.

The next morning, television news channels reported that a young woman had lost her life in a collision with a truck the night before.

'She was drunk, and her red Scooty was smashed as it banged head-on with a truck. She didn't have her headlights on,' the anchor elaborated.

Most people evinced only passing interest at the routine news of an accident caused by drunken driving, but for one person in particular, it was the culmination of weeks of careful strategizing—the first step to becoming a billionaire. The die was cast and the gamble had paid off.

The next step had to follow.

Chapter 1

Vijay, superintendent of police, fought to concentrate on his workout. He went through the motions, at times unmindfully falling into phases of non-activity. He lifted a dumb-bell with his left hand and then placed it back. He stood on the weighing scale. At twenty-six, his six-foot tall and muscular frame tilted the scales at eighty-three kilograms. He ran his fingers through his thick black hair, massaging it gently with his fingertips.

He ended his workout prematurely.

His mobile trilled. Inspector Madhukar Dalvi was trying to reach him. Irritation coursed through his veins. A lovely day was about to be ruined.

'Morning, Sir.' Dalvi's enthusiastic voice cheered him up. 'The students' union has changed their venue of protest. They have now decided to picket the Secretariat.' He stopped.

Vijay understood the rest.

The venue fell within his jurisdiction, so the headache was his. The site was sensitive, and the slightest of transgressions would be blown up. Reporting in Nagpur had become florid and intrusive.

'I will be at the site in fifteen minutes,' he told Dalvi. 'Keep water cannons and barricades ready.'

'A fifty-strong cavalry is already at the site. Barricades have also been erected. I am also at the site. I do not think you need to come.'

'What a blessed soul I am to have an inspector like you!'

Dalvi hung up.

Vijay decided to go. Although Dalvi could be trusted, Vijay liked being with the boys. He drove himself.

As soon as he reached the site, he put on his dark glasses. He always felt that dark glasses accentuated his impact. A smiling student leader was negotiating with Dalvi, who was shaking his head to disagree. Even at forty-one, Dalvi's six-foot-three frame was all sinew, and passed skinfold tests with flying colours. He was still strong enough to finish third in a half marathon. A dedicated officer, he would lay down his life for Vijay.

Vijay walked briskly and gave a long hard stare.

Unperturbed, the student leader extended his hand. 'Sir, I am Rajat Sharma.'

Vijay was impressed with his calm, confident demeanour. He asked gruffly, 'What is going on?'

Rajat smiled. 'We are protesting against the repeated hike in bus fares.'

'Do not,' Dalvi warned, 'do it here.'

Nearly five hundred students were squatting on a makeshift podium. Most citizens seemed to be supporting them. Girls apologized to pedestrians and motorists for the inconvenience. A group of boys requested passers-by to register their support for the cause by signing on huge posters affixed to cardboards. Leaflets were distributed, anti-government slogans were shouted and banners held aloft.

Rajat folded his hands respectfully. 'Sirs,' he said humbly, 'we will not indulge in any violence.'

Vijay spoke affectionately, 'Why don't you choose some other venue?'

Rajat smiled. 'Sir, we need media coverage, and there is no better place for that than the Secretariat.'

Vijay put a comforting arm around Rajat's shoulders. He had started to like the boy. 'The problem with this venue is its sensitivity. Any slip and I am impaled.'

Rajat waved off other student leaders converging on them. He could exercise hypnotic control over his followers. 'I can understand that an award-winning cop must have many enemies waiting to pounce at the first opportunity.'

The comment cut Vijay to the bone. This youngster was mature beyond his years.

'Sir,' Rajat explained, 'any violence will hurt our movement because attention will be diverted from the core issue.'

Vijay relented and wished Rajat all the best.

Egged on by Rajat, the students shouted, 'SP Sahib Zindabad!'

Dalvi whispered in his ear, 'Sir, this could boomerang.'

Vijay grinned. 'Relax. This boy,' he said pointing at Rajat, 'is a leader to watch.'

Dalvi took off his cap and put it back on.

Vijay knew that this was his subordinate's way of registering his disapproval. He smiled affably. Dalvi had spent a decade wrestling with the filth and squalor of Mumbai's underworld. His wide exposure to the evil in human nature had made him suspicious.

Vijay prepared to leave.

A tall, lissom young woman walked confidently towards him. She was wearing black denims and a white top, her deep blue eyes brimming with life. She smiled, revealing her pearly whites. 'You are a risk-taker.'

He swatted her off.

'I am a crime reporter, not a student,' she clarified.

'I am not giving interviews!' he snapped and walked towards his jeep.

She followed him. 'I am not asking for one.'

'Then?' Vijay put on a stern face, 'What do you want?'

'I want to compliment you and wish you good luck.'

Vijay was too stunned to speak.

'You have taken a bold gamble. I hope it comes off.'

'Thanks.' Vijay's tone softened. 'By the way, what's your name?'

'Padmini Jain.' She waved and went away.

Vijay could not stop thinking of the woman. She was different—bold, intelligent but not intrusive. He tried to believe that he was not momentarily infatuated.

Chapter 2

Back in his office, Vijay took out his planner and looked at the first item. A government official had complained that the nearest police station was not responding seriously to the hotline drills. He picked up the landline and called the station house officer of Dharampeth, a newly promoted sub-inspector.

'If you do not participate in hotline drills, then you will be hauled up if the office is robbed. Who knows, the manager might himself rob the treasury and lay the blame at your door!' Vijay inhaled after this breathless sermon.

The officer promised immediate action. After fifteen minutes, he reported compliance.

Vijay cross-checked with the government official who corroborated the station house officer's claim. He crossed off the item and peered out of his office window. It was an expansive one that opened out to a magnificent view of the town. He could hear the rumblings of the local trains rushing past. His own train of thought was jolted by the buzzing of the intercom.

A polite voice said, 'ACP on line, Sir.'

'Come to my office immediately!' was the terse order from Assistant Commissioner of Police Madhav Godbole. Vijay immediately set out for Godbole's office. After marking his entry in the visitors' book, Vijay entered his office with a polite knock.

Godbole pretended not to notice him and kept reading a file.

Vijay coughed twice to attract his attention.

Eventually, Godbole looked at him. 'Yes?' he said, in an enquiring tone.

'You...' Vijay paused.

'Ah, I called you. Yes, I called you.'

A constable smiled at Vijay as he placed two cups of tea on the table. Vijay smiled back.

'What is the meaning of all this?' Godbole thundered.

Vijay convinced himself to remain calm. 'Of what, Sir?'

'You allowed student protesters to gather so close to the Secretariat.'

'Sir, there was no violence...'

Godbole raised his hand to arrest Vijay's sentence. 'The political affairs secretary rang me up. He is furious!'

'Why should he be?' There was indignation on Vijay's face.

He was interrupted by the abrupt entry of Rathore. This sudden appearance of his former roommate—and lifelong rival—seemed pre-planned to Vijay. 'Very bad, very bad,' he muttered under his breath.

'The government has received adverse publicity, all thanks to our hero here.' Godbole fumed. He sank backwards in his revolving chair.

'There was no violence and everything went off peacefully.' Vijay's voice became louder. 'I have a clear conscience.'

'Who is bothered about your conscience?'

'Sir, our department,' Rathore butted in, 'has been smeared.'

Vijay turned around to look Rathore in his eye. 'You are plain jealous.'

Rathore smirked.

'Do you realize how wild the government is at us?' Godbole sounded angry.

'I think that our department has come in for a lot of praise,' Vijay responded.

'Yes, but by students and certain sections of the media. The government is livid.'

'But why?'

With a cunning smile on his face, Rathore intervened. 'Because the students have seized the day and struck a chord with the common man on the street. Our masters,' he said, the smirk reappearing, 'have been let down.'

'In a democracy, we are responsible to the common man.'

'Behold the new Mahatma Gandhi!' Godbole mocked as he clapped his hands dramatically.

Rathore laughed at the supposed joke.

Vijay placed his elbows defiantly on the table. 'I work to ensure safety of the common man.'

Rathore was about to interrupt, but Godbole silenced him with a wink.

Vijay went on. 'I ensured that legitimate democratic methods were followed by the protesters.'

Rathore and Godbole looked at each other.

'I'll take your leave,' Vijay declared, and got up.

'Take a biscuit.' Rathore stretched one arm out towards Vijay. Vijay's eyes gored into Rathore. Intimidated, Rathore looked away.

After Vijay left, Rathore whispered impatiently, 'I have lost count of the number of times that toad has outsmarted you?'

Godbole replied, 'I have been consistently poisoning the commissioner's ears and someday my efforts will bear fruit.'

'Someday!' Rathore mocked.

'Every time,' Godbole lit a cigarette, 'I say something negative about Vijay, a seedling of doubt, however small, is planted in the commissioner's mind.'

Rathore lifted his hands in despair and shook his head. 'Then we are forever losers.'

'No, his luck will run out.'

Rathore sighed.

※

The effeminate-looking Sikh at the paid telephone booth looked flustered. His mobile phone trilled, even as he was speaking on the landline. He told the caller on the mobile, 'Chakravak, I will call your cell.' He disconnected the mobile and spoke into the payphone mouthpiece. 'You are a bloody coward. You have blown your last chance to avenge your sister. I am going to kill him myself today.' He banged the phone down, paid the attendant, and left the booth.

He heard a remark that pleased him immensely. 'This is the first effeminate Sikh I have come across. They are usually muscular and manly.' Then he promptly hailed an autorickshaw and got off at Orbit Mall.

Chapter 3

Vijay sat waiting for Birender, a friend who ran a travel agency, at a table very close to the road. Vijay preferred such tables in restaurants because he could see what was going on and also save on crucial seconds if intervention was needed. Last year, Vijay had dived just in time to prevent a stabbing, thanks to the location of his table.

Although thronged by youngsters, it was an age-old restaurant, spartan in decor. The tables and chairs were comfortable and the arrangement provided ample legroom. The tables were arranged in a manner to ensure reasonable privacy at an affordable cost even on a busy street.

Vijay belonged to the new generation; yet, he found that things had changed. Six years back, Facebook or Twitter on mobile was relatively unknown. The lingo too had changed. In fact, some of the slang sounded alien to him.

But then, there were some things that remained unchanged—boys showing off, giggling girls faking admiration and egging them on, Birender being behind the clock.

Across the road, a black Nano wedged itself into a tiny parking space sandwiched between the restaurant gate and the pavement. A limping parking attendant who had shooed other vehicles marked this one for special attention. The driver, who stayed put in the car, wasn't visible, but the registration number stuck in Vijay's mind: MH-26-AH-1986—his age and year of birth.

'Hi, absent-minded professor!' Birender panted.

Vijay was still eyeing the car. *Quite unusual. Why was the Nano getting such special attention*, he wondered.

'You are off duty, pal,' Birender reminded him.

Vijay shook his head.

'A cop is always on duty.'

'You live on the edge.'

Vijay handed over the menu card to Birender.

The waiter smiled. 'One idli and vada, followed by masala dosa for Sahib,' he said, pointing at Vijay, 'and onion uthappam and coffee for Sahib,' he said, looking at Birender.

Glancing at the waiter, Birender nodded his head in admiration and put away the menu card.

Vijay's eyes were intent on the road. He tapped Birender's wrist. 'That man,' he said, pointing to a tall, lean, respectable-looking bespectacled man with unkempt hair, 'has a gun in his jacket pocket and wants to shoot someone.'

'Ha ha ha!'

Vijay smiled. 'Maybe I am overly suspicious.'

The waiter brought the sambhar and chutney first. Birender sniffed and savoured the aroma.

Soon, the idli, vada and utthapam arrived. Birender slid the laptop back into its holder. He kept away the fork and spoon, then rolled a piece of idli round and round in the sambhar bowl and ate it with his hand.

'Tell me,' Birender's eyes twinkled mischievously. 'When will you find a girl?'

'I am actually infatuated with one,' Vijay blurted out.

Birender leaned forward in anticipation, 'Who? Who?'

Vijay could not bring himself to meet Birender in the eye. 'She is a crime reporter. Has a nose for news and is quite sharp.'

'Great! Great!'

'Her name is Padmini.'

Birender smiled enigmatically.

Vijay craned his neck and shifted in his chair to get a better view of the road. Birender tapped his shoulder.

Vijay stood up, wrote a few telephone numbers on the paper napkin, and addressed Birender, 'I don't have time to explain, but call these numbers immediately.'

'Whose numbers are these? What should I tell them?' a flummoxed Birender enquired.

'These two numbers belong to an ambulance service and those three to the police control room. Tell them that I asked them to come over immediately!' He added impatiently, 'Don't forget to give this address.'

Vijay weaved his way past a waiter carrying a tray laden with three glasses of fruit juice and a couple entering the restaurant. Once on the road, he began to shout at people, flashing his identity card. 'Make way!' He was now convinced that the man in the red jacket was a gunman. He never took his eyes off his target. Surprisingly, the red-jacketed man seemed oblivious to Vijay's moves.

The man stiffened—a giveaway that he was readying.

Vijay decided to move in a circular way and ambush. His eyes kept scanning a wide horizon. *What is this man doing with a gun in the middle of a busy street?*

That the man would have no chance to escape was clear. If he was hiding the gun in his jacket pocket, it could not be a big one. Vijay's guess was that it was a Swiss revolver.

Vijay feared that this could be a daring daylight robbery. The targets were many. The road was full of shops with flourishing businesses and bulging treasure chests. It was not well guarded. This man could be a part of a gang.

Vijay observed him. He did not seem to be communicating with anyone. He hardly took his mobile out. If he was a part of a gang, then it was one that did not believe in verbal communication.

Vijay had now come behind the man. He probably was just four or five steps away now. From his peripheral vision, he noted that the black Nano was raring to go. He roughly brushed a pedestrian's shoulder and subdued his default reflex to apologize.

The gunman who had been near motionless suddenly moved. His hind leg moved backwards towards Vijay. Vijay was momentarily distracted and in a reflex action, he retreated.

The man's shoulders were taut and moving rapidly. Vijay realized that the man had pulled the trigger. He studied the distance between himself and the gunman. He lunged forward, with perfect timing. He landed heavily on the man, who by now had thrown off his jacket. Vijay immobilized him quite easily. The man was not trained in fighting, nor did he seem to have the willingness to fight. The gun fell out of his hand. He made no attempt to retrieve it. Vijay held him in an armlock.

The bullet, whose sound was drowned amidst blaring horns, found its mark. The victim had been hit on the shoulder. He lay in a pool of blood, surely unconscious.

Vijay was relieved to hear an ambulance van announce its arrival. A minute later, the police siren wailed. Birender had done his bit.

The police van parked itself on the other side. Policemen stood on both sides of the victim and stopped vehicular traffic. The ambulance stationed itself next to the victim, with the police van adjacent to it.

Two male nurses ran with a stretcher. A doctor in his white overalls felt the pulse. Vijay recognized him as Dr Amarnath.

The doctor too recognized Vijay. Dr Amarnath walked up and whispered, 'It is a murder.'

The ambulance left with the victim. Although the medical team had not officially declared the victim dead, Dr Amarnath had given the game away.

The police cordoned off the area with barricade tapes.

※

Vijay spotted Birender arguing with a constable guarding the cordoned area. 'Let him in,' he shouted.

Birender looked disconsolate.

'What is the matter?' Vijay asked with concern.

'I feel responsible for his death.' Birender broke into tears. Vijay embraced him; Birender's neck perched on Vijay's shoulders. 'Had I not mocked your initial suspicion, you would have saved that man's life.'

Vijay, too, felt the same way. Still, he said firmly, 'No, I could not have done anything.'

'Really?'

'Yes, because this killer was weird. He made no attempt to escape. He was desperate to kill him.'

'I feel drained out.' Birender said.

'Go home,' Vijay advised.

'Yeah,' Birender agreed

Vijay was a little upset. The events were dramatic and unexpected, and tired him out mentally. Once the situation seemed under control, he left for a nap.

Chapter 4

Vijay's mother had a surprised look on her face as she opened the door. 'I have not made lunch,' she admitted.

'Amma, I want to sleep.'

Concerned, she placed her palm on his right cheek. 'Normal temperature.'

'Plain exhausted,' Vijay explained.

He changed into pyjamas and hit the bed. In less than five minutes, he was snoring.

When he got up, it was early evening. His mother served him aromatic filter coffee. He popped a delicious barfi into his mouth and whistled. 'I am off.'

He dashed to the garage. The purple Victor motorbike appealed to him more than the car. He loved the breeze on the face as he rode. He looked at himself in the side-view mirror while waiting at the lights.

In his list of most-hated things, morgues were close to the top. His scalp prickled as he parked his motorbike. He took off his helmet. The guard, who knew him well, ran forward to take it. He promised to keep it safe.

The glass doors parted to the strong smell of formalin. If he were ever kidnapped, gagged, blindfolded and dumped, he would still figure out that he was in the morgue—so revolting was the smell of the disinfectant. A morgue attendant was diligently cleaning the scalpel and scraping the saws.

The only thing that Vijay liked about his visits to the morgue was talking to the forensic head Dr Ayushman Gaikwad. He took out his diary to take notes.

Dr Gaikwad spoke like a professor delivering a lecture, 'The death was caused by a bullet fired at close range.' He beckoned Vijay to follow him.

The room was an eerie reminder that death could come in myriad ways. A face, crushed by a rock, had been disfigured beyond recognition. Another had its mouth gaping open, probably screaming for help that never arrived. Bodies that had spent days in water were boldly labelled in blue. Each body had an unknown story to tell. All the formalin in the world could not mask the odour of death.

Dr Gaikwad offered a pair of gloves to go with the sole coverings. As he lifted the white linen covering the corpse, Vijay had his first look at the man whose life he had tried hard to save. The victim was around five feet eight in height. Untrimmed facial hair covered most of his face. He probably had not cared much for his appearance. His belongings, which included his glasses, were all in a sealed transparent bag.

Dr Gaikwad's forefinger rested on the corpse's neck, and he gently massaged a point with his finger, saying, 'The bullet entered from the left side.' He lifted his fingers. Vijay saw it from close quarters.

Dr Gaikwad moved over to the other side. His finger now zeroed in on a point on the right side of the corpse's neck. 'The bullet severed the carotid artery in his neck. The loss of blood would have caused loss of consciousness within three minutes, brain death within two or three minutes.'

Vijay asked whether photographs were available.

Dr Gaikwad replied in the affirmative. 'Death,' he said contemplatively, 'would have occurred within minutes of the infliction of the wound.'

Vijay's mind raced back to Dr Amarnath pronouncing him as dead straightaway.

'Young man, you're lost in thought.'

Vijay smiled sheepishly. 'Happens.'

Dr Gaikwad pointed to a bump near the left bicep. 'That is an injection shot, not long before his death.' He lifted a hand lens from the tray and zoomed it on the corpse's chin to reveal a chessboard-like mark under the stubble. 'I am told it is a lip tattoo, used by models and fashionable young women.' A small plastic box labelled 'Case 108, 2012' contained the blood samples, skin, hair, and teeth belonging to the corpse.

శ్రీ

Vijay shook hands with Dr Gaikwad, who saw him off as far as the parking lot.

Vijay rode straight to his office.

Dalvi was waiting there, bursting with news. 'The murderer is a record clerk in an export firm. This murder is a revenge killing!'

'For what?'

'The murderer's name is Karun. He claims that the victim raped his sister a couple of weeks back although we have no such information. His sister committed suicide soon after.'

Vijay thought for a moment. Then he turned to Dalvi. 'Take me to the murderer.'

Dalvi shouted orders. The police jeep waited at the door.

'I fancy,' Vijay said thoughtfully, 'that the killer was a novice shooter. He nearly missed from point-blank range.'

॰

Vijay had never seen a murderer like Karun before—a frail body, bespectacled eyes, an earnest bearing and a ready smile. Somehow, evil did not emit from him.

Karun's smile widened. To Vijay, it was the smile of a satisfied man. 'A burden has lifted off my chest. My sister Kumudini's soul will now rest in peace.'

Vijay observed him intently.

Karun was jubilant. He wasn't denying his crime. He raised his chained hands in triumph. 'God is great.' Then he folded his hands and thanked the heavens. 'I am a novice with guns, but my bullet found its mark.'

There was an earnestness in Karun's eyes that floored Vijay. There was surely more to his words of confession that he so readily uttered. Yet, how could a man caught red-handed for murder appear so innocent and pure.

'How are you so sure that he raped your sister?'

Karun laughed derisively. 'Why are you wasting your time?' He looked at Vijay. 'You need not have tried so hard to catch me. I was going to surrender anyway.'

Dalvi communicated through his eyes that they were dealing with a mule.

Vijay walked back, head bowed down.

Dalvi missed a step and nearly tripped. He steadied himself and looked at Vijay and joked, 'Tripped over the sharp edge of realization.' He laughed.

'Why this philosophical crap?'

'A realization hit me that it is not as simple as it seems to be. Karun is a pawn in a larger game.'

The old wooden stairs creaked under the weight of the two large men.

Vijay dug his hands in his pockets. 'Some questions need answers.'

'Let me,' Dalvi volunteered, 'frame the questions. One, why did he choose such a busy spot? He could have done it in lonelier places.'

Vijay raised his eyebrows in approval and nodded.

Encouraged, Dalvi went on. 'Two, how was he so sure that the victim was going to be there at that moment? It's all the more fishy because Karun did not use his mobile. It seems that an accomplice must have informed him in advance.'

They had reached the parking lot. Vijay sat on a bench and spread his arms. Dalvi remained standing.

'Good questions,' Vijay said, 'but I have some more to add.'

Dalvi whisked a diary from his trousers' pocket to take notes.

'A black Nano with the registration number MH-26AH-1986 was around the murder site making suspicious movements. The man you are referring to as the accomplice might have a motive of his own and could be the mastermind.'

Dalvi flailed his hammer-like fists in the air, almost jubilantly.

Vijay cast him a startled look.

'After a long time,' Dalvi said, elated, 'a case that will challenge us.'

Vijay could not agree more as he took leave of Dalvi.

Dalvi lost no time in proceeding to the crime scene to find an answer to Vijay's question.

A man with a limp in his leg was waving at Dalvi. Dalvi recognized him as Madan, a man who had once been a witness in a theft case, investigated by Dalvi, many years back.

Looking at his legs, Dalvi asked, 'What happened?'

'Operated for gangrene. My diabetes was uncontrolled.'

Dalvi raised his eyebrows in surprise.

'At your age? You are barely thirty-five.'

'Ill health can strike at any stage,' Madan laughed.

Dalvi asked, 'You have the contract for managing parking slots for vehicles, don't you?'

'For sixteen shops. From Krishna Textiles to Deccan Medicines.'

Dalvi consulted his diary.

'I want to enquire about a black Nano with the registration number MH-26-AH-1986, which was parked here yesterday.'

'Yes, it belonged to a lady,' he replied straightaway. 'She had reserved the slot in the morning itself.'

'Do you reserve parking spots?'

'Not really, but she wanted one right next to Padma Jewellers. I charged her five hundred extra.'

'Thanks Madan.'

Dalvi crossed the item. It was a false lead. The woman was probably buying expensive jewellery and was therefore nervous. She chose a Nano, to avoid attention.

Chapter 5

Rangarajan, Vijay's father, had purchased a new pizza-maker to try out his culinary skills.

Vijay's mom whispered, 'Son, do not break his heart. Somehow eat whatever he dishes out.'

His father wore a chef's hat. He served the pizza with infectious enthusiasm. He tasted a piece from Vijay's plate. 'A little burnt at the edges, but otherwise yummy.'

Vijay faked enthusiasm. 'Excellent, Dad.'

His mom rewarded him with a loving glance. Vijay loved

his parents dearly, but today his patience was being tested.

The doorbell rang. Mrs and Mr Vidhyanathan had dropped in unexpectedly. Vijay had never been so pleased to see them. He vanished after exchanging pleasantries.

He slipped into his nightclothes. Then, slouched on a chair, he watched some television. There was nothing remotely interesting playing. Shortly after, the manservant of the household brought him his bedtime glass of milk.

Vijay slid into the bed and closed his eyes, but it was a disturbed night. He woke up, not fully refreshed with a vague feeling that it was not going to be his day.

His father was up and about. From the look of things, it seemed that a very important business meeting was scheduled. He was sporting a grey suit, the one he always wore when his chairman visited the plant. Anyhow, that would keep his mother from enquiring about his being ill at ease.

Vijay could not fathom the reason for the doomsday feeling he had since morning. There was nothing visibly wrong, but the feeling persisted.

※

In his office, Vijay looked at the planner. A meeting with two public prosecutors had been scheduled in the afternoon. Most of these were open-and-shut cases where the suspects had been caught with their hands in the jar. Sex crimes were increasing too, and the victims seemed to get younger and younger. Uncles, cousins, close friends, teachers—the offenders were often known to the unsuspecting victims.

He felt disgusted. How sick society had become. He had done his bit by making streets safer: super-fit constables on motorbikes equipped with walkie-talkies and night vision optics now patrolled all night. He himself carried out surprise checks. The control room, so fine-tuned that a cavalry could be dispatched within minutes of receiving an SOS, received high praise by a top Swedish policeman.

But this emerging breed of criminals made him feel helpless; they operated within the supposed safety of four walls, where the police could not intrude. This neutralized all his preparations that catered to crimes on the streets.

Godbole sent an SMS demanding Vijay's immediate presence in his office.

Vijay drove himself.

※

Godbole was puffing on a cigarette and blowing out smoke rings. He seemed to be admiring his own ability to do this. There was a newspaper on the table. He pushed it towards Vijay. He placed his ring finger on an article and yelled, 'Read!'

The article titled 'Police Incompetence' attributed the loss of life to Vijay's slow reflexes. Although the superintendent of police was within a hundred yards, he could do nothing to protect the life of an innocent citizen.

Rathore walked in. He looked cocky.

'You have tarnished the fair name of Nagpur Police,' Godbole howled.

'Sir,' Rathore pleaded, 'be a little charitable.'

Ignoring him, Vijay replied, 'I could not have done anything more.'

'You should have nabbed him earlier.'

'I just guessed that he had a gun. I went around him and got within four feet of the murderer. I could not have nabbed him on a vague suspicion.'

Godbole took out a marker pen and underlined a portion of the article. 'Read.'

The article stated: 'The award-winning cop was too immersed in his girlfriend to notice the gunman. At least ten people complained to the super cop, who refused to listen.'

Rage seared through Vijay, almost blinding him. 'That is crap! No one complained to me because nobody knew I was a policeman. I was in plain clothes. By the way, I was with Birender, not some girl.'

'Whom should I believe,' Godbole remonstrated, 'a reputed newspaper or a controversial officer?'

Vijay's eyes spewed fire.

Godbole looked directly at Vijay, locking eyes.

A thought came into Vijay's mind, that he was exceeding his brief. He took two deep breaths and calmly said, 'Sir, the article is factually incorrect.'

'My dear,' Godbole spoke comfortingly, 'our commissioner is very sensitive about media reports.' He sipped water and continued. 'He has advised me to shift you from crime to traffic.'

Vijay was aghast that the department trusted an irresponsible reporter more than a celebrated officer.

Godbole bent down and retrieved a file from the drawer. The file contained the letterhead of the commissioner. Indeed, Vijay's transfer orders had originated from the commissioner.

Vijay sunk in his chair, his senses numbed from shock. It took him two minutes to recover. He told himself that he should take the setback sportingly. He got up, saluted Godbole, and then congratulated Rathore.

Rathore smiled snidely. 'All the best in your new assignment.'

Vijay left for his new office.

※

Rathore dipped a teabag into boiling water and chuckled.

'It pays to have a brother in the media.'

Godbole lit a cigarette. 'True, but that was never going to be enough. You have no idea of the effort I had to put in to convince the commissioner.'

Rathore offered his hand, 'You are great.'

Godbole clasped his hand tightly.

Chapter 6

Vijay drove for around twenty minutes to reach his new office. Deshpande, the smart inspector, with two other officers, stood at the door and saluted him smartly. A constable opened the door and took his briefcase.

Inside his office, Vijay told Deshpande, 'I need a formal introduction with my staff.'

'I will take care,' Deshpande promised and waited. 'Sir...' He hesitated. 'We all love and respect you. None of us liked the way you were transferred from the crime branch.'

'Doesn't matter,' Vijay said in a matter-of-fact voice.

'Still, Sir,' Deshpande protested, 'an able officer like you should not be treated like this. The entire police force is with you.'

Vijay smiled encouragingly. 'Anyway, it is an opportunity to work with you guys.'

※

After Deshpande left, Vijay checked his mail. The first one was from Birender. He had been queasy after witnessing the shootout—the first murder he had ever seen. He was taking time off. He had gone to Ooty to recover.

The last line of the mail, however, surprised him. It read, 'The victim was the man I was standing behind in the post office a good two hours before. I am very sure because he had submitted a visa application to travel to China a few days back at our office.'

Vijay was in a quandary. Logically, he should be forwarding this information to Godbole and Rathore. This was an important link to the case. He thought of calling Godbole, but decided against it. After all, it was Godbole's duty to seek a takeover of all information from him.

He continued browsing. The second mail was from Dalvi. This also related to the murder. Dalvi had not cc'd the mail to either Godbole or Rathore. The mail read:

> The victim is Anirudh Babu, a scientist. He works in Amrit Laboratories as understudy to the great Samir Mashelkar. He is known to have a glad eye. He has been at the wrong end of many incidents involving women, but no rape or police case registered yet. He is known to flirt around excessively.

Deshpande cried excitedly, 'Sir! Please put on Zee News on television. There, Sir,' he exclaimed, 'the pride of Nagpur!'

Renowned scientists Dr Samir Mashelkar and Dr Bharat Rao, the founder patrons of Amrit Laboratories and Research Center, were addressing a press conference. The scientists had made a breakthrough in the cure for diabetes.

Bharat Rao was explaining, 'So far, diabetes could be managed or controlled, but never cured.' He turned to his understudy, who inserted a pen drive into the computer. A diagram lit up the giant monitor.

Bharat Rao continued. 'Our formula regenerates the pancreas so diabetes is reversed and cured.'

'Reversible and curable!' Mashelkar interjected.

'It has been tried and tested on monkeys, and the results

have been encouraging.'

'We have,' Mashelkar announced, 'been awarded a patent of one billion dollars—the highest for any Indian scientist.'

Deshpande had tears in his eyes. 'What a day for Nagpur!'

Vijay began to ponder. Anirudh Babu, assistant scientist to Mashelkar, had been murdered a day before the billion-dollar contract. Also, hadn't Birender mentioned millions being stashed in his account? Was this a simple case of revenge over rape, or something deeper than that? Vijay's instinct told him that it was the latter. If that were so, more murders could follow.

He hesitated to call Godbole. He knew that Godbole would take this as encroachment. Vijay reasoned with himself. *Preventing loss of lives is a noble cause. Who cares for insults if I can save lives.*

He rang Godbole. 'Sir,' he began tentatively, 'I want to share some information regarding—'

'Do not waste my time!' Godbole snapped.

'Sir, this is important. Lives are at stake.'

The sound of laughter echoed through the phone.

'Please…'

'You,' Godbole said in an imposing voice, 'could not save a man from being murdered in broad daylight!'

'I beg of you—'

Godbole interrupted him again. 'Once and for all, I do not want to hear anything from you. Rathore is perfectly capable. You manage the traffic.'

Vijay slammed the telephone back into the cradle with such force that it slid off its position. He replaced it properly.

Chapter 7

Padmini had acquired a membership in a new club that had opened up in the neighbourhood. The tennis court was excellent. She had heard that nothing else in the club was worth talking about.

At six o'clock on a Saturday morning, she was hardly hoping to find someone to knock around with, but she was pleasantly surprised to see Vijay limbering up at the court. He looked tall and athletic; his elegantly sculpted musculature even more impressive in shorts and a T-shirt.

'Hi!' He waved at her. 'You play tennis?' he asked.

She just smiled. 'I can smell the whitewash,' she said, sniffing.

Vijay knocked a ball. Then he asked, 'Do you come often to play tennis?'

'Only with men.'

'You must be walloping women,' he commented dryly, amidst a rally.

'Shall we have a match?' she chimed in.

Vijay pretended to think and then nodded.

He served powerfully, but booming serves from strongmen did not intimidate her. She did not take her eyes off the ball. On nimble feet, she moved right behind the serve. The backhand return made a sweet sound of the middle of the racquet meeting the ball. Padmini's strength was in her timing. Vijay's pace was back at him, and he did not seem ready for it.

His technique was sound, but he was out of touch. His strokes were power-packed but awry. Padmini broke him twice and led 4–0.

Vijay showed no signs of panic or insecurity, and Padmini could not cease admiring him for it.

He reduced the power but still served deep. She tried to advance to the net, but was kept pinned to the baseline. He dropped one close to the net, and she was too leaden-footed to reach it. He had changed tack and was playing the waiting game. It worked, as she was tiring. Despite her best efforts, Vijay won the first set, 7–5.

In the second set, rhythm flowed for Vijay and Padmini. He won comfortably, 6–2.

Padmini walked up to the net and offered her hand. 'Well played!'

He shook his head. 'You were the better player.'

She gave a self-deprecating laugh. 'The loser at 5–7, 2–6!'

He raised his eyebrows and exclaimed, 'Boy, you are graceful'.

Padmini's pulse galloped. Adrenaline hit her like never before. She groped for words. At last, they came out. 'But you won easily.'

'By sheer power.' He emphasized the word 'power'. 'You were better tactically. You have a greater range of shots. I am just stronger.'

They walked towards the car park. Suddenly, he suggested, 'How about lunch at Ravenous today?'

She thought about the offer. 'Okay, by one o'clock in the afternoon.'

Vijay raised his thumb.

She reciprocated.

૱

Padmini entered the fine-dining restaurant ten minutes ahead of time, but she was surprised to see Vijay signalling to her, his level of excitement exceeding hers. *This is interesting.*

An IT company was celebrating its foundation day. They

had reserved most of the tables, and the remaining ones were pushed tightly together. Vijay and Padmini sat cheek by jowl with another couple.

Vijay was peering over a menu card that had a Laughing Buddha on its cover. 'Lemon coriander soup to begin with?'

She smiled an approval.

Vijay toyed with his fork. 'I suspected the article to be a planted one. Do you know for sure?'

Padmini smirked. 'Rathore's brother wrote that article. He calls himself Sadashiv.'

Vijay muttered something to himself.

Padmini noticed the waiter hovering near the table. 'I am a pure vegetarian,' she told Vijay.

'So am I.' He smiled at the waiter.

'A roti basket, dal tadka, dum aloo Kashmiri along with a green salad?' He asked, looking at Padmini. She nodded.

The waiter took down the order on a notepad and repeated it.

Padmini took a deep breath. 'I am not convinced that the murder of Anirudh Babu is as straightforward as it seems.'

Vijay took out a visiting card. He wrote something on it and showed it to Padmini.

She smiled. The card read: 'Great minds think alike.'

Padmini urged, 'Now, maybe we need to act in unison.'

Vijay drawled, 'How?'

The food arrived. Both finished the meal without talking.

Vijay gulped down water clumsily from a glass, spilling it all over his clothes. Padmini's lips curved in an endearing smile. Vijay was drilling himself into her heart.

Padmini reached for the credit card inside her Gucci bag.

Vijay put his palm over her bag. 'Please.'

She acquiesced, smiling.

When they came out of the restaurant, Padmini pointed to a park. 'Let us go there. I have something important to discuss.'

Vijay hesitated, and then agreed. They crossed a fountain and stopped near a bench. Padmini sat on one end. Vijay sat at the other end. They faced each other.

'It is,' she said slowly, 'about the Anirudh Babu murder case.' She paused.

Interested eyes looked back at her.

She lowered her voice and asked, 'What is your take on the case?'

Vijay seemed to be rehearsing his answer.

'This is not a media briefing,' she quipped teasingly.

Vijay laughed. 'Just arranging my thoughts.'

'Take your time.'

Vijay shuffled across the bench and now their elbows touched each other. 'Anirudh was a scientist and a junior member of the Mashelkar–Bharat Rao team.' He crossed his arms. 'His murder just before a billion-dollar contract sounds fishy.'

'What is the fallout?'

'I expect,' he said meditatively, 'that more crimes might follow.'

'I apprehend that Mashelkar and Bharat Rao can come to harm.'

Padmini dug into her purse, fished out a photograph and handed it over to Vijay. Vijay studied it. 'It is Anirudh Babu falling down at Laxmi Road.' He continued to study the picture. A puzzled look came over his face. He looked enquiringly at Padmini. 'Something is funny,' he observed. 'This is surely the picture of Anirudh's murder. It is the same place, same dress, but one thing does not fit in.' He closed the fingers of his left hand into a fist. He locked gazes with Padmini. 'I am certain that Anirudh fell to his right. This indicates that he collapsed to his left.'

Padmini handed another photograph to him.

Vijay reflected. 'This is more like what it is etched in my memory.' He put both the photographs side by side on the bench and scrutinized them intensely. Occasionally, he looked skywards. Suddenly, his face lit up. 'I got it!' He pointed to the time inscribed on the top right-hand corner of the two photographs. 'This'—he held the first photograph—'was taken a split second before the gunshot. He was falling over to his left like this.' He leaned downwards towards his left. He clutched his left shoulder.

'Then,' he patted his own shoulder, 'the bullet hit him here. The impact...' Vijay now leaned rightwards, almost falling over.

Padmini gave a mini applause.

He gasped. 'Where did you find these photographs?'

'It pays to social network.' She secured her hair with a band. 'They are uploaded on YouTube, if you had cared to see them.'

'I can't waste my time on the crap that is uploaded on social media.'

'You have to come out of your shell.'

Vijay ignored the last comment. 'I could not have seen the first fall to the left because Karun unsighted me.'

She smiled understandingly. 'YouTube, Facebook and Twitter are all speculating on a theory that there were bullets fired from two different points.'

'I see.'

'I do not,' Padmini admitted, 'buy that.'

'Yeah, someone would have seen that. Anyway, let me get Dr Gaikwad.'

'I have already called him.'

Vijay looked skywards. The sun was high and directly above them. The rays were beginning to scorch. 'Why waste time?' He looked at his watch. 'You park your car here and let's go.'

※

Vijay unlocked his car into gear and drove.

Padmini found his driving too cautious. 'You drive like a fifty-year-old.' She sighed impatiently as he stopped at a red light although no other vehicle was in sight. 'Superintendent Traffic,' she remarked acidly, 'leads by example.'

Vijay smiled and drove on. A black Santro turned right after signalling left, almost causing a collision.

※

Vijay was well recognized at the forensic lab, but Padmini did not appreciate the attention bestowed on her. She glared at a tall man who had been staring at her for two minutes now. He immediately lowered his gaze.

Dr Gaikwad was holding a feng shui crystal in his hand. His hair dye was almost a reflection of the coffee-brown tabletop. 'Where is east?' he wondered aloud.

Vijay pointed a finger. 'Wardha is to our east.'

Dr Gaikwad placed the crystal in the direction that Vijay pointed. He took Vijay aside and whispered, 'You are taking a risk by openly associating with her.'

'I see her as an asset,' Vijay replied

Dr Gaikwad shrugged his shoulders and said, 'Don't blame me for not warning you.'

Vijay ignored him and walked towards Padmini. Dr Gaikwad followed him.

'Something remarkable,' the doctor said, his voice rising, 'has happened.' He pressed Control+P on his keyboard and punched the number '2' for copies. He handed a printout each to Vijay and Padmini.

He looked at Vijay. 'Do you remember that I said he had received a shot shortly before his death?'

'I do,' Vijay said flatly.

Dr Gaikwad took a deep breath. 'Someone pricked Anirudh with ricin.' He measured every word he spoke. Continuing in the same vein, he said, 'Ricin is a poison. It must have taken around twenty minutes for the toxin to work. Anirudh was probably dead, more precisely, brain-dead, when he was falling to his left.'

Padmini was trying to decipher the situation.

Vijay surmised, 'That means Anirudh's death was caused by two factors almost simultaneously.'

'Exactly! It is difficult to categorically establish that he died as he was falling. In any case, he would most certainly have died very soon after.'

Three coffee cups were placed on the table.

Vijay blew the froth from his cup. 'So, what happened first—death by gunshot or death by poisoning—cannot be established. But certainly the *act* of poisoning happened earlier.'

Dr Gaikwad nodded vigorously.

'As a detective,' Vijay said, sipping his coffee, 'it can be reasonably assumed that the poisoner was a cold-blooded killer with a different motive.'

'That,' Dr Gaikwad replied, raising his hands in abdication, 'is your domain.'

Vijay stood up. 'So, what next, Doc?'

'Taking a vacation.' He also got up. 'Grandparenting in Seattle. Will be there for a month.'

Chapter 8

Vijay pulled into the parking lot just opposite Birender's travel agency.

It was still quite sunny, and Padmini could not fathom why the street lights should be on. 'What a colossal waste of electricity!' She looked behind and noticed one light off. 'Maybe that one is fused,' she said. 'Let us,' she proposed, 'try to re-enact the murder scene.'

'We have no idea about the man who injected the poison. So, where should we start?'

Padmini smiled. 'We know something about the victim. Maybe that will help.' She looked at her watch. 'Anirudh,' she said, looking away from Vijay, 'left the post office at 12:10 p.m., but reached Laxmi Road at 2:00 p.m.'

'He was walking.' Vijay remembered

'Even if he walked very slowly,' Padmini conjectured, 'it could not have taken him more than twenty to twenty-five minutes.'

'In that case, he might have gone somewhere else in between.'

Padmini wondered aloud, 'So, which trail do we take?'

'I think,' Vijay cupped his chin with his palm, 'towards Laxmi Road.' He paused and then explained. 'We came from the other side.'

'Also,' Padmini interrupted, 'there was no place where he could have spent an hour and a quarter.'

'Unless, of course,' Vijay countered, 'he had friends in those residential apartments.'

'That needs to be checked out, right?'

'Yeah.'

Padmini pointed to a superstore. 'Do you think he would have gone in there?'

Vijay stood and thought. 'No, he did not have anything with him.' He added, 'He also did not look like someone who would window-shop.'

They marched ahead.

'Wait,' he said, a little excitedly.

Padmini traced Vijay's eyeline. There was intensity in his eyes. 'That could be it,' she remarked.

Vijay looked excited. 'Are you thinking what I am thinking?'

'Sneha Massage Parlor.' She smiled broadly.

'I will look at journalists with great respect from now on and that is a promise.' He lifted his head towards the parlour. 'A man who loves female company could certainly spend an hour in there.'

Padmini proposed, 'I think that you can go as a decoy customer.'

Vijay dug his muscular hands into his pockets. 'Not necessary.'

'Then I'll go and quiz the girls.'

Vijay speculated, 'This could be the crime scene. If you do not come out in ten minutes, I will charge in.'

'Aren't you getting carried away?'

Vijay looked dead serious. 'There is no other place where someone could have pricked him with a needle.'

Padmini added, 'No other place where a woman could get intimate with him.'

She walked slowly towards the parlour. She surveyed the scene. It was located on the first floor. The staircase leading to it was narrow, but well lit. It did not look insecure. She waved back to Vijay and tiptoed on to the staircase while Vijay stood at the foot of the stairs. Twelve steps took her to the parlour. A teenage girl smiled from behind a counter. She shoved a chair towards Padmini.

Two more girls, in their early twenties and wearing aprons, came from inside. Padmini reckoned they were therapists.

One of the therapists spoke. 'Have you received any training?'

Padmini smiled. 'I have not come here for a job, or for a massage.'

The girls looked startled. They exchanged glances.

'Relax.' She took out three five hundred rupee notes. They were brand new and crisp. 'Just answer my questions and you get these as a prize. I am Padmini.' Her countenance was warm and affectionate. 'Tell me your names.'

One therapist said, 'My name is also Padmini.'

Padmini put an arm around her.

'I am Sneha,' the second therapist said.

'Karuna,' the receptionist introduced herself.

Padmini took out a photograph of Anirudh Babu. She placed it on the counter. Looking at all three of them, she asked, 'Have you seen him?'

Sneha answered, 'Someone like that was here.'

Excitement coursed through Padmini's veins.

The therapist Padmini giggled. 'He came just when we opened, around ten thirty, but he did not bother for a massage. He just wanted female hands all over him. He was Ummaid's friend.'

'Ummaid?' Padmini echoed.

'A male therapist had joined us,' Sneha clarified. 'He used to be very aloof.'

Padmini got impatient. 'Where is he now?'

Karuna looked at Sneha. 'He hasn't come to work since that day.'

Padmini looked at the three of them as though they were students in a detention classroom. 'Was Ummaid alone with the customer?'

'For about an hour after the massage.'

Vijay climbed a couple of stairs and then climbed down. Then he looked at his watch. He realized that he had climbed up and down more than five times now. He took out his mobile and then put it back in his trouser pocket. *Maybe, this is why smokers can handle such situations better. They have something to occupy a restless mind.* He looked at his watch again and started running up the flight of stairs.

Padmini heard someone running up the staircase. She turned around. It was Vijay. She signalled him to go back. She told Karuna, 'Go on.'

'They were talking in hushed tones. The stranger had a bag with documents. He showed them to Ummaid. Ummaid told me not to charge him for the massage.'

So, Anirudh had been here, that too just before the murder. Anirudh was probably blackmailing Ummaid. So, Ummaid called Anirudh to the massage parlour, where he could have easily pricked him with a needle during the massage. Padmini was well on her way to become a Miss Marple. The first case had been solved in half a day! She felt heady—the same sensations she'd felt three years ago when she'd lifted the Mumbai Open Lawn Tennis Championship title.

Smiling happily, she gave her mobile number to the three girls. 'Call me whenever you please.'

When Padmini exited the parlour, she found Vijay pacing back and forth and looking at his watch. She filled him in on the details.

He asked, 'Where did you get Anirudh's photo?'

'From his visa application form.'

Confusion clouded Vijay's eyes.

'I met your friend Birender,' she laughed. 'He looked at me as if I was from another planet.' She hastily added, 'He was sweet and gave me what I wanted.'

Vijay fixed her with an admiring gaze. 'You are streets ahead of me.'

She relished the magnanimity and honesty behind the compliment.

He led her to the ice cream shop and ordered a raspberry stick for himself and a strawberry cone for her.

Padmini's mobile trilled. It was Sneha.

'I need to meet you.' The therapist's voice was panic-stricken.

'I am at the Baskin Robbins ice cream parlour in front of the parlour.' She disconnected and inched closer to Vijay. 'I think the massage parlour girl has a secret to reveal.'

Padmini left her bag on the table and went out. In two minutes, Sneha appeared, nervous and frightened. Padmini hugged her and took her in. 'Don't worry.' She pointed to Vijay—'He is the superintendent of police. Nobody can dare touch you.'

Vijay motioned her to sit.

'I cannot,' Sneha said humbly, 'sit before such a big man.' Her voice fell to a whisper. 'Sir, Ummaid was specially recommended by the manager. He did not do any work. He would be on his mobile all day long.'

Although, they were probably of the same age, Padmini tended to her like a child. 'What else do you want to say about him?'

'Something strange. Ummaid had disguised himself as a Pathan. He wore a turban, a false beard and a false set of teeth.'

Padmini eyed Sneha furtively. She noted that Vijay wore a deadpan expression. She envied his composure.

'His appearance, when he left for good,' Sneha continued, 'was totally altered, but I recognized his jeans. I never shared this with the other girls. Ummaid knew very little about massages, but he read a lot of big fat books.'

'Do guys like Ummaid come to your parlour often?'

Sneha took a deep breath. 'Men do come, but mostly it is to hide from the police. Once they get bail, they go away.' She adjusted her apron. 'But Ummaid was different. He belonged to a very decent background. He ordered food from expensive restaurants. He drank only mineral water. He wore good clothes.'

'What kind of interaction did you have with him?'

Sneha pondered. 'We rarely talked to him. He had a separate room. One day, I came in early and peeped into his room.'

'Why?'

'Only out of curiosity,' Sneha replied a little defensively. 'His beard was false, so were his teeth. He is not a Pathan. He had disguised himself as one.'

Padmini's mind ticked furiously. Suddenly, she asked, 'What did he do on that day?'

Sneha replied in an irritated voice, 'He kept peeping through the curtain. As soon as a customer came, he would rush in. Finally, his friend came. He told Padmini to give him a nice massage.'

'Give me your manager's address,' Padmini said.

'I do not have it. I have only his mobile number.' She parted with it. Then she held out her hands beseechingly. Tears rolled down her cheeks padded with heavy make-up. 'My manager, we call him Ustad is very well connected. If he gets angry, he will kill me.'

Padmini wiped Sneha's face with a tissue. She tucked her arm into Vijay's elbow and thrust him before Sneha's face. 'No! He won't dare touch you as long as this cop is around.'

'Can you,' Vijay asked, 'recognize Ummaid if he came without his false beard, teeth and turban?'

Sneha answered immediately, 'Yes.'

'Go home,' Vijay said. 'We will call you when we need you.'

'Madam, please help me,' she squeaked. 'This place is bad. Only men looking for cheap sexual thrills visit the outlet. I am a good beautician.'

Padmini suddenly remembered a conversation she'd had with Lalli, her friend's elder sister. 'An acquaintance of mine runs a beauty parlour. I will recommend you to her.' Padmini immediately called Lalli. She smiled at Sneha. 'The deal is done,' she said. 'Report to 1/17 Accolade, Viman Nagar at ten o'clock in the morning tomorrow.'

Sneha prostrated herself at Padmini's feet. Padmini felt embarrassed. She gave a tired but relieved smile.

Vijay dialled Ustad's number on his mobile. Ustad revealed that someone had paid him ₹20,000 for employing Ummaid.

Vijay barked, 'Didn't you smell a rat?'

'Sir, my brother owns the shop on the ground floor and my brother-in-law the next shop. We have a lot of well-wishers in the government. We are a formidable force there.'

'Has anyone,' Vijay asked, his anger mounting, 'ever made such requests to you before?'

'Plenty,' he answered matter-of-factly. 'A lot of men need shelter 'til they manage bail in dowry cases.'

'Was it the case this time round?'

'I never exceed my brief,' he boasted. 'People come to me because I never ask unpleasant questions.' He laughed, 'I only charge unpleasantly high!'

'I will get back when I need you.'

'At your service, Sir.'

Vijay looked long at his mobile after the conversation ended. He filled Padmini in.

'I think he is not speaking the truth,' she concluded.

Vijay shook his head.

'On the contrary, he might be. Dowry is a non-bailable offence, so people need to duck somewhere before bail is arranged.'

A coffee-stained cup and a half-eaten vada littered the pavement. Vijay walked past, hardly noticing the trash.

Padmini shook her head ruefully. 'Typical Indian boy, spoilt by mama.' She bent down, wrapped the trash in a napkin and took it to where it belonged—the waste bin.

Vijay waited for her to join him.

She cleared her throat. 'The pieces do not fit. Ummaid had no business poisoning Anirudh, the man who in all probability had arranged his bail.'

'What you say makes sense. Anirudh might have been blackmailing Ummaid, who in turn might have suckered Anirudh to visit Sneha Massage Parlor and accosted him there. That,' Vijay said, pursing his lips, 'does not prevent Ustad from believing that Ummaid was seeking a shield from an arrest warrant, so Ustad might be telling us what he knows.'

The day had passed. Twilight had dissolved into darkness. Vehicles had switched on their headlights and from a distance, looked like a flowing river of brightness.

'I guess that wraps up the day.' Padmini waited for a response.

'I will drop you home,' he offered.

'My car,' she suddenly remembered, 'is parked at Ravenous.'

'I will have it sent to your home,' he promised.

Chapter 9

Vijay typed a paragraph. He made deliberate errors in spelling and grammar. He folded the paper into an envelope. On it, he pasted a paper with Commissioner Patel's address typed out. He had the letter dropped in the letter box. He had done his duty.

Commissioner Patel read the anonymous letter with its numerous mistakes in spelling and grammar. But, its message was clear. He folded it neatly and inserted it into a fresh envelope. He then rang his peon bell. A peon answered almost immediately.

'Get me three copies of the letter in this envelope.'

The peon disappeared.

Patel summoned Godbole and Rathore.

Both Godbole and Rathore were provided with a folder. The folder contained the anonymous letter.

Patel read the letter aloud, moving his finger along each word:

> The lives of the great scentists SAMIR Mashelkar and BHARAT Rao are of DANGER. The murder of Anirudh BABU, a junior scintist, were a forerunner.

'Now,' Patel said, looking squarely at both of them, 'this could be a hoax, but let us err on the side of caution; take as many men as you want, use whichever equipment you wish, spend as much money as required...' He paused. 'But there is zero tolerance for any slip-up.'

Rathore had a condescending look.

'You will pay dearly if you fail,' Patel warned, 'and none of your political godfathers will be able to save you.'

Rathore was about to react angrily, but Godbole pinched his elbow. Godbole replied courteously, 'Sir, we will live up to your expectations.'

Chapter 10

Rathore couldn't take his eyes off the ICICI Direct trading terminal screen. 'A good day for margin traders,' he exclaimed, even as he clinched another deal.

'Stop that, will you?' Godbole snapped.

Rathore whistled. 'Boss, what is cooking?'

'I am worried about that death threat.' He stood up. 'And you,' he accused, 'are busy playing the stock market.'

'Boss, you underestimate me. Foolproof arrangements have been made.'

Godbole shifted his weight to the other foot and looked expectantly at Rathore.

'Really!'

'Why don't you see for yourself,' Rathore offered, 'and judge.'

'Let us go.'

Rathore drove Godbole in a direction opposite to where he was expecting to go. Still, Godbole said nothing, smoking a cigarette along the way.

Rathore flashed his identity card to gain access through a security cordon. They passed through another highly guarded gate into a car park adjacent to a lawn. The lawn had a circular construction of concrete with the letter 'H' glowing in the sun.

Godbole exclaimed, 'It is our helipad.'

'I am a licenced pilot.' Rathore displayed his licence proudly. 'Let us make an aerial survey of our arrangements.'

A smartly dressed, clean-shaven man saluted the duo as they disembarked from the car.

Rathore had a conversation with the man and then beckoned

Godbole to follow him. He climbed into a MBB Bo 105 helicopter and turned to Godbole.

'Hop in.'

Godbole looked worried. 'I hope it is safe.'

Rathore said nothing and opened the throttle fully. With one hand, he slowly pulled up a handle that was labelled 'Collective', and with the other hand gripped something labelled 'Cyclic'. He simultaneously operated both the foot pedals. Rathore pressed the left foot pedal forcefully and gradually pulled up on the Collective.

The helicopter skidded and rose slowly. Godbole saw intense concentration on Rathore's face. He wished Rathore could replicate it in police work.

As the helicopter gained altitude, Rathore eased into a smile. He pointed downwards. 'Can you see the jeeps down there?'

Godbole could appreciate that by cutting out the noise, headphones and microphones had made conversation simpler inside the helicopter. 'Yes, they look like our jeeps.'

Rathore hovered. 'Two patrol jeeps with three men disguised as telephone linesmen and electricians guard the entrance and exit to Mashelkar's house.' Rathore propelled forward. 'We are over Bharat Rao's bungalow.'

Godbole saw patrol jeeps there as well.

After a swoop over Godbole's office, Rathore touched down, albeit with a jerk.

As they drove back, Rathore exclaimed, 'I have ten patrol vehicles with fifty men, all equipped with helmets, gas masks, automatic weapons, bulletproof and fireproof clothing, four sniffer dogs, eight tear gas experts, five explosive experts and two frogmen. We would'—he took a deep breath—'be able to storm any part of the city in ten minutes flat. Of course, this helicopter would be used for aerial surveys.'

Godbole stared at Rathore for one full minute. Then he said, 'I am impressed. Style is Rathore's middle name.'

Rathore bowed in appreciation.

Chapter 11

As far as Dalvi was concerned, his worst fears had come true. He had no doubt that Godbole and Rathore would not be able to prevent the renowned scientists, Mashelkar and Bharat Rao, from being murdered. Mashelkar had died and Bharat Rao had nearly lost his life. His heart pined for Vijay as he accompanied Rathore to the forensic laboratory.

Dr Gaikwad was on a vacation. Dr Salpekar, his deputy, was efficient and looked every bit an eager beaver salesman. 'I have analysed,' he read from a report, 'both the blood samples. Dr Mashelkar has some unidentified proteins, no real poison. Something actually turned toxic due to some reaction.'

Rathore barked, 'I do not want medical jargon.'

Dr Salpekar controlled himself. 'Sir, I found no poisonous substance in the blood test.'

He placed the report back on the desk.

Rathore flipped through the report. 'Did he die of yoga?'

Dr Salpekar was losing patience. 'Sir, poisons are difficult to identify during a post-mortem. Either there was an allergic reaction for Mashelkar, or it was a poison that I do not know about.'

'Tell me,' Rathore said, trying to be nice, 'how is it that Bharat Rao, who drank the same potion from the same glass, should live and not Mashelkar?'

Dr Salpekar held Bharat Rao's blood report in his hands. 'We found proteins and vitamin B in his blood also, but I am told he regurgitated.'

'You mean vomited.'

Dr Salpekar nodded.

'You have,' Rathore said, wagging an admonishing finger at Dr Salpekar, 'been of no use.'

'That,' Dr Salpekar protested, 'is unfair. I did my best.'

'Nonsense!' Rathore fumed. 'I am not able to decide whether it is a murder or an accident.'

'That is not my job,' Dr Salpekar snapped. 'You are shirking your responsibility.'

Rathore's eyes reddened, his face contorted, and his voice rose. 'Who the hell do you think you are?' he screamed.

'That is what I must ask you.'

Rathore muttered angrily, 'I will fix you! I will fix you, good and hard.' He then left, helmet in hand.

Dalvi sighed. His yearning for Vijay only increased.

Chapter 12

The proximity of his house to the main road and the esteem in which Mashelkar was held—in fact, his entire family, since his father had put the city on the scientific map—had churned up a mixture of emotions, and a huge crowd had gathered outside. Some lined up to pay their respects, others because their curiosity was piqued, and many simply because it gave them something to talk about. The body had been preserved and kept encased in a glass box for admirers and well-wishers to pay their last respects to the great man.

Traffic jams had been caused for the second consecutive day. The nature of the murder—right under the nose, blatantly in the open, in front of a hundred witnesses—and the curious fact that two men drank the same liquid, poured from the same bottle at the same time, and yet one died, the other survived led to wild and unending speculation by the media. It could have been put down to allergy, but then every media man worth his salt was aware that the police commissioner had received a tip-off. Rathore had opened his mouth, only to put his foot into it. The media loved it and lapped it up.

The forensics team had not been able to demystify the mysteries that surrounded the case.

Godbole felt the heat. He sat pensively on his chair. Occasionally, he looked out of the window. 'Rathore,' he said, 'we have to make progress on this high-profile double murder.'

'I thought,' Rathore replied, 'only Mashelkar is dead.'

'But,' Godbole countered, 'the attempt was to kill Bharat Rao also. He escaped miraculously.'

Rathore shook his head defiantly. 'The forensics are unable to explain how the same drink from the same glass could be deadly for Mashelkar and non-toxic for Bharat Rao.'

'The chief minister has ordered the commissioner to nab the culprit.' Godbole stood with his palms on the table. 'He urged me to show results. We are being tested,' he emphasized fearfully.

'The forensics are not supporting us adequately,' Rathore repeated.

'Now,' Godbole snapped, 'the commissioner will replace you with Vijay.'

Rathore frowned. 'That rat,' he muttered. He sat on the sofa and fiddled with his Blackberry.

Godbole smiled affectionately. 'Rathore, dear, we have to move before the commissioner calls. Let us try to find out the possible suspects.' He lit a cigarette and taking a long, deep drag, closed his eyes.

A polite knock forced his eyes open.

It was Dalvi. 'Sir.' He saluted them both.

'Dalvi.' Godbole turned on the charm. 'Give us your take.'

Dalvi cleared his throat. 'The poison was prepared by an expert, so he must have needed access to a laboratory.'

Rathore shrugged his shoulders. 'A motive is needed.'

Godbole straightened himself with a jump.

'The murder most certainly is for the billion-dollar contract,' Dalvi affirmed. 'Only a professional rival can realistically hope to benefit from the death of these scientists.'

Rathore looked disinterested. He checked his mail on his Blackberry.

'The professional rival,' Dalvi continued, 'can only be a scientist because only a scientist can prepare this potion.'

Godbole drummed his fingers on the table. 'These scientists, I understand, are absent-minded. Mashelkar would not know even if a volcano burst.'

Dalvi smiled knowingly. 'His concentration was legendary.'

'So,' Godbole deduced, 'to insert drops of poison into the energy drink would not have been a very difficult job. Do you have any suspects?' His voice was more optimistic than before.

Dalvi's eyes riveted on Rathore.

Rathore fumbled for words.

Godbole's eyes darted from Dalvi to Rathore and back to Dalvi.

'I scanned the videographic recordings,' Dalvi said. 'I have also spoken to eleven witnesses. The bottle was opened in front of everyone. The drink was poured in the open hall. No scope of anyone tampering with the drink.'

'Anything more to add?' Godbole asked curtly. 'Right under our nose,' he muttered under his breath.

Dalvi saluted both the senior officers.

Godbole signalled that he was free to leave.

'Shall we arrest a couple of guests who were at the party?' Rathore proposed.

Godbole gave a perplexed look.

Rathore said airily, 'We need to be seen as acting.'

'It would boomerang.'

Rathore wrung his hands in exasperation. 'So we are just sitting tight?'

'To be a good detective,' Godbole lectured, 'requires hard work and loads of patience.'

'Patience is not my way. I am the angry young man.'

Godbole's face was creased with worry as he saw Rathore depart.

Chapter 13

Godbole sat chewing his nails. Rathore had let him down. Someone knocked politely. 'Come in,' he roared.

It was Dalvi. 'Sir, I forgot'—he panted—'to give you this file.'

Godbole motioned for him to sit.

The file contained a news item that mentioned that senior microbiologist Srikanth Mahapatra had fallen out with Mashelkar and Bharat Rao. Mahapatra had cited his disillusionment with Mashelkar after working together for two decades.

Godbole jotted down points in a diary. He flipped over a couple of pages. There was another news item. 'Srikanth Mahapatra terms Bharat Rao's act of rejoining Mashelkar as great betrayal,' he read.

Dalvi got up. 'See the last page.'

Srikanth Mahapatra had questioned the methods used by Mashelkar as well as his claims.

Godbole closed the file. 'Nothing to follow up,' he said blandly. 'Srikanth Mahapatra is too renowned a man to indulge in such acts.'

The colour drained from Dalvi's face. 'But, Sir,' he protested, 'he has a strong motive.'

'Do not even mention it,' he suggested. 'Otherwise, we will be roasted for harassing a famous citizen.'

Dalvi nodded, saluted and left.

Godbole smiled slyly. The country bumpkin had stumbled on the jackpot. Now, he was going to snatch it.

Chapter 14

Padmini stood outside Anirudh's home. She had done many difficult interviews, but talking to a recently widowed woman was never going to be a welcoming prospect.

An immaculately dressed woman answered the doorbell. A bright red sari, with a dazzling golden border, accentuated her glowing complexion. The hair was conditioned. She was readying to go out. Her eyes looked hollow from lack of sleep. Otherwise, she seemed to be dressing up for a party. She looked at Padmini and said, without a hint of a smile, 'Come in.'

Padmini removed her footwear before entering. She extended her hand. 'I am Padmini, a crime reporter.'

An amazingly strong hand for a petite body clasped her hand. 'I am Vasudha.'

The telephone rang in the bedroom and the woman sauntered in to answer it.

A sudden rush of current, almost like an electric shock, ripped through Padmini. She had often felt such shocks when she encountered liars, thugs and cheats. A psychologist laid it down to strong intuition. Unexplained tremors were not new to her, but the scale, intensity and duration of this quake was unprecedented. It was many times more than all her past experiences put together. She clutched the sofa armrest for support. It took her a few minutes to recover. Mercifully, Vasudha was still on the phone.

'If you do not mind,' Padmini hesitated, 'I want to talk about your husband's—'

'Murder,' Vasudha interrupted. She smiled. 'You are surprised at my demeanour.'

'Indeed,' Padmini acknowledged.

'Our marriage,' Vasudha reminisced, 'was over long ago. We lived like co-tenants in a guest house, hardly talking or fighting, but generally cooperating.'

Padmini nodded her head sympathetically. 'Have you come to terms with the loss?'

'What loss?' Vasudha sneered. 'He ceased to be mine long ago. He belonged to a host of women.'

Padmini was astonished at Vasudha's calm countenance, even when emotions must be stirring up inside her. The people she had encountered in the past spoke their heart out in such circumstances. Vasudha was different; she was composed, cold, confident and sort of eerie.

'Did you,' Padmini asked slowly, 'ever confront him over his roving eye?'

'I do not deny,' she said with candour, 'that it hurt me initially. First, it was with a colleague, then a neighbour, then my son's teacher. It was unbearable.'

Padmini looked at her with a straight face.

Vasudha poured water into two glasses. She offered one to Padmini. She continued. 'Each time, the story was the same. I would hear from friends. He would deny it and then apologize when caught red-handed.'

Padmini found it hard to believe. 'How did so many women get attracted to him?'

Vasudha sighed. 'He picked woman with unhappy marriages, looking for a fling. He had a great eye for spotting such women,' she said, her voice displaying grudging admiration. 'He would move slowly, soften them up, and they would simply flutter around him.' She went into the kitchen.

Padmini heard the sound of the electric kettle buzzing. She could see a Lenovo flat-screen computer monitor through the curtain partings. On a table, placed perpendicular to the computer, stood a colour printer. A colour printout popped out like a periscope.

Padmini's journalistic eyes scanned the living room. Photographs of Vasudha in flowing robes, walking on the ramp wearing designer outfits and participating in rock climbing, apart from receiving awards, stared back at her. The furnishings were modest, but carefully chosen. Not a speck of dust, not a scratch or dent on the furniture, not a drop of water in the form of seepage on the roof, could be sighted.

'I take great care in everything I do,' the hostess said, returning with a tray of biscuits and two mugs of coffee. She almost read Padmini's mind. I am blamed for being an impatient perfectionist, but I am always flawless.'

Padmini picked a framed photograph of a younger Vasudha accepting an award from the legendary Amitabh Bachchan.

She gloated. 'I won the best actor award in an inter-collegiate competition a few years back.'

Padmini popped a biscuit. 'You lead a colourful life.'

'I also lead a successful life.'

Padmini's eyes followed Vasudha's. Prizes, medals, trophies and mementos awarded to her jostled for space on the mantelpiece, which had no room for any other showpiece.

Padmini created a circle with her thumb and pointer finger to indicate that she was impressed. Then, she moved in her chair. 'Did you not try to sort out your differences?'

'Little point, if he never kept his word. He never meant it; he never tried.'

'I understand.'

'I soon learned to cope. I want to concentrate on my career, on bringing up my son.'

Padmini liked the aroma of the coffee. She enquired, 'Is it peaberry?'

Vasudha smiled. She put a cushion, which had tilted slightly, back in place. 'I believe that a rapist deserves death penalty. I will maintain that, even if my son is on the wrong side.'

'How are you so certain about that?'

Vasudha had a faraway look and a pleasant smile. 'A woman is never wrong about her husband.' She looked at her watch as she finished speaking.

Padmini got the hint. She got up. 'Thanks, and all the best.'

'Show me the draft of the interview that you are about to publish,' Vasudha cooed.

Padmini stood up, stupefied.

'Which publication do you work for?'

'I am a freelancer,' Padmini replied.

'Do not forget to show me the draft,' Vasudha repeated.

Padmini nodded as she left. She stood about a hundred metres away from the apartment. She looked around and something remarkable struck her. The post office, the massage parlour and this flat were like the three corners of an equilateral triangle, all equidistant from each other. Ten minutes from one other.

She shook her head sadly. If the marriage had been a happy

one, Anirudh would have headed home from the post office instead of the massage parlour or Laxmi Road. Neither the poisoner at the parlour nor the clumsy gunman would have got to him.

She thought of Vasudha, Anirudh's widow. Her confidence and verve were chilling, but admirable. However, Padmini needed to discuss her psychic experience with Vijay.

Chapter 15

Bharat Rao stared at the ceiling as if in a trance. He sat up and shivered. The nurse draped a blanket around him. He lay down again. The room was dark except for a red light that blinked. Another nurse pricked the forefinger of his left hand. Godbole glanced at the values shown by the glucometer. On checking the readings on it, a look of concern clouded the nurse's face. She said, 'Sir, please have a snack.'

Bharat Rao did not respond. The nurse placed a tender hand on his forehead. 'Sir, your sugar level is dropping.'

Bharat Rao got up. A bowl of rice gruel with a spoon was placed on the tray beside him.

Godbole turned to Dr Tripathi, who looked out of place in the sombre atmosphere of the hospital in his purple stripes and brown corduroy trousers.

'I want to know—When exactly can I interview Bharat Rao?'

There was silence and stillness for a minute. Then Dr Tripathi laughed. 'You better consult an astrologer.' He laughed again.

'What really is wrong with him?'

Dr Tripathi echoed the words, 'What really is wrong with him?' Then he said, 'Physiologically, nothing much.' He paused and scratched his head. 'He is scarred psychologically.'

'Is it the effect of the poison taking its toll?'

Dr Tripathi pulled up his trousers. 'No, there is no poison, just proteins and vitamin B. He took an energy drink, something I am told he has been taking for years.'

'So,' Godbole enquired, his voice rising, 'why is he in this state?'

'The shock of losing his friend,' Dr Tripathi replied, 'and almost his own life.'

'Is his brain affected?'

Dr Tripathi shrugged. 'There is nothing physiologically wrong,' he said, enunciating each word for effect. 'He is neurologically okay, only psychologically depressed.'

'Is there no hope then?' Godbole asked, with feeling.

'Don't be so impatient.' Dr Tripathi smiled. 'He will recover suddenly. It could happen any day.'

Chapter 16

Godbole was pleasantly surprised to get a phone call from Dr Tripathi three days later.

'It is a miracle,' Dr Tripathi cried excitedly, 'Dr Bharat Rao has recovered!'

'Indeed.' Godbole tried his best to sound composed. 'When can I interview him?'

'Maybe today itself.'

'Really?'

'We are discharging him today.'

Godbole called the constables guarding Bharat Rao. 'Do not leave him alone for a moment, and call me when he is home.'

Godbole was halfway through his lunch when he was

informed that Bharat Rao was home and more than willing to talk. Godbole left his lunch unfinished, washed his hands, gargled and set off. He combed his hair in the car. He was shocked to find strands of hair sticking to the comb each time he brushed. When he looked at the mirror, he caught sight of wrinkles that he hadn't noticed before. This case was ageing him. Godbole instructed his chauffeur to park the car outside the bungalow.

One of the constables was standing near the outer door. He ran up to Godbole and saluted him.

'How is Bharat Rao?' Godbole asked, as he walked briskly.

'Fine.' The response beamed from another corner.

Godbole looked up in the direction of the voice. He saw Bharat Rao standing with his arms outstretched, as if he wanted to embrace Godbole. Godbole walked straight into his arms.

Tears rolled down the scientist's cheeks. 'I know how much you have done for me.'

'It is my duty,' Godbole replied calmly, 'to guard such a VIP.'

'I am forever indebted to you.'

Godbole stood still.

'Let us sit on the lawn,' Bharat Rao suggested.

One constable immediately ran and brought two chairs. A middle-aged man stood humbly beside Bharat Rao.

'Ramu,' Bharat requested, 'can you get us two cups of special ginger tea?'

'Sure, Sir.'

Godbole swallowed. Then he said haltingly, 'I want to get to the bottom of this business.'

Ramu placed the tray jerkily, and tea spilled on to the tray from the cups.

Godbole sipped the tea. 'It is refreshing to have freshly cut ginger.'

Bharat acknowledged the comment with a dip of his

head. Suddenly, he yelled, 'Forget about me, but don't spare the murderer.'

Godbole straightened himself and spoke in a voice that displayed his determination, 'I will bring the killer to justice and I will also not allow any harm to befall you.'

Uneasy silence prevailed for a couple of minutes. Then Godbole said, 'You must be having so many fond memories of Mashelkar"

Like magic, Bharat Rao's face brightened as he thought of Mashelkar.

'Around a decade back, Srikanth, Mashelkar and I attended a conference in California. A scientist told us that Edison drank a juice made of crushed pearls to increase his memory and concentration. Another circulated a draft paper on how Einstein boosted his mental powers by sucking nectar from select flowers.'

Bharat rested the fingers of his left hand on his chin. His eyes widened as he continued, 'Srikanth discounted the theory, but Mashelkar and I took it seriously. Five years back, we developed our own power drink, a combination of vitamins, enzymes and proteins. We called it Gandhiv.'

Godbole exclaimed, 'What an apt name. I am sure, it...'

'Not really,' Bharat interrupted, 'The original version was just passable and Srikanth poked fun at us,' he paused and looked at Godbole and said, 'A month back, I tweaked the formula and lo and behold!' he stood up and spread his arms sideways like Jesus the Redeemer, 'I had stumbled upon a drink that would add not just power to the brain, but also imagination!'

Godbole chipped in, 'I remember, Einstein had said that imagination and knowledge are two sides of the same coin.'

'No, the correct phrase should be "imagination is more important than knowledge".' Bharat Rao closed his eyes. He was beginning to tire.

'Weren't you excited about the new Gandhiv?' Godbole asked.

'I was, I was,' Bharat chirped like a child, 'I always carried the bottle containing the potion with me because I didn't want to lose it.'

'But you know the formula, you can always make it again.'

'These formulations take six weeks and I didn't want to wait that long, but alas...'

He broke down as he spoke.

Godbole offered his handkerchief, but Bharat ignored him and sobbed. Ramu came over with another manservant. Bharat got up. The two servants supported him and carried him in. Godbole followed them.

A doctor was present in the living room. He examined Bharat. 'He is okay, but let him rest now.'

Godbole, however, did not go. He sat on a chair, newspaper in his hand.

By and by, Bharat resurfaced. 'Sorry, I got emotional.'

'No, I understand,' Godbole responded with empathy. 'You have lost a dear friend.' Godbole retraced, with a serious face, 'Sir, what could have caused your dear friend's death?'

In a tone that sounded conspiratorial to Godbole, Bharat asked, 'What do the forensics think?'

'They think it's an allergy due to some impurity in the energy potion.'

'Typical.' Bharat sneered. 'How can he be allergic to something he has been consuming for years? I only made a small change in the tonic.'

Godbole sighed in exasperation. 'I am going around in circles. Nobody is able to even zero in on the precise cause of death.'

'You,' Bharat accused, 'have never asked me. In fact, no one approached me.'

'I pray to you. I beg of you,' Godbole beseeched.

'In my opinion'—Bharat assumed an air of importance—'the death was caused due to ingestion of poison two hours prior to the drinking of Gandhiv. I think Gandhiv had nothing to do with it!'

Godbole jumped like a jack-in-the-box. 'You mean,' he cried, 'we were all barking up the wrong tree?'

'I am certain.'

Godbole curled the fingers of his right hand into a fist.

'I am certain that the death was an impact of something administered upon him earlier. The consumption of the Gandhiv was probably your red herring.'

Godbole felt as if his shovel had hit a buried treasure chest. 'Why,' Godbole asked, in an incredulous voice, 'could not the forensics detect any poison?'

'The forensics department is manned by fools, not scientists,' he screamed.

'Godbole, unless they use Scarob's technology, As^{+3}—an inorganic arsenic—cannot be separated. It is believed to be fifty times more toxic than As^{+5}, the popular arsenic.'

Godbole twisted in his chair. 'What makes you suspect As^{+3}?'

'Mashelkar had complained of drowsiness and dizziness just before the party began. At that time, I put it down to tiredness, but in hindsight, I know it was the effect of As^{+3}.'

'Whom do you suspect?'

'We have a long list of enemies.' He almost seemed to be boasting—'Rival scientists, pharmaceutical companies, physiotherapists, the list goes on.'

'No particular person?'

Bharat shook his head.

'Are you sure that arsenic would have been used only on that day?'

'Poisons,' Bharat stressed, 'act either within two hours or a maximum of four hours.' He put his hand on his heart. 'I can vouch that he was administered the poison two or three hours before the death.'

Godbole had now got the answer he wanted. He called Ramu, 'Your master needs rest, take care of him.'

'Come again,' Bharat said.

'I will,' Godbole promised.

Chapter 17

Vijay and Padmini were sitting very close to the kitchen of a popular restaurant, a price they had to pay for arriving late. Padmini heard the rhythmic slice of knife on board. Onions were being chopped. She tapped her feet to the beat of an old film song that was playing in the background. A waiter wiped their table with a sponge.

Padmini recounted her psychic experience with Vasudha and waited for Vijay's response.

The one thing that Vijay did not do was to scoff at her intuition. Vijay heard attentively every word of her experience and processed the information in his own way.

'So, Vasudha,' Vijay surmised, 'is not at all aggrieved at the loss of her husband?'

'Not at all.' She coughed. 'In fact, her older photographs do not even show a wedding ring or chain. She knocked off his family name from her name after using it for barely six months. If my intuition is anything to go by, then we needn't go further.'

The strong smell of garlic floated in the air. The exhaust was ineffective, and the smell grew stronger.

'Intuition has its place,' Vijay explained, 'but in a murder, motive and evidence form the fulcrum.'

Padmini said, 'She suspected and accused her husband of infidelity.'

'Not strong enough,' Vijay dismissed. 'Anyway, she had learnt to cope with it, and how do you connect that to the Mashelkar case?'

Padmini didn't answer that. She sat with her cheeks buried in her hands. 'What is the latest on Mahapatra?'

Vijay's eyes darted around the hall. He was checking that nobody was even remotely in the overhearing range. He spoke in a low tone designed to keep it confidential. 'Godbole made a complete dossier of his whereabouts. He has been abroad for the last two months, but Godbole reckons that it is a created alibi.'

'Token 107,' a frantic voice called out. The number '107' flashed on a moving red display. Padmini went to the counter and lifted a tray. She elbowed a glass door on her way back to the table.

'That also means,' Vijay wailed, 'that I am stuck in my present posting. Godbole will be the toast of the town.'

'Not so fast.' Padmini clutched his arm. 'He could be totally wrong. He just has had an initial hypothesis, nothing concrete.'

Vijay did not respond.

Neither spoke for the next ten minutes. They ate their dinner in silence. Vijay paid with his credit card.

'Look!' Padmini pointed skywards. 'The perfect crescent of the moon.'

'I like it when it is round and full.'

'How romantic.'

Vijay squeezed her neck.

She faked pain and laughed. A few metres ahead, two mongrels fought bitterly over a bone. Padmini stood and watched the dogfight intently. 'We should,' she gushed, 'imbibe their fighting spirit. Cops are losing it too quickly.'

He put an arm around her shoulder.

She wrapped her arm around his waist. They both looked at each other and smiled.

Vijay asked, 'Why did you get such a violent sensation this time round?'

Padmini tightened her arms around his waistline. She liked sliding her fingers over his rocky abdominal muscles. 'I have seen people with shades of evil, but this one was diabolical: not a single good cell in her body. If you ask me for a rational explanation, I have none; it's just a strong intuition.'

'I will,' Vijay offered, 'get Dalvi to get a lowdown on Vasudha.'

Padmini's face glowed. 'I wouldn't be surprised if she had a hand in the murder of Mashelkar, but again I can't back my gut feeling with logic.'

Vijay propped his shoulder against her car. 'We will need evidence.'

Padmini boxed his ears playfully. 'That is a cop's job.'

Vijay smiled and walked towards his car.

Padmini kept staring at his back. With each passing minute, he had become an obsession. She had started avoiding her friends, parties and shopping binges. Even if she attended them, she missed Vijay. He was a shadow in the dark, but in her mind, he shone brighter than the sun. Any doubts she may have had on whether this was her man, had vaporized by now.

Chapter 18

Police Commissioner Patel growled at Godbole, 'Read!'
They were all clippings from popular newspapers.

Police, brawn, no match to criminal brains

Nagpur police incapable of spotting an elephant in a dog show

Mashelkar murdered right under police's nose

Inept police makes Nagpur insecure

Godbole mumbled as he read the headlines. 'Every newspaper has hauled the force over the coals.'

'What else do you expect?' Patel bellowed. 'If we fail to avert an important murder despite a tip-off! Darned, all the media men knew that we had a tip-off.'

Godbole felt like he was in a bullring, where Patel was charging like a bull. Much against his counsel, Rathore had arrested two maids and an aged manservant working in the Mashelkar house. The manservant had been dragged along the pavement long enough for cameras to click and splash it round. The maids had been picked up by a team that did not include a woman officer, a serious violation. Human rights activists were having a field day attacking police brutality.

Patel's table had the cover page of *Nagpur Midday*. Godbole glanced through the article, most of which had been underlined by Patel.

> A slick murderer is on the prowl. Samir Mashelkar, the pride of Nagpur and India, paid with his life. Bharat Rao, the other prize winner, nearly did. The incident that shook the country, possibly the world, is a fortnight old, but the police have no clue. How many more will he kill? Can

Bharat Rao escape again?

People want assurance, but the police have no answers. Instead, they pick up innocent servants, lock them up, subject them to third-degree tortures and extract confessions. The arrested people, two women and a man, were not produced before a magistrate, nor were they given a chance to call for a lawyer, and this constitutes a gross violation of human rights and is not in accordance with Criminal Procedure Code. Can a police that concentrates on extra-legal quick fixes be trusted? Shouldn't the errant cops be booked?

Godbole could feel the rage fuelled by the report in *Nagpur Midday* in Commissioner Patel's mind. He sat with his head bowed down in shame.

'I could wring Rathore's neck with these arms,' Patel said, almost convulsively.

'Sir, Rathore had made elaborate arrangements.'

'What was that fool planning?' Patel howled. 'Storming a fort?' He banged his fist on the table. 'I want you to suspend that idiot straightaway.'

'Sir,' Godbole registered a feeble protest, 'he is a dynamic young officer who may, in his enthusiasm, step over the line.'

'What rubbish! He hasn't followed even basic practices.' The landline rang. Patel ignored it. 'The blasted phone,' he shouted, 'hasn't stopped ringing. Pressmen, human rights activists, nosy television anchors haven't given me a minute's peace. I want,' he repeated, 'Rathore suspended forthwith and Vijay to be reinstated in the crime branch.'

'Sir, sir,' Godbole pleaded, 'I hold no brief for Rathore, but Vijay's return so quickly will give him a larger-than-life image, and my own authority will be totally eroded.'

Commissioner Patel considered for a moment. 'Nor do I want anyone to think that Nagpur Police is a one-man army, but at the same time, you guys do not look capable of locating an elephant in a dog show.'

'Let me,' Godbole pleaded, 'update you on the considerable ground that I have covered.'

Patel seemed satisfied with Godbole's take on the murder. 'Okay, you have your way on the Vijay issue, but Rathore is being suspended right away.'

Chapter 19

At home, Vijay checked his personal mail. Birender had sent an interesting message.

A spa in Israel had put a unique spin on the standard massage procedure. Instead of soothing music or scented candles, snakes would be slithering up and down the body. The owner claimed that the calming effect could not be exaggerated. He also planned to use defanged venomous snakes for greater impact soon.

Vijay smiled reading the message. Birender had an eye for the unusual. He logged out of his personal e-mail and checked his official one: three routine messages, none worth a second look. A new message had landed. He clicked it mechanically. It had an attachment, but no subject, no body. He clicked open the attachment. It was a list of men who were charged with dowry harassment. The name Umakant Sharma was highlighted. A scanned photograph had also been appended. It was Ummaid!

Vijay picked up his mobile and rang Ustad, the massage parlour owner. 'I want both you and Ummaid in my office at 11:00 a.m. sharp,' he ordered.

'But—'

'No ifs, ands, or buts! 11:00 a.m. sharp at my office, you and Ummaid.'

※

Vijay stood under the shower for a long time, allowing the lukewarm water to trampoline over his hair, shoulders, chest and back. He felt fresh and optimistic. Something would give today.

A quick breakfast and he was at the office at nine. Two more hours to wait before Ummaid came. In his mind, he ran through the questions he would ask. He fidgeted nervously and browsed the internet, but he could not really concentrate. A few files for sanctions of bills for expenses were signed without any scrutiny. He picked up the latest edition of the *Police Journal*. He flipped through the pages, hardly reading a word. He slammed it shut. At quarter to eleven, a constable informed him that the two men had arrived.

Vijay said excitedly, 'Usher them in.' His excitement and anticipation reached a crescendo as soon as he saw the man accompanying Ustad. He was a replica of the scanned photograph sent to his mail.

'Sir,' he said feebly, 'my wife had an affair with her boss and then to intimidate me, she filed a false dowry case. Sir, I had to hide somewhere before I could manage an anticipatory bail.'

Vijay placed Anirudh's photo on the table and looked threateningly at Ummaid. 'What were you doing with him?'

'Sir'—Ummaid trembled—'I do not know this man, but a lawyer friend resembling him arranged my bail.'

Vijay looked searchingly. 'Call him right now.'

'Sir,' Ummaid said brightly, 'he is registered with the Bar Council. His registration number is 61452.'

Vijay clicked open the Nagpur Bar Council website and scrolled the cursor to the menu option Registered Members. A double click later, an option to key in the registration number blinked on the screen. Vijay punched 61452 and a man's face popped up. He resembled Anirudh at first glance, but a closer scrutiny would reveal the differences. The therapists had gotten only a glimpse of this lawyer, and they could not be faulted for mistaking him for Anirudh. So Ummaid was a false lead. Vijay sat with his head buried in his hands.

'Sir,' Ummaid offered, 'I have all the documents.'

Vijay had lost all interest. He was hardly listening. 'It is okay, you may go. All the best.'

The two men looked at each other, confused.

'Please, go,' Vijay repeated.

Vijay was gutted. He had to start afresh. He had been cocksure that Ummaid was his man. It was now established that his hypothesis was off the mark.

'It is back to square one,' he wrote in his diary.

The day passed uneventfully for him.

Chapter 20

At Vijay's behest, Karun had been assigned a single-occupancy special cell in the first-time offender section. He had been provided with a mattress, pillow and blanket. The lice-infested blanket troubled him initially, but soon he got used to it. The sanitary facilities were what he detested most. Toilets had to be shared and water was scarce. Fellow inmates were mostly pavement dwellers who had spent their lives defecating on the streets. Karun could not eat after a visit to the toilet.

Life otherwise was slow. A very good yoga teacher visited every morning. Karun attended the sessions regularly and practised the exercises diligently. This had instilled a new sense of inner peace in him. He was slowly regaining an urge to live. Initially, he had only wanted an early trial and death sentence. He had even planned to request the judge for immediate hanging. Now, he was longing for a delayed trial. He prayed for a miracle that could save him.

The yoga guru had taught him to relax and visualize future scenarios. The yoga guru asserted that if done diligently and faithfully, these visualizations could become reality. Karun started the process. He took deep breaths. He counted backwards—10, 9, 8, and so on, up to 1. He started relaxing every part of his body, toe upwards. He imagined the stress leaving his body in the form of black smoke. He had reached the lower abdomen in his relaxation routine when a sentry tugged him on the shoulder, 'The superintendent himself has come.'

Karun got up, smoothened the crease on his clothes, and stood up tall. The sentry led him respectfully along the narrow corridor into a part of the prison that he had not seen before. The lights were brighter, and Karun found his eyes struggling to adjust.

He eventually ended up in what looked like a living room in an upper-middle-class home.

'Please sit here.' A guard pointed to a sofa. 'Sir will soon be with you.'

Another guard came with the prison medical officer. 'Follow me,' the new guard ordered, in a baritone voice.

Karun was led into a small cubicle.

'Take off your clothes.'

Karun was aghast.

The doctor laughed. 'It is just to ensure that you do not have any secret weapon.'

Karun was relieved. He had heard that sodomy was rampant in certain wards of the prison. The doctor's kind words put his fears to rest. He complied. They gave him a quick pat down. He raised his arms and legs. His armpits and even his rectum were not spared. A guard declared that he had thoroughly checked the clothes.

'Okay, you can go. The superintendent awaits you,'

Another chuckled, 'With your clothes on,'

※

Vijay was apprehensive and jittery. In his brief career, studded with awards, he had arrested and killed many criminals, terrorists and Naxalites, but had never sought cooperation from a murderer. He walked tentatively towards Karun. He readied for a physical attack. *I will dodge, but not hurt him*, he told himself.

He stood gingerly in front of Karun. They were alone in the room. *He can*, Vijay speculated mentally, *make a grab for my legs*.

Expectedly, Karun aimed at Vijay's feet, but to Vijay's surprise, he just touched them respectfully. There was no aggression in the act; it was plain reverence.

Tears blotched Karun's face. 'You are a great soul who never shirks his duty.'

Vijay smiled wryly and asked, 'Do you not want to kill the man who has ruined your life?'

Karun brushed away a tear that had leaked. 'I am doomed. Even a noble soul such as you thinks so lowly of me.'

Vijay bent forward and gave him a comforting hug. He helped him sit on the sofa and ordered tea.

Karun sobbed for a few minutes more, sipped tea and occasionally looked towards the ceiling. He regained his composure. 'I have great regard for people like you, who lay their lives for duty.'

'You too did,' Vijay reciprocated, 'for what you thought was your duty.'

The compliment brought lot of cheer to Karun. He blushed. His voice choked. 'Thank you.'

'I know,' Vijay said sympathetically, 'that prison life is not a pleasant one, but I will make it as comfortable as possible. I will pass instructions to the jailer. You can call me on my mobile.'

'Thank you, Sir.' There was gratitude in the voice. 'The sanitation bugs. I could'—he halted—'do with a cleaner toilet, and if I may ask, access to the prison library.'

Vijay heard him attentively. He knew that this was no more his case and the jailer could very easily refuse the request, but he knew that he had earned a lot of goodwill. As expected, the jailer was eager to comply with Vijay's requests regarding Karun's stay in the jail.

Vijay smiled at Karun. 'Who is your defence lawyer?'

'Ajith Menon,' he replied flatly, 'had approached me, but I refused.'

'Why?'

'Mine is a hopeless case.' The sadness glinted in his eyes. 'At least a hundred people, including you, witnessed the murder.'

'You did not seem to be eager to live when we met last time,' Vijay recollected.

Karun nodded in assent. 'The yoga guru and prison life have opened my eyes. The yoga guru instilled inner peace in me and taught me forgiveness and compassion. In prison, I see that people do not want to leave, as they are guaranteed meals and shelter. What poverty exists in our country!'

Vijay was impressed. Karun sounded sincere and convincing.

'Sir,' he pleaded softly, 'conditions are appalling in certain wards. Three hundred people are lodged where only fifty people can stay. Forced sex is rampant, as is also the threat of AIDS and other communicable diseases. Please do something.'

Vijay placed a comforting hand on Karun's shoulder. He

looked directly into his eyes and smiled. 'What you say,' he said softly, 'is true, but prison reform is a monumental task, and I am too small a fry.'

Silence prevailed. Vijay clicked his fingers. 'I do not want to raise false hopes, but all is not lost for you.'

Karun leapt out of the sofa and threw his arms around Vijay's shoulders. He grinned sheepishly. 'Sorry, for a dying man, such words are too much.'

'You cooperate with me,' Vijay said, tapping his pen on the table, 'and I will explain to Ajith Menon. I am reasonably certain that you will get away with a light sentence.'

'Really?'

'*Provided*,' Vijay stressed the word, 'you cooperate with me and also appoint Ajith.'

Karun nodded excitedly.

'Tell me, Karun'—Vijay's tone was conversational—'why did you take this extreme step of murder?'

'In hindsight, I regret it. We lost our parents early.' Tears welled up in Karun's eyes as memories of his sister resurfaced. 'And my sister was my most precious possession. She was pretty and good in studies. She had secured a decent job in Safer Insurance. I was thinking of her marriage when...' Karun broke down.

Vijay allowed him to calm down on his own.

'Sorry, I got emotional,' Karun said.

'Never mind.' Vijay smiled. 'Tears wash away our pent-up stress.'

The sentry came with another round of tea. Both Vijay and Karun gulped it down.

'I got a mail from her wherein she said that she had been raped and that she was ending her life.'

Vijay sucked in a lungful of air. 'How did she die?'

Karun's breathing became rapid and shallow. He struggled to stand.

Vijay supported his shoulder.

'I am okay.' Karun resettled himself on the chair. 'She used to ride a Scooty. She had a head-on collision with a truck. Post-mortem found alcohol in her body.' Karun broke down again.

'Could it be,' Vijay suggested, 'that your sister began to like the modern lifestyle?'

'Never!' He gritted his teeth fiercely. 'My Kumudini had imbibed all the morals and values of our parents.'

Vijay did not dwell further on the topic. 'Did you register a case?'

'Yes, with Wardhaman Nagar Thana, but no progress.'

'I will personally follow up that case,' Vijay promised.

'I tried to somehow forget the incident and move on.'

Vijay leaned forward in anticipation. 'Then what happened?'

'I came to know the identity of the rapist. That enraged me. I wanted to kill him, but I have never hurt anyone in my life.'

'How,' Vijay asked, 'did you get to know the identity of the rapist?'

Karun exhaled noisily. 'I received a photograph of my sister being raped, in an envelope. The name and address of the rapist were mentioned.'

'Who sent it?'

'I do not know. However, that man would often call me on my mobile and inform me about the whereabouts of the rapist.'

Vijay raised his arm to stop Karun from proceeding further. 'Where is your mobile?'

'With the warden.'

Vijay ordered for the mobile to be brought. Karun showed him the call log. A call had come just two hours before the incident, probably when Anirudh was in the post office.

'He would even tell me that Anirudh was alone in his home and that the time was ripe for the strike.'

Vijay's concentration flagged. He requested Karun to repeat what he said, which he did. 'Why did you not strike when things favoured you?'

'I am not a killer'—remorse filled his voice—'although I killed.'

'Do not let that bother you.'

Karun cleared his throat and spoke. 'I could not bring myself to kill. He chided me. He said I was a lady-boy, unfit to be a brother or even a man.'

'I can understand how you felt.'

'He once,' Karun continued, 'told me that Anirudh was a heavy diabetic who needed three injections a day, and he would be sending Anirudh to Parul Medicos in half an hour.'

'That pharmacy that opens to Ambajari Garden?'

'Exactly. It is a deserted place at times.'

'Did he ever tell you where his clinic was?'

Karun shook his head to indicate a negative reply. 'On the ill-fated day,' he revealed, 'that man threatened that this was my last chance to avenge my sister's insult. He said he would kill him otherwise.'

'Kill him himself?' a surprised Vijay echoed.

'Yes, that galvanized me. I was petrified that my sister's soul would never rest in peace. So I went and waited for the rapist to arrive.'

'Did you tell him that you were ready this time?'

'He used to ring from a public booth. I could never call him.'

'You have kept your word,' Vijay gratefully said. 'Now, I will keep mine.'

'Sir'—he clung to Vijay's elbow—'how can I possibly escape?'

'Firstly,' Vijay replied, exhaling deeply, 'you have helped the law in investigations. Also, yours is an attempted murder, not murder, because Anirudh was already dead when you shot him. He had been poisoned.'

Karun closed his eyes, folded his hands and prayed for a good five minutes.

The warden announced that a new cell with an attached toilet had been readied for Karun. He stood with a new set of mattress, pillow and blanket.

Vijay asked, 'Where is the photograph kept in your house?'

'On the second shelf of my PC table.'

'By the way, Karun,' Vijay said as he rose, 'you may soon be bailed out.'

'You know,' Karun said, smiling wryly, 'I have used that expression "bailed out" countless times, but never did I imagine that I would be using it literally.'

Vijay felt a lump in his throat. He just pressed Karun's hand, and for the second time, tears flowed down from Karun's eyes.

Chapter 21

Vijay adjusted the rear-view mirror before turning on the ignition.

Padmini asked, 'Where to?'

'Somewhere.' Vijay whistled. He drove past the well-known school Learners Paradise, which was celebrating its foundation day. The air was pulsating with the shrill shrieks of excited children. The decorative lighting had ratcheted up the atmosphere. The outdoor lights looked like a lighted palm tree but they were actually hollow, hard, coloured plastic stems with mini bulbs.

Vijay thrummed with excitement. 'Watch out for the fireworks. They are a joy to behold.'

With a fizzing sound, sprays of coloured sparks shot upwards in a fan pattern.

Vijay parked his car on the side and watched the display.

Another aerial spark flew, lighting up the sky. It exploded, and then the shell broke into large falling stars. Smoke spread.

Vijay drove on. He and Padmini barely exchanged words. The moon was full, round and luminous. He was on a joyride with a ravishing girl who had sluiced through his heart. The roads were now wider and bereft of potholes. Interspersed with well-maintained parks and avenues of trees were independent bungalows with large compounds.

There was no one at home. Her folks were also away; everything tailor-made for a romantic night. He looked at her from the corner of his eye. Her body was stiff, tense. She did not lock gazes with him. Most of the time, she lapped up the scenery; at other times, she talked on the mobile. Indecision at that end as well.

Vijay drove past the most exclusive club in town that housed a golf course. He stopped in front of a massive black gate. He alighted and pressed a red button on the wall. The gates parted. Vijay drove the car over and down an incline into an open garage. Padmini looked skywards on alighting from the car and then followed Vijay.

She stood at the foyer, surveying the house, especially the staircase leading to the bedrooms. Her hair, smooth and glistening, cascaded down her shoulders, her lustrous skin reflected in the black outfit that fit so well on her. She was irresistible, but the fear of losing it all kept Vijay's passion at bay. Vijay had never been so cavalier in his life. He was going wild, but this waywardness gave him a pleasure he had never imagined. He had to flee the scene. He went for a wash. He wore blue jeans and a black T-shirt, mirroring her outfit.

He had splashed cologne all over his body.

Padmini was leafing through a magazine. Carrying the periodical, she walked towards Vijay and sniffed. 'Nice fragrance.'

Vijay stepped closer to her. Curbing his 'basic instincts' required every ounce of his willpower. He managed it for now, but his tank was empty.

She moved a step closer and inhaled his perfume deeply, openly savouring every moment.

Vijay's defences crashed. He grabbed her breasts and kissed her, twice on her lips and once on the forehead.

Padmini seemed to have braced herself for a violent demonstration of passion. She cocked her head and smiled bewitchingly.

Suckered, Vijay picked her up in his arms, ran up the stairs, and deposited her on the bed. He felt stupid, nearly guilty.

She took his hand gently and kissed him softly. Then, she turned off the lights.

※

Padmini wasn't sure what woke her up, probably a telephone ring in her dream. She sat up, glassy-eyed. She felt for the bedside lamp. It wasn't there. The bedroom was strange, surely not hers.

She groped around. Then it all came back, like a cascade on her blank brain. She had spent the night with Vijay. She ran her fingers over her body. She was nude.

A barrage of questions overwhelmed her. What would happen if Vijay's mother stood at the bedroom door? How could she face her? How would she face her own parents?

Vijay was snoring, without a care in the world, one leg diagonal and the other bent at the knee. She remembered that she had been awake when the clock struck two. Gradually, her eyes had adjusted to the dark. It was a quarter to five.

Despite feeling drowsy, her brain began to tick in the thinking mode. It flashed in her still-sleepy mind that physical activity would get her blood circulation flowing and kick her out of the dreamy state.

She gently folded the bed sheets. Then she went to the bathroom and rinsed her mouth, washed her face and brushed her hair. She was back to her senses. No more did she feel guilty. She would tell Vijay's mother and the world that she had done no wrong. She loved Vijay and he loved her equally and dearly. Still, it would help if she could make an uncomplicated exit.

She switched on the lights of the bedroom and quickly slipped into her jeans and T-shirt. Vijay tossed over in the bed, still sleeping. Padmini loved him even more. She packed her things into her purse and buckled her watch. She made a quick search.

Satisfied that no trace of her visit remained in the room, she shook Vijay. 'It is five.' Vijay sounded drugged with sleep. She poked his nose with an earbud.

Startled, he got up.

Padmini, half spoke, half yawned, 'I have to scoot before anyone sees me.'

Vijay pulled her back to the bed. 'We have not sinned. I am ready to own you anywhere, anytime.'

She planted a kiss on his cheeks. 'Still, I better leave.'

Vijay wrapped a towel around his waist and led her to the back door. He opened the door slightly and peeped. 'The coast is clear.'

※

Padmini hired an autorickshaw. She messaged Vijay. Although she had gone past a line in the sand, guilt did not prick her heart, nor did regret rear its head. The only regret was the few minutes of irrational fear, immediately after waking up.

She had crossed the border of no return and Vijay came along on his own. Had Vijay sown the smallest seed of doubt in her mind, she would have withdrawn. She still felt that a trophy man like Vijay deserved a much better girl, but she had not forced herself on him.

It was love, pure love, not lust. She was proud of herself and of Vijay.

Chapter 22

Godbole got down from his car and walked angrily into the forensic laboratory. Seeing Dr Gaikwad, he passed an acid remark, 'So, you are back.'

Dr Gaikwad took no notice and continued browsing the internet.

Godbole stood close to Dr Gaikwad. 'I am talking to you.'

Dr Gaikwad turned around. 'What do you want?' he asked gruffly.

'I need,' Godbole said, in a half-pleading, half-demanding voice, 'some help on the Mashelkar poisoning case.'

'I think,' Dr Gaikwad reflected, 'you have been briefed that we suspect the death was due to an allergic reaction. No poisonous substance was found anywhere. The potion was a mixture of proteins and enzymes.'

'So, it is not murder.' Godbole sounded exasperated.

Dr Gaikwad fingered a pendant that he was wearing. 'Looks that way to me.'

'What about the arsenic theory floated by Bharat Rao?' Godbole prodded hopefully.

Dr Gaikwad smiled patiently. He beckoned Godbole to follow him and took him into a room that had chemicals linked up in bottles with labels. He shouted orders to a young male chemical analyst.

Dr Gaikwad held a beaker in his hand. 'This is called the Reinsch test.' Dr Gaikwad opened a case that had the label 'Mashelkar Stomach'. Dr Gaikwad turned to Godbole. 'I am taking a twenty-gram sample of the stomach contents of Mashelkar.'

His assistant put that in a fifty-millilitre Erlenmeyer flask and added four millilitres of concentrated hydrochloric acid.

'Add ten millilitres of water,' Dr Gaikwad advised. The male underling did so.

A young lady, who reminded Godbole of his neighbour's daughter, held a twenty-gauge copper wire and prepared a spiral by winding it closely over a piece of glass rod.

She announced, 'I have done it ten times.'

The copper spiral was then washed with alcohol and ether. The lady immersed the spiral copper strip into the flask and her male partner placed it over an electric burner and lit the fire.

Dr Gaikwad turned to Godbole. 'This solution will be boiled for an hour. Then the copper strip will be removed and washed. The depositions on the strip will be checked. A dark discolouration indicates arsenic.'

An hour later, the procedure was completed.

'There you are,' Dr Gaikwad held the copper strip against the light and showed it to Godbole.

Distress tightened Godbole's features. His voice sounded dejected. 'I know that there won't be any arsenic because there is no dark discolouration on the strip.' He left, walking heavily.

Godbole stood, smoking one cigarette after the other, and watched the rings of smoke rise in the air. The day had promised much but fulfilled little. He was weary, both in the bone and in the brain.

The next day held a frightening prospect for him. He would have to concede that, for all his efforts, he had nothing to show. Commissioner Patel, he imagined, would look through his half-moon glasses and get Vijay back. What a calamity it would be to lose to a man younger by twenty years.

Godbole lifted his right foot, threw the butt under his foot and stomped on it three times. He walked a few paces and stood right opposite the Nasheela Bar. He knew that people wouldn't recognize him there. He paid his driver a hundred bucks and told him to come to the bar exactly two hours later.

Godbole tiptoed into the bar, hoping not to be recognized. Fortunately, no one did. He sat in a corner and drowned his sorrow in whiskey.

Chapter 23

For Vijay, life had never been punctuated with so many shades. The transfer from the crime branch to traffic in an unceremonious manner was a double whammy. First, it was an unjust insult; second, he could not concentrate on the murder cases.

Then, he thought of the biggest prize the events had brought about—Padmini. Life would never be the same again. The setbacks on the career front were nothing compared to the reward. He had no doubt that he did not deserve the stepmotherly treatment that his department meted out to him. On the other hand, a dream girl like Padmini had walked into his life. Vijay slipped into sleep in an extremely pleasurable state.

※

Vijay felt his mother's hand on his cheek, gentle to begin with, but gaining steadily in roughness. Soon, he felt her shaking him violently. 'Get up, son, get up! There is an urgent call for you.'

He half opened his eyes. It wasn't a dream.

Seeing his half-open eyes, she shouted in his ear, 'The commissioner called you twice.'

Vijay growled from under the bed sheet. 'Why at three in the morning?'

She replied frantically, 'Ask him. It is five, not three.'

His father too had come in. He put on the lights and turned on the music system at full blast. Vijay sat up. His father quickly turned off the music.

'That was fast,' Vijay commented. The landline rang again, the sound resonating in the silence of the hour. Vijay ran down the stairs.

'Vijay,' Commissioner Patel spoke in an apologetic but urgent voice, 'be at my office before six.'

'Sure, Sir.' He could not stifle a huge yawn. 'Sorry.' He struggled to stifle another yawn.

'Never mind,' Patel grunted, 'but I must tell you that the Union home minister and the chief minister of Maharashtra will be having a video conference with us.'

'Us?' Vijay echoed.

'You, me and Godbole,' he clarified. 'Another murder took place yesterday in Nagpur.'

'Who, Sir?'

'It was David,' Patel said, taking a deep breath. 'The junior scientist of Mashelkar and Bharat Rao.'

'Oh God!' Vijay exclaimed. 'The entire team is being wiped out.'

'Okay, come over.'

Vijay heard the click of the disconnection. He placed the receiver on the cradle. His mother had already prepared filter coffee. He gave her a peck. He brushed his teeth, shaved, shampooed and blow-dried his hair in quick succession. He chose an officious-looking black suit and a red tie, and brushed his hair carefully. He took the car keys and ran down the stairs.

Suddenly, he turned and ran back. He panted. 'Mom, come to Dad's room.'

His mother obeyed unquestioningly. He bowed before his parents. They blessed him.

'Now that I have my parents' blessings, I am sure of success,' he pronounced.

Vijay drove past joggers wearing tracksuits, walkers with pet dogs on leashes, milkmen, and newspaper vendors on cycles, already on their daily routine. Vijay's heart went out to a few school children who stood waiting for the bus.

It took Vijay less than fifteen minutes to traverse ten kilometres. Godbole's car was parked between the commissioner's and Dr Gaikwad's Honda City. Two motorbikes stood towards the far end. Vijay guessed that the video-conferencing technicians had also been summoned. He entered a room.

Dr Gaikwad acknowledged Vijay's entry with a wink. Godbole had his head buried in his hands. For all the enmity that existed between the two, Vijay felt sorry for him.

'Got a jolly pasting from the chief.' Dr Gaikwad whispered and chuckled.

The commissioner's face wore a scowl that Vijay thought could be the 'frown of the year.' Hot cardamom tea was served. Godbole declined it.

'Vijay'—Patel swivelled towards him—'you have to take charge of the Mashelkar and David homicide cases. I am…' He stopped. 'I am recommending you to the home minister and chief minister.'

'No problem, Sir.' Vijay sounded bright and energetic.

'By the way—,' Dr Gaikwad started, but immediately stopped as the video screen showed the home minister of India.

The home minister was informally attired in an open-collared light blue shirt and spotless white dhoti. The chief minister of Maharashtra, wearing a formal suit, was also hooked in from Mumbai.

The home minister's wide grin eased nerves. He apologized for the early morning conference and attributed his busy schedule for the next three days as the reason for calling them at this 'unearthly hour,' as he put it.

'Despite the unflattering media coverage in recent times I am proud,' he said, placing his hand on his heart, 'of the police force, but you need to do something to turn this tide of adverse publicity.'

Vijay surmised that he was a left-hander because he placed his left palm over his heart.

'The two murders,' he said, stressing every word, 'have shaken the conscience of the nation. Who could have killed these jewels? Only a traitor!' His voice boomed towards the end.

He sipped water. 'Question marks hang over our efficiency and commitment. We have,' he said, looking everyone in the eye, 'surmounted bigger challenges in the past, but in a week's time from now, the parliament's winter session is underway.' He smiled, 'It seems I will be another murder victim.'

The chief minister cleared his throat. 'I assure you, Sir—that will not happen.'

The home minister looked enquiringly; first at the chief

minister and then at Police Commissioner Patel.

Overwhelmed by the occasion, Patel fumbled. 'We will surely catch the murderers, Sir.'

'Remember, you have only one week.' The home minister signed off after wishing them good luck.

It was now the chief minister's turn to hold forth. 'So far, things have been sloppy.'

He pointed his index finger at Patel. 'I want results.' The voice was demanding.

'I am putting my best officer on the job, Sir.' Patel pushed Vijay in front.

The chief minister smiled. 'Isn't he too young?'

'Sir,' Patel replied, 'He was honoured with the bravery award last year.'

'Good.' He smiled appreciatively. 'Vijay, what do you want from me?'

'A free hand and full support, Sir.'

The chief minister seemed to like the reply. 'I will grant you more.' He smiled. 'You can tap any telephone, go anywhere, spend any amount, interrogate anyone, and of course, you report to me directly.' The chief minister coughed twice. Then he said, 'I hope Patel has no objection.'

Patel stood ramrod straight and said, 'Absolutely, Sir.'

The chief minister asked, smiling, 'What does that mean?'

'No objection, Sir.'

'Good.'

'One more request, Sir,' Vijay said.

The chief minister's eyes widened.

'Sir,' Vijay began in a deferential tone, 'I might sound silly, but we need out-of-the-box solutions.'

'Don't worry, go ahead,' the chief minister said in a cheerful voice.

'I want to include a crime reporter in this team and...' Vijay hesitated.

'Go on,' the chief minister prodded.

'She should be given the powers of a police officer till the end of the case.'

'Are you sure this girl will add value?'

'She has loads of imagination, plenty of pluck and a never-say-die spirit. People talk more willingly to her. In fact, she might turn out to be our trump card.'

The chief minister pondered.

Vijay's heart skipped a beat. Had he overreached? The silence was killing him. He looked around. Patel was emotionless. Godbole was plainly disinterested, and Dr Gaikwad was holding back a mischievous smile.

'I am taking a huge risk, maybe such decisions have very few precedents,' the chief minister drawled. 'But I do not want to deprive you of any resources.'

Vijay heaved a sigh of relief.

'Okay, guys,' the chief minister signed off pleasantly.' You have only a week. Your time starts now!'

Patel affected a smart salute. Godbole jerked himself into the same pose. Vijay followed his seniors.

'Yes, Sir,' they said in a chorus.

It was Patel's moment in the sun. 'Godbole, do not sulk, and hand over the transcripts of all your interviews to Vijay, straightaway.'

Godbole looked ready to burst into tears. He squeaked, 'I will get my diary, my notes and give them to Vijay.' He slunk away quietly. Vijay felt even sorrier for him.

'Hot cardamom tea and biscuits are on their way,' a peon announced, with a broad smile.

A boy wearing a worn-out denim shirt and torn T-shirt

came in with a kettle. He had three very small plastic cups, into which he poured tea. The video technicians left immediately after Godbole. That left a constable, a peon and the three of them. The tea was consumed, and a second round followed. It was refreshing. Salt cookies were placed on a tray.

'I do not,' Patel said, as he munched on a biscuit, 'like the idea of involving that crime reporter.'

'Why, Sir?'

'Call me sexist, call me old-fashioned,' he said, leaning back on his chair, 'but women at work are a serious distraction.' He paused for effect. 'You will be flirting more, working less.'

Vijay resisted the urge to retort. He waited for his nerves to calm. Then he said slowly. 'Sir, I assure you that both Padmini and I are thorough professionals. I cannot gamble away my career for a fling. Have faith in me, Sir.'

Patel laughed. 'I have been your age and I know what damage pretty women can do.'

'No, Sir,' Vijay said firmly. 'My focus will not waver.'

Patel sat in his chair and stretched his legs. 'Of what use would a reporter be to us? We are a crack police unit; we do not need nosy reporters. Rather, I would want to avoid them like plague.'

Vijay flicked a glance at Dr Gaikwad over Patel's shoulders.

'Patel,' Dr Gaikwad said slowly, 'Why are you disobeying the home minister?'

Rattled by the counterarguments, Patel gave the matter an alarmist twist. 'This will set a bad precedent. Everyone will make different demands. Discipline will go haywire.'

'Sir,' Vijay replied evenly, 'this is a crisis. Desperate situations call for desperate measures.'

Patel was annoyed. He walked in a semicircle, hands in his pockets and head down. Vijay knew that Patel would now concede.

Patel took off his half-moon glasses. 'All right, if you desire.' He looked at Dr Gaikwad. 'You will also be full-time with us, no lectureship for this week.'

Dr Gaikwad shot back, 'I know my responsibilities.'

Vijay calmed him with a restraining raise of his palm.

Looking at Vijay, Patel said, 'The official letters for you and that reporter…'

'Padmini.'

'Yes, they will be ready by noon. Just update me in the evening.'

'Sure, Sir.'

'All the best. May God bless you!'

Patel was seen off by Vijay and the constable. Once Patel left, Vijay asked Dr Gaikwad, 'What happened before I came?'

Dr Gaikwad was enjoying himself. 'Godbole was given a hiding. Patel said that even a high-school kid could have deduced that David would be the next target.'

'No argument on that,' Vijay concurred.

'Godbole was an asshole,' Dr Gaikwad remarked. 'Anyone could see that David was a logical end to Anirudh, Mashelkar and Bharat Rao.'

'To be fair to him,' Vijay said, 'he thought that Anirudh had been shot by Karun.'

'My left foot,' Dr Gaikwad cried. 'I had sent the second forensic report to his office. He never cared to read it.'

'You know, Doc,' Vijay confessed, 'I felt bad for Godbole today.'

'This is a man's world. Grow up.'

'Soft skills are the cutting edge for mankind.'

'You youngsters exasperate me.'

Vijay smiled. The two men took leave of each other.

Chapter 24

Day 1

Vijay's mother answered his doorbell. He gave her a quick hug. 'I will take a quick nap.'

He ran up the stairs to his bedroom, with his shoes on. He realized this only when he reached his bedroom. He changed into shorts and a T-shirt and kicked off his shoes. A manservant placed them in the shoe rack.

Vijay got up after an hour. He was refreshed. He had a quick shower and gobbled up the idlis that had been laid on the breakfast table.

'Mom, I will be coming and going at odd hours,' he informed her, 'so do not wait for me or involve me in your plans.'

'You look excited.' Maternal affection overflowed. 'May success be yours.'

Vijay took care to remove the front door key from the key stand and put it in his trouser pocket. He went back to his bedroom and rang Padmini. 'Come to my office.'

૱

Padmini looked a little different when she brushed back her hair. It made her look older. He updated her on the morning's events.

She listened with excitement written all over her face. She clasped his hands tightly.

'I will not let you down.'

'Let us,' Vijay suggested, 'visit Hotel Heaven, the site of David's murder and then chalk out an action plan.'

She nodded and got up. Both got into their respective cars. Padmini had reasoned that two vehicles would increase their mobility. Vijay had acquiesced, although he thought time could be better spent discussing the strategy. It was embarrassing as traffic lights did not work in two intersections. Traffic policemen were absent and it was all chaos. Pedestrians cursed the police; little did they know that the superintendent of traffic too sailed in their boat. He resolved to fix things, once this triple monkey was off his back.

A police car stood outside Hotel Heaven. The policeman thankfully was alert and active. He recognized Vijay and ran up to him with a pleasant smile.

'Sir, Dalvi Sahib with the manager and two constables are in room 701, the murder site.'

Vijay looked around. 'Tell Dalvi that I am here.'

Padmini inched closer to him. 'David was in the seventh—the top floor,' she observed, 'and it's quite possible for someone to enter from the top.'

'He would need a rope.'

Dalvi came out, bright and effervescent. 'Glad to have you back in the saddle.'

He bowed respectfully to Padmini. 'Welcome to the police force.'

'I hope,' she replied, 'I am worthy of it.'

Dalvi lead them into the lobby. 'Sir, this case is baffling.'

Vijay did not react.

Padmini scampered towards the lift. Vijay followed her. Dalvi told the liftman to take them to the seventh floor.

'We are in seventh heaven,' Vijay joked. No one smiled.

Room 701 was situated almost next to the lift; maybe ten feet or so in between.

A quick getaway is possible, Vijay thought.

It was a suite with a lobby. A fruit basket with a knife, a plate and a napkin were placed on the table. The lobby opened into the main suite. A heavy chair, with a back slanting at an obtuse angle, leaned against a double bed. The room was musty. It emitted a foul odour akin to rotten eggs.

Vijay's nose wrinkled at the unpleasant smell. Three deaths, a narrow escape for the fourth, clueless forensics and a deadline that demanded telescoping a year into a week—overwhelming odds, but with Padmini and Dalvi at his side, he stood an outside chance.

He frowned. Padmini held her nose.

The manager turned to Vijay. 'We have been ordered,' he explained, 'to keep everything as it is. So we have not touched anything.'

'That,' Dalvi said, pointing to a chair, 'is where David was found dead.'

'I suppose,' Padmini interjected acidly, 'the death was on account of poisoning, and we have no clue how the poison was administered.'

Dalvi laughed. 'Madam, that is how it is.'

'David,' Dalvi sneezed again and continued, 'checked into the hotel before the normal check-in time of noon. The room was ready and they allowed him.'

'Why are we all standing?'

Vijay sat on the bed. Padmini sat next to him. Dalvi continued to stand. Vijay signalled him to sit. A boy who sported a French beard brought two chairs. Dalvi and the manager sat on them.

'Where was I?' Dalvi asked.

'David checked in...'

'Yes, Sir. He then ordered orange juice after about five minutes. The orange juice was never consumed by David. He died two hours later—of poisoning.'

'Are the forensics examining the orange juice?' Vijay inquired.

'Yes, Sir.'

Padmini was deep in thought. Vijay walked round the suite. He knocked on the panels and floors. He asked Dalvi to get the walls, ceiling and floor checked for secret entrances.

'Who entered his room,' Vijay asked the manager, 'while he was here and who all did he meet?'

'Give me a minute,' the manager pleaded and whispered into his mobile.

Three boys clad in hotel uniform stood like students in a detention room. Vijay wondered whether they were underage. One of them had carried his luggage to the room. The second one had supplied water. The third had brought in the orange juice.

'Did you,' Vijay asked the boy who had brought orange juice, 'notice anything unusual?'

'No' was the instantaneous response. The boy had been asked this question several times. He continued. 'I just kept the tray with the juice on this table.'

'Then...?'

'I came back after two hours to clean the room. I rang the bell. Nobody opened. I turned the handle—it was not bolted—and then I saw him with his head on one side.'

'How did you know that he was dead?' Padmini asked.

'I saw my grandfather die two weeks back. Somehow, it looked similar.'

Vijay found the boy to be courageous. He had not been overwhelmed by the circumstances. He asked the boy, 'How many times did you ring the bell?'

'Many times,' he said. 'I have seen guests struggle to open our bolted doors from inside.'

Vijay went over to the exit door. The lever needed to be pulled to the right and pushed forward. The directions were illustrated in a pamphlet pinned to the door. Vijay reckoned it was a complicated process that many would not be able to fathom.

'When I saw him,' the boy continued, 'I lifted the lampshade and brought it near him and flashed the light in his eyes.'

Three voices spoke in a chorus. 'Why did you do that?'

Vijay looked around. The hotel manager and his two friends had a concerned look on their faces. Even Dalvi looked stunned. The boy was probably revealing this bit of information for the first time.

'Sir,' the boy who supplied water, fell at Vijay's feet. Vijay placed his hand on his chin affectionately and lifted him up. 'Sir, my friend did not kill anyone.'

Vijay laughed. 'I know that.' He smiled at the talkative boy.

Padmini asked, 'What is your name?'

'I am Sudarshan and this is my elder brother Ritesh.'

'Yes, Sudarshan,' Padmini gestured with her hand, asking him to continue.

'I had seen a doctor flash a torchlight into a man's eyes, and when the eyes did not blink, he declared him dead.'

Padmini tucked a strand of hair behind her ear. 'You wanted to confirm that he was dead?'

'Yes, because my next move would depend on that.'

'You over-smart bandicoot,' the manager screamed. 'You will get all of us into trouble.'

'No,' Padmini cut in sharply, 'he is your pride. He might lead us to the real culprit.'

'Relax,' Vijay advised. 'We know that no one from the hotel is involved.'

Relief was palpable on the manager's face.

Sudarshan's confidence grew. 'If he was alive, I would have called a doctor, but because he was dead, I told the manager to call the police.'

The manager glared at Sudarshan and muttered something under his breath. Vijay realized that he did not appreciate the room boy stealing his thunder. Vijay told the manager and the three boys that they were free to go. Vijay stretched his legs.

Someone knocked politely. Dalvi yelled, 'Come in.'

A senior constable came in with a packet. It was addressed to Vijay. Vijay opened it. It contained two more sealed envelopes, one addressed to Vijay and another to Padmini. Vijay handed over the envelopes to Dalvi and asked him to make five copies of the letters inside them. The constable also handed over a diary. He said softly, 'This is from Godbole, Sir.'

Vijay leafed through the diary. It contained transcripts of Godbole's interviews with Bharat Rao, Dr Tripathi and Dr Gaikwad. Godbole had also penned down his own take on the cases. Vijay handed it to Padmini.

Dalvi came back with the photocopies.

Padmini smiled reading it. 'I have the powers of a superintendent of police.'

Chapter 25

Vijay called Dr Gaikwad, who promised to meet them for lunch.

Padmini went through Godbole's transcripts. 'Godbole seems to believe that the poisoning in both cases was done elsewhere, and not at the murder site.'

'Any basis for his conclusions?' Vijay asked.

Padmini was still leafing through the diary. 'Not really, apart from elimination.'

'I suppose,' Vijay said, contemplatively, 'since there is no evidence to establish that the poisoning took place in the hotel or at Mashelkar's home, it has to be elsewhere.'

There was silence. Then Vijay took another round of the room. He checked the washroom, the balcony and the cupboards, almost aimlessly.

Meanwhile, Dalvi came with three other officers. 'Check every inch for secret passages,' he ordered.

The men went about it diligently. The beds were pulled apart and the floor under it scrutinized thoroughly.

Vijay said, 'I have full faith in you guys. Padmini and I will take a look at the terrace.'

The terrace had a rugged floor, with criss-crossing water pipes. All the tanks, but one, were Sintex and black in colour. Two were overflowing and one was leaking.

'What a waste of water.' Padmini did not conceal the disgust in her voice.

Vijay did not want a discussion on this subject and waste precious time. He stood bang above room 701 and peered downwards.

'Careful,' Padmini shouted.

Vijay turned around. He was amused to note creases of worry on her face. He fondled her nose. She pushed him away. He smiled.

'A sure-footed man,' Padmini suggested, 'could go to room 701, if he had a rope.'

Vijay shook his head. 'The only problem is that he would have had to come up here unseen, then secure the rope—'

'There are many places for that,' Padmini butted in.

'Agreed, but the balcony door needed to have been kept open for that.'

'Maybe it was.'

It was gusty at the top of the hotel. Padmini pulled back her hair, which had blown on to her face.

Vijay meditated on Padmini's logic. 'If he could enter the

room, then we also can. We will try re-enacting it.'

Having surveyed the terrace, Vijay walked down the stairs, followed by Padmini. Dalvi and his team were still knocking around looking for possible secret passages to the room.

Seeing Vijay, Dalvi said, 'Sir, no chance in the lobby, or the room. We will now check the balcony.'

'Not necessary,' Vijay advised.

Dalvi and his men looked relieved. Coffee was served and everyone consumed it silently.

'Call the manager,' Vijay said, 'and find out if they have television footage of movements in the hotel.'

The manager came with the tapes. Two men brought two chairs with slanting backs. The cassettes were placed on the glass table before Vijay. Vijay was about to ask them to leave when Dr Gaikwad arrived.

The manager recognized him. He held out his hand. 'Sir,' he addressed Vijay, Dalvi and Dr Gaikwad and marked Padmini for special attention, 'Madam, please have our buffet lunch. It is fabulous.'

The invitation was accepted.

Dr Gaikwad fiddled with a breadcrumb in his soup. 'There is no chance of poisoning at any other site. He was poisoned in this hotel only.'

'How was the poison administered?' Padmini sprinkled pepper in her soup. 'What poison was used?'

'Cyanide.' Dr Gaikwad answered the second question first. He looked heavenwards. 'It was fed to him. The poison was on his lips, tongue, throat—everywhere.'

Vijay was thinking hard. 'Cyanide imparts an almond-like smell, I guess.'

Dr Gaikwad laughed. 'That part is exaggerated in books. It is only a faint smell, if at all. I think twelve milligrams of cyanide was used. So, he would have died within two hours. Initial symptoms would have started within twenty minutes.'

'So, there could be no way for him to have been poisoned before entering the hotel,' Vijay surmised.

Dr Gaikwad lifted a spoon and wiped it with a napkin. 'The poison was not in the orange juice that he had ordered, nor on the glass.'

'What about the Mashelkar murder?' Padmini asked softly.

'No,' Dr Gaikwad replied contemptuously. 'Godbole put forward that arsenic poisoning theory. I did the chemical tests in front of him.'

Vijay sighed in despair. Then his face brightened. 'Could it be possible,' he asked, 'that something he ate in the hotel before the orange juice was poisoned?'

Dr Gaikwad waved his hand violently to negate the possibility. 'There was nothing in his stomach.'

'So, Doc, Godbole was right,' Dalvi butted in, 'you are of no help.'

Vijay put a pacifying left hand on Dr Gaikwad's shoulder and followed it with a glare at Dalvi. Padmini also put her index finger on her lips to signal Dalvi to keep his trap shut. She walked towards the buffet, plate in hand, followed by Dr Gaikwad.

'The detectives have to put forward a hypothesis.' He halted. 'The forensics can confirm or deny the hypothesis. We cannot do your work. This is the file we have built on the case.'

Vijay leafed through the file Dr Gaikwad had just handed him. He held up an enlarged image of David's face. 'The mouth seems unaligned with the rest of the face. It is too small.'

Dr Gaikwad snatched a cap from a puzzled constable and put it on. Then he took it off and bowed. 'Hats off.'

Vijay laughed. 'Cut the drama.'

'This is a medical condition, known as Meige's Syndrome. These patients have difficulty in eating and swallowing and suffer from spasms of the jaw. It is not life threatening.'

The buffet had a wide array of dishes. Everyone quietly satiated themselves gastronomically. Dr Gaikwad gave a loud burp. He rolled his hand over his abdomen to indicate his satisfaction. Vijay, too, complimented the food. Padmini smiled. Dalvi did not react.

Dr Gaikwad left. Dalvi waited in the lobby. Padmini followed Vijay into room 701.

'Same story,' Padmini remarked. 'No clues.'

They alighted from the lift and went to the room. One of the officers informed him, 'Sir, we have scanned every inch of the room. There is no secret passage.'

'I will call if you are required,' Vijay told them, 'and well done.'

The officers beamed and ran down the stairs.

Vijay sat down with a paper and pen. 'Let us now plan every moment.'

Padmini had another quick glance at the transcripts. 'Nobody has talked to the wife and daughter of David.'

'Where are they located?'

'At Wardha.'

Vijay looked at his watch. He said, 'Wardha is a good two hours' drive. So the exercise will take six hours.'

Padmini nodded.

Vijay walked round the room. Then he said, 'You go to Wardha. I will go through the footage.'

Padmini got up.

Vijay pulled her back. 'Go in a police car,' he suggested. 'You can keep thinking during the drive.

Once Padmini left, Vijay called Dalvi. 'Have you recorded the statements of everyone in the hotel?'

'Yes, Sir,' Dalvi replied. 'I even cross-checked the list of statements from his employee payroll.'

'Why did you need to do that?'

Dalvi scratched his head. Then he replied, 'In case someone was present on that day but isn't there now. I don't want anybody to be left out.'

Vijay nodded appreciatively. Then he inserted the tape into the video player and flicked it on.

David came in a taxi. A concierge picked up his suitcase. He went through the security checks and reported to the front desk. The receptionist smiled and requested him to sit, which he did. Some documents were brought to him, presumably the check-in formality papers. He was handed a card key and he boarded the lift and checked in. As reported, only Sudarshan with the orange juice and with water bottles visited him. Vijay would have loved a spy camera to have been placed inside the room, but he knew it was an infringement of privacy rights and not permissible by law.

Nothing was out of place. So, something happened in the room. Vijay went out and checked the cameras. Every camera was functional and it would be very difficult for anyone to have dodged the camera and entered through the front door. If that was the case, then the route from the terrace, using a rope via the balcony door, was the only option available.

Vijay had already visited the terrace along with Padmini. He took another look. Then he asked Dalvi to check whether anyone had been seen using this route. None had.

'Sir,' Dalvi said, 'it would be very difficult for anyone to secure the rope, climb down, poison him, climb back, untie the rope and scoot.'

'You need rest.' Vijay smiled appreciatively. 'You have worked your butt off. Just hand over the call logs.'

'Sure, Sir.'

David had received two calls from a PCO just minutes after he checked into the hotel. Vijay watched the tapes again. Indeed, David was wearing earphones and speaking on the mobile. It probably got disconnected in the elevator, so he was called again.

Vijay could see a distinct pattern. The murderer used poison in all three cases. He did not leave any trail, for he understood the power of electronic surveillance. PCOs were used. He was probably known to all the victims. The pattern was slightly different in the Mashelkar murder because the circumstances were different.

Vijay looked at the other numbers in the log. Once he traced them, he found no reason to suspect any of them.

He called the manager. 'Get me a strong rope.'

The manager shouted instructions. Then he said hesitatingly, 'May I ask the reason?'

Vijay laughed. 'I am going to Tarzan my way into this room from the terrace.'

A pensive expression overcame the manager's face. 'Sir, please allow Ramakant to do it. He is very good.'

Vijay relented.

Ramakant was a small, wiry lad with Jim Kelly-like hair.

Vijay said, 'When I say start, you begin. You have to enter room 701, touch the bed and come back.'

The lad smiled.

Vijay winked. He put his mobile on stop clock mode and said, 'Go!'

Ramakant tied the yellow nylon rope to a water pipe close to the wall. He tied a navy knot and tugged at the rope, feeling and judging it. He wore gloves to protect himself from rope burn. Holding the rope in his hand, he went up to the parapet and slowly lowered himself. He was suspended mid-air at a height of seventy metres from the ground. He showed no signs of nerves. Vijay's heart pounded.

Ramakant kept his feet close to the wall. He slid down by jumping off the wall at short distances away from it and then back on to it. There was a languid elegance in him. The boy swung himself quite effortlessly on to the balcony. He secured the rope to the railing of the balcony. He ran in, probably touched the bed and came back. He quickly untied the rope, held it and climbed on to the railing. He leant back and made sure that his whole body was in the same angle as the wall. He firmed his grip more.

Ramakant received a splendid round of applause on completion of the task. Vijay presented the boy with two crisp five hundred rupee notes. The boy saluted him.

Once the crowd dispersed, Vijay realized that this route was not the one employed. The uphill climb was too steep and dangerous. His adversary was a brainy, not brawny, one.

Chapter 26

A girl, about Padmini's age, ushered her in. She had a wooden expression on her face and spoke nothing while leading Padmini to the living room.

Curled up in a corner of a sofa with deep cushions, David's wife, Lucy, flanked by other women, was crying inconsolably. Tears soaked her sari and blouse. The woman sitting on the right of Lucy walked up to Padmini. On knowing the purpose of Padmini's visit, she relayed the message to Lucy, who was weeping non-stop.

Lucy wiped her face and turned to Padmini. 'Please do your duty.'

Taking their cue, the other women left the two of them alone.

'I am really sorry. I can understand your emotional state,' Padmini began, 'but if you tell the truth, we will nab his murderer.'

With anger and rage in her eyes, Lucy spoke in a trembling voice. 'I know it is Vasudha.'

Another spell of weeping.

Padmini let her cry. She too felt like crying, but she reminded herself to behave like a consummate professional. 'We understand,' Padmini offered, 'that he died a painless death due to cyanide poisoning.'

'My husband...' Lucy faltered, 'was a pawn in her hands. He would have drank poison if she had said so.' Lucy broke down again.

Padmini's thoughts drifted to the changing contours of Indian morals. Vasudha, who had accused her husband of infidelity, was being blamed for breaking up another home. There was, however, a difference. Vasudha was nonchalant, even relieved, at Anirudh's death, but Lucy was inconsolable.

Lucy recovered herself to speak. 'My David was like a child, and although he was under her hypnotic control, he loved me and our daughter.'

Padmini asked, 'Did anything disturb him lately?'

'He was upset with something concerning Mahapatra and Patterson Labs,' she replied. 'He went to meet Bharat Rao in Nagpur and never returned.'

Yet again, the pendulum of suspicion swung towards Bharat Rao.

Lucy wept again. Anger was simmering in her voice. She

opened her heart to Padmini. 'I scolded him,' she said, and pointed to a washbasin, 'for inserting the nozzle into his mouth. He was like a child. He loved to play Ludo, Scrabble and hated to lose.' Lucy held Padmini's hands. 'Believe me, it is that bitch. I am confident that you will appreciate what I say, because only a woman can see through her. Men get suckered.'

More mourners began to troop in. Padmini walked off.

※

'The car ride was awful,' Padmini complained.

Vijay looked at her with surprised eyes. 'The road is good; so is the driver.'

'The driver,' she said with cold anger, 'cannot drive without the radio and that conversational patter of radio jockeys gets on my nerves.'

Vijay laughed. 'Any worthwhile leads?'

She smiled vaguely. 'As usual, Bharat Rao is the suspect. David was having sleepless nights, sandwiched between Bharat Rao's perversity and his extramarital affair.'

Vijay's eyes widened.

'David,' she continued, 'found solace in Vasudha's companionship.'

'The wife told you.'

'Yes, amidst sobs, she told me that.'

Vijay was emotionally drained. He sat on the chair and closed his eyes. Soon, he dozed off.

Padmini tickled his armpits and he woke up with a jump. 'Fagged out?' she teased. 'Let us leave the room.' Seeing Vijay's bemused expression, she said, 'I am going to take a room in this hotel itself and stay here. It will allow me to work without any distraction and at the same time, I may stumble on to something.'

They locked room 701 and stepped out to speak with the manager. The manager booked room 702 for her.

Padmini checked into her room with a suitcase and a bag. It was eight in the evening. 'I will have a quick dinner and hit the sack,' she said.

Chapter 27

At home, Vijay retired to his bedroom. His mother came to check if everything was okay. 'Yes, just very busy,' he told her.

He could not sleep. He took off his pyjamas and pulled on a pair of jeans. Then he put on his sneakers and slowly slipped out of the house. He put his mobile on silent mode. He wandered aimlessly. The revolver inside the waist holster felt cold against his skin. He noticed pavement-dwellers keeping themselves warm around a fire. Most of them wore long shawls.

As he walked down Shivaji Ring Road, he found it desolate. He knew that Gowardhan Das Jewellery Mart was situated at the turning. The oldest jewellery shop in the city boasted of a lineage that had been family jewellers to the royal family. They had even installed a private checkpoint with a guard.

The rumbling sound of approaching motorbikes shattered the tranquillity. *Youngsters coming back after a late-night show.*

There were two motorcycles, as per his assessment. The bikes stopped. Then he heard noises. Vijay concentrated hard. It was the sound of a scuffle—a brawl. Then he remembered the jewellery mart. It was a burglary! The scuffle was probably between the guard and the burglars. The motorcyclists were burglars.

Vijay ducked behind a tall dustbin just in time, as one of the burglars appeared with a gun in his hand and stood at the intersection. Vijay sent a message to the 24/7 cavalry with details of his location. The jewellery mart was right at the turning, so one accomplice had been posted to keep watch at the intersection while the others looted. The guard must have been overpowered. He had not heard gunshots, so he must be alive.

Vijay crouched behind the dustbin. He wasn't far from the gunman keeping watch. As a rule, Vijay refrained from using guns. He could dash forward, grab the adversary's legs in a rugby-style tackle, fell him, snatch his gun and then get close enough to pump his knee into the opponent's groin.

The gunman was still looking the other way. He was sixty metres away and Vijay could reach him in less than seven seconds. In less than a minute, the gunman would be dispossessed of his weapon. With two guns, he would back himself to hold the burglars until reinforcements arrived.

He noiselessly lifted himself to an upright position and prepared to sprint. In his mind, he said, *On your mark, get set*—

The gunman whirled around abruptly. He was a baby-faced teenager of light build, with white patches on his face. The white patches, more than anything, disoriented Vijay, causing his concentration to lapse. The boy fired instantaneously. Vijay froze, taken aback by the viciousness of someone so young. The bullet headed for his chest. Images of past events in his life flashed in his inner eye as death stared at him.

A piercing hoot, sounding like an owl in pain, followed by a feathery thud, registered in Vijay's semi-conscious mind and jolted him back to complete alertness.

He was still alive and standing. A dead owl lay two feet ahead of him, in a pool of blood, his large eyes surrounded by disks of feathers.

Things became clear to Vijay. The boy was a good shot and the bullet was on its way to its target—Vijay's heart. At that precise moment, an owl tracking its prey, a rat, came in the way, flying noiselessly and sacrificing its life while saving his.

The unexpected turn of events numbed the boy. Vijay was taking no chances with a ruthless opponent, who was no mug with the gun. He aimed at the right wrist of the boy. The shot was deadly accurate. With a curse, the boy let his gun fall. His left arm supported the bleeding right wrist. A moment later, the boy howled in pain, so loudly that the entire neighbourhood would have woken up. He fell on his back, his head taking a knock on the cold, hard surface. With supreme effort, he got back on his feet. Had it not been for the viciousness displayed minutes ago, Vijay would have walked over to the victim. Not this time though!

Vijay fired again, aimed at the knee but got the thigh instead. The impact sent the boy reeling across the pavement, his trousers smeared with blood. Vijay sprinted, gun in hand, and grabbed the fallen boy's gun. A shot rang out through the half-open glass door of the jewellery mart. It missed him by a mile and hit the fence behind him. The steel wires reverberated.

The marksman had been laid low. Barring a freak bullet, the guns posed no threat.

Feeling more secure, Vijay rolled forward and shot towards the door. One burglar who came out rushed towards his vehicle. Vijay aimed at the base of the tyre of the first motorcycle. The tyre exploded like a bomb, and then it hissed as air escaped. The bike fell and upset the balance of the adjoining bike, toppling it over.

The boy whom Vijay had shot had lost consciousness and lay in a pool of blood. Both the bullets had targeted the limbs and hands, so the wounds should not be fatal, but you never know with bullets. If the bullet had punctured a major artery or a vital organ, it was curtains for the fallen boy.

Vijay surveyed the scene. One burglar too injured to make

a difference, two of them holed up inside the jewellery mart, probably waiting for him to make the next move. The security guard lay unconscious on the ground. The fallen motorcycle made any escape complicated.

Vijay expected reinforcements to arrive any moment. He was worried about the fallen security guard, who had been knocked on his head.

Vijay said to himself, 'They dare not make an aggressive move. Even if they do, they cannot go far.' He lay on the ground, waiting for the next move.

ॐ

Inspector Arun heard a beep. The red light on the emergency call flickered. His mobile neighed, calling his attention. He paused to read the message.

'SP Vijay needs our help,' he cried. 'He is at the jewellery mart in Shivaji Ring Road.'

Sub-Inspector Waghmare and a head constable set off on their motorbikes. Two jeeps, with five men each, followed.

Vijay heard the distant sound of motorcycles. He smiled. It was game, set and match. He placed his curved palm near his lips and shouted, 'The police have surrounded you. Give yourselves up.'

The wailing sound of the police sirens filled the air and as it grew louder, people began to wake up in the middle of the night and pour into the streets in their nightclothes.

Waghmare had come with a megaphone, but he did not use it. He cried out loud and clear, 'Surrender or we fire.'

The first jeep too had arrived, and the burglar who was injured by Vijay was nabbed. Two more came out of the jewellery mart with their hands raised. They were disarmed and handcuffed.

'Call a van and get those motorcycles cleared,' Vijay advised. He looked around. In the confusion, no one cared for the fallen guard, who was just coming around. Vijay made him gently sip water. The guard stood up groggily.

Vijay said, 'Rush him to the hospital.'

Two policemen were on it straightaway. Vijay requested a constable to drop him home. He was convinced that his team would handle the rest.

Chapter 28

Day 2

Vijay's father, Rangarajan, wanted to be kept abreast of the latest news. He normally alternated between *Times Now* and *Headlines Today*, morning and evening. Coffee cup in hand, he watched *Times Now* today. The news anchor focused on water cannons and lathis being rained on protestors who had converged in New Delhi's Jantar Mantar. The anchor said that the police action was provocative, since the protests had been largely peaceful. The anchor promised a round-up of the business news after the commercial break. This was what he had been eagerly waiting for.

The doorbell rang—unusual for this hour. The maid, who was mopping the floor, left the duster on the ground, placed the bucket of water near the wall, and opened the door. She engaged in a long argument. Rangarajan could not see the visitor through the half-open door.

His wife, meanwhile, shouted to the maid, 'Who is it?'

'Some ragtag who insists on seeing Vijay Sahib.'

'Usher him in,' Rangarajan said urgently. 'He could be in some trouble.'

A frail-looking man wearing a torn shirt entered with folded hands and a panic-stricken face.

'Please sit down.' Rangarajan smiled welcomingly.

His wife also greeted the man cordially and asked, 'Tea?'

The man continued to stand near the door, trying to occupy as little space as possible.

Vijay had by now woken up, and he came down from his bedroom, still in his nightclothes.

Rangarajan turned to Vijay. 'This man wants to see you.'

'Why are you standing there? Please come and sit here.'

The man trembled. Then he spoke in a shaking voice, 'Sir, I am a poor snake charmer. I have never seen such grandeur except in movies. I do not want to spoil the chair or soil the floor with my dirty clothes.'

Vijay went up to him, gently pulled him and seated him on a sofa chair. The maid brought him tea. The man poured tea on to the saucer and lapped it from there. Then, without a warning, he fell at Vijay's feet and sobbed noisily, 'You are like an angel to me...You saved my son's life.'

Vijay now understood the context. 'I suppose,' he said, 'the security guard at Gowardhan Das Jewellery Mart that saw an attempted robbery was your son.'

The man bowed his head. 'Sir, if not for you, my son would have died.'

'No, I just did my duty,' Vijay said.

'Just like your brave son.'

Vijay looked back. His father had spoken those words.

Rangarajan walked towards the snake charmer and shook the hand of the visibly embarrassed man. 'Both of us should be proud of our brave sons.'

'How is he now?' Vijay enquired.

'Out of danger,' the snake charmer replied, 'but he will be

in hospital for a couple of days.'

'You look tired and haggard,' Vijay's mother butted in, 'so have breakfast and go.'

A quiet breakfast followed. Vijay told the snake charmer that he would visit his son in the hospital.

'By the way,' Vijay said, 'what is your name?'

'Kalu.'

Vijay visited special ward number 210, where Kalu's son was admitted. He was conscious and cheerful. The doctor assured Vijay that he would be discharged in a day or two.

In the adjoining bed, the boy whom Vijay had shot lay unconscious, innocence emitting from his baby face. Inspector Arun had WhatsApped that one of the burglars was an employee of the jewellery mart and had clandestinely made duplicate keys.

A nurse commented flatly, 'Out of danger, but on crutches all his life.'

Vijay blamed himself for the boy's fate. If only if life was gentler...if only the bullet didn't damage to this extent...if only an eventful night didn't leave a permanent scar. He buried his head in his arms.

A constable whispered, 'The chief medical officer is here.'

Vijay wiped his eyes and faced a short man with a big jowl, kind eyes behind steel-rimmed glasses and betel-stained teeth. 'Not your fault.' He gave Vijay a fatherly hug. 'If you didn't react in time, he would have shot you like a dog.'

Vijay nodded slowly.

'My son,' Kalu chipped in meekly, 'would not have lived either.'

Kalu's quip had the impact of a judge in a court acquitting him honourably. He had saved a law-abiding young man's life—never mind the collateral damage.

Vijay was about to take leave when a sudden curiosity

overcame him. 'Where do you stay?' he asked Kalu.

'At Koradi, Sir. Close to the forests that abound in snakes.'

Vijay looked at his watch. It was around eight. A trip to Koradi, a look around the snake charmer's house and back would mean until lunch. 'I have never seen a snake charmer's home or a snake being captured,' he said sheepishly.

'You are welcome anytime, Sir.' Kalu blushed.

'Can we go now?'

'Sure, Sir.'

Chapter 29

Padmini hardly slept. She tossed over from side to side. She even tried changing pillows, but to no avail. She was surprised, almost scared, that the Anirudh, David and Mashelkar poisonings had become embedded in her mind like glue. She thought of nothing else. She got up later than usual. It was around seven in the morning. The sun's rays entered her room in a weird angle. She made her morning coffee, strong in caffeine, with a bit of milk and sugar.

She scanned through the morning's newspapers. Newspaper could be read in minutes these days, unless one was interested in the advertisements. The second newspaper, a Mumbai edition, contained a news item: 'Srikanth Mahapatra to Inaugurate the National Biological Museum's Golden Jubilee.'

This suggested he was back in Mumbai. She called Vijay. The mobile was switched off. She called again, but no reply was forthcoming. Puzzled, she sat down and stretched her legs. Then she decided to take another look at room 701.

The room emitted a foul smell; it hadn't been cleaned. The linen was getting dirtier. Padmini wondered whether the room could be freed. What further investigation was to take place in the room? The poison had been ingested, so somebody had fed him the poison, but when, where and how?

Padmini wore gloves and began to search the room afresh. She began with the far corner. Suddenly, she recalled that a hand lens was there in her kit. She ran over to her room to get the magnifying glass. It was like searching for a needle in a haystack. Padmini's back and knees ached. She sat, rested and ordered coffee. Having finished the floor, she scanned the walls. This could be done standing. The upper part of the walls and the roof were beyond her reach. She called for a ladder. The search continued to be fruitless. She finished her coffee and stared into the depths of her mug. No inspiration there either.

The washroom had been bolted from the outside, but in a moment of casual absent-mindedness, she pushed the door. It opened with a whoosh sound, the entrapped air escaping gleefully. She held her nose, fighting the foul odour. She rushed out and opened the balcony door.

She was about to call the housekeeping, but she stopped.

How did this stench come about? Water and dust can't emit such a foul smell, she wondered. She pressed a handkerchief over her nose and went back.

A dead lizard was tucked in the corner of the washbasin. Padmini looked long and hard at the lizard. With her mind focused on the lizard, she no longer felt the stench. It did not have any injury signs visible on its body.

Padmini remembered that she had placed a pair of forceps in the first aid kit that she carried with her. She went to retrieve it.

Slowly and carefully the lizard was lifted and examined. No signs of injury or crushing. Then what could have caused its death?

She wondered whether it was worthwhile to spend so much

time on pondering the cause of a lizard's death when the causes of deaths of human beings were yet to be established.

She closed the balcony door and the bathroom door as well as the outer door to the room. She went to her room and took a shower and shampooed her hair. The white fluffy towel that smelled of lemon was wrapped on her head.

Later, a hungry Padmini gorged on the well-laid-out buffet breakfast. The dead lizard preyed on her mind. *Could the lizard have died of poisoning?* She rang Dr Gaikwad.

'You need,' she said excitedly, 'to send your team to Hotel Heaven.'

'I thought that was done and dusted.'

'If you come,' there was a distinct edge in her voice, 'I will be able to explain my discovery.'

'I will be there,' he promised, barely concealing his excitement.

Sure enough, he was there sooner than expected with three other evidence collectors.

Padmini led them into the bathroom. 'There.' She pointed to the dead lizard. 'I think the lizard has been poisoned.' She looked at Dr Gaikwad and postulated, 'The whole washbasin and the tub need to be examined.'

'Do not leave any corner,' Dr Gaikwad cried. 'Check the taps, shower caps, nozzles, everything.'

Cotton swabs were rubbed and inserted into bottles with labels, numbered serially. Larger swabs were used for the floor. It was painstakingly pursued and in an hour's time, the job was done. The lizard itself was inserted into a bottle.

'It might take until evening,' Dr Gaikwad informed as he departed.

Although the forensic results would take until evening, she was reasonably certain about the outcome. If David had touched the washbasin nozzle with his fingers and licked them, then poison would have entered his body that way. But people generally touched knobs of taps in order to open and close them.

Padmini rang David's wife. 'I am sorry to embarrass you,' she said, 'but I need to confirm this to reach your husband's murderer.'

'No problem.'

'Did you tell me that your husband was in the habit of thrusting his mouth into the nozzle of taps?'

'Yes,' was the instantaneous response. 'My husband suffered from Meige's Syndrome and had difficulties in eating and swallowing. He preferred sucking, especially when his mouth went dry. Dryness was something he had to avoid at all cost.'

'Thanks.' Padmini hung up. She had her answer.

Excited, she rang Vijay. 'Damn it,' she cursed, 'it is switched off.'

Padmini was now assessing the situation. Although Dr Gaikwad's confirmation was awaited, she was certain about her conclusions. They were as follows:

» *the lizard had died due to cyanide poisoning, just like David;*
» *the bathroom was the source site for the poison; and*
» *David had thrust his mouth into the nozzle and got poisoned.*

The big question now was to figure out how the poison come on to the tap. She had no doubt about the mastermind, but as Vijay said, evidence was needed.

It was clear that someone in the hotel, staff or guest, had to do with it. The closed-circuit television should give a clue.

Chapter 30

Navigated by Kalu, Vijay drove to a part of town that he didn't imagine existed. As they left the town behind, they seemed to be going back in time, from civilization to primitiveness. Roads more mud than tar, declined in width with every metre advanced.

Vijay could see dark, though not dense, clouds hovering on the horizon. The first raindrops fell without a warning, just as his wipers gave way. He dismounted and tried righting them with force. It worked fortunately, for the nearest garage was miles away. He continued driving on what he called the 'mudway'.

He lowered the windows and sniffed. The fresh scent of rain on earth—petrichor, a heavenly fragrance that was a refreshing contrast to the metallic smell in cities. Puddles of muddy water filled up ditches that seemed to have sprouted every furlong. The municipality was remotely bothered, maybe blissfully unaware.

The rain had eased into a drizzle, and Vijay winced every time his car threw up a splash of slush. Fortunately, he was driving on a deserted road, where there was nobody to complain about a ruined outfit.

Kalu lived on the edge of the forest. This part of the town was sparsely populated; probably only occupied by the tribe of snake charmers who lived there. Around ten families lived in primitive hutments, with thatched roofs and mud kilns.

Vijay was amazed that such a dwelling existed just fifteen kilometres outside the city. 'Will there be cobras?' he asked, a little scared. 'Slithering all around the place?'

Kalu laughed. 'No, Sir. We keep them in closed containers, jars, bottles and baskets.'

Vijay did not conceal his relief.

'Sir,' Kalu explained, 'we cannot afford to allow our source of livelihood to escape.'

Vijay nodded.

Kalu's dwelling was no different from the others. Kalu stored most of his pets in transport bottles. The coiled serpents, mostly cobras, wriggled. Occasionally, they would stick their tongues out, but they had no conceivable chance to escape.

'I keep them in bottles rather than cane baskets,' Kalu explained, 'because then I can see them all the time.'

Vijay was both fascinated and scared; the fear less than the fascination.

'Don't others of your ilk,' Vijay asked, gazing nervously at a bottle, 'want to see their pets?'

'It is not that,' Kalu said, 'but if a bottle breaks, the snake might escape or get injured. I am,' he said, with his chest welling with pride, 'very, very careful.'

'Can we catch a snake today?' Vijay asked, his eyes shining,

'No.' Kalu laughed. 'They come out during monsoons. In autumns and winters, they stay in their pits, warm and cosy.'

Disappointment etched on Vijay's face. 'How do you normally spend your day?'

'These days, I spend time training Dharmendra.'

'Dharmendra?'

Kalu pointed to the biggest jar in the room. He removed it from the ledge. The snake occupying it looked big and strong; maybe that was why it was named after the muscular Bollywood hero who often played the role of a strongman in yesteryear films.

Kalu carried the jar to the cement-floored backyard. 'I spent a lot of money on this.' He pointed to the cemented floor. 'It is ideal to train snakes on a smooth surface.'

Vijay stood exactly where Kalu instructed him to be. Kalu

placed the jar on the floor. He went in, followed by Vijay. He brought out his *been*—the snake charmer's flute—which resembled a long clarinet with a bulging end. Kalu took a handkerchief and stuffed it in his pocket.

'What is that for?'

'In case the snake is too fast,' Kalu explained. 'I need a second line of defence.'

'How does the handkerchief help you?'

Kalu waved it. 'I will distract the snake using this handkerchief, and then grab it by the neck.'

Vijay admired Kalu but also pitied him. Kalu was very proficient in his trade, but his skills fetched him very little earnings. No wonder he had prevailed upon his son to relinquish the ancestral trade. Other youngsters were also following suit. This skill was a dying one.

Kalu surveyed the entrapped serpent from where he stood. He slowly extended his left arm and removed the lid of the jar. The serpent shot out like a spring and hit out at Kalu. The serpent was not a cobra; it was longer and bigger and surely stronger.

Kalu, unperturbed, played the *been*. The snake again darted at Kalu, but hit the *been* instead.

Vijay felt as if a hammer was pounding inside his heart; his pulse racing at 200 beats per minute. He wondered whether Kalu needed help. But Kalu seemed calm. He was a picture of concentration. Upsetting his concentration could be fatal.

The routine continued: Kalu moving the *been* as he played it, the serpent moving alongside and then striking. The snake's movements were now getting slower. Vijay attributed the sluggishness to tiredness. Reptiles, being cold-blooded, had little stamina.

In a sudden unexpected moment, Kalu lunged at the snake, held it by the neck and thrust it into the jar, head first. He used a stick to poke the snake's tail, which forced the snake to coil itself into the jar. He replaced the lid. He turned round and smiled at Vijay.

Vijay was perspiring and panting.

Kalu said gently, 'Routine training.'

'What were you doing?' asked Vijay, as he regained his composure.

'This snake,' he said, 'is very swift and strikes differently from our cobra.'

'I could see that it was not a cobra,' Vijay said.

'The training methods are the same.' Kalu caressed the fur of a cat that had strayed in. 'We make the snake react to the movements of the *been*. Hard stones are glued to the sides the *been's* head. When the snake hurts itself after repeatedly striking at a hard object, it learns to refrain from doing so.'

Vijay listened, spellbound. These illiterate tribesmen had developed training methods based on scientific and rationalistic assumptions.

'I neither sew the mouth of the serpent, nor remove its fangs, like most others do. This method is time consuming,' he accepted, 'but it gives me infinite pleasure.'

'Where did you find Dharmendra?'

Kalu laughed. 'Someone brought it from another country.' Kalu walked with the jar holding Dharmendra back into the hut and replaced it on the ledge.

A framed photograph of a cultural troupe lay in a corner. Vijay had a good look. It was a younger Kalu in New York.

'I was a part of a cultural troupe that visited three countries.' Pride shone through Kalu's eyes. He had a large bottle containing a brownish liquid and a very small one containing an orangish liquid.

A tiny flutter of excitement shivered at the base of Vijay's spine. The orange liquid most definitely resembled the Gandhiv that caused Mashelkar's death. No, it could not be! How could Kalu be connected to Mashelkar? He was getting far too ahead of himself.

Kalu pointed to the orange liquid. 'That is Dharmendra's venom.'

Vijay looked transfixed. Epiphany was coming in waves. He felt like crossing over to another world. The mystery of Mashelkar's death had probably been solved, but Dr Gaikwad would have to confirm his hunch forensically. Vijay hardly registered whatever Kalu spoke. He told Kalu, 'Bring Dharmendra with you. We have to go.'

Kalu fell at Vijay's feet. 'If I have broken any law,' he beseeched, 'please pardon me.'

'No, you will be rewarded,' Vijay assured, 'but quick.'

Kalu placed the jar carrying Dharmendra in a pot hanging from a bamboo pole and slung it over his shoulder.

Vijay smiled. 'We are going by car. Carry Dharmendra in a pouch.'

'Should I carry the milked venom as well?'

Vijay nodded affirmatively.

Kalu sat on the back seat of the car. Vijay drove fast and halted near a school building.

Vijay took out his mobile to call Dr Gaikwad. The mobile that had been switched off when he entered the hospital had now been turned on. 'I am bringing a live snake,' he announced, 'and you have to identify the snake.'

'What the hell is going on?' Dr Gaikwad thundered. 'First it is a dead lizard, now a live snake. This is not a zoo.'

Vijay protested 'I do not know about the lizard.'

'Padmini has made my boys work like mules today, and now you.'

'No jokes, doctor. It is urgent.'

'Let me call a herpetologist friend of mine,' Dr Gaikwad suggested. 'He would be a better bet. I will call him.'

Vijay hung up. What was all this about Padmini and the dead lizard? He would catch up later. Right now, he had enough on his mind. He turned the car towards Shankar Nagar and parked it outside Birender's office. He told Kalu to wait.

Birender was selling a specialized holiday product to a senior citizen. 'We offer greater care, lesser cost as well as personalized service.'

Vijay waited for the customer to leave. Then he plunked down opposite Birender. 'Get me a cup of masala tea. I am dying for one.'

Birender studied him. 'You look like you have survived an air crash!'

Masala tea with biscuits was served. Vijay gulped down the tea and ordered for another. Birender extended his cup, which had been untouched.

'Birender,' Vijay growled, 'do you remember you sent a mail regarding a contact of yours who had set up a spa in Israel using slithering snakes as a relaxant?'

'Ali Nasiri,' Birender said, matter-of-factly and punched a few keys on his terminal.

'There.' He rotated the monitor screen towards Vijay. The page had all the details of Nasiri, his photograph and his address. He stayed in a villa outside the city.

'He owns a villa. He is an entrepreneur who sets his spas in different countries.'

'Give me a printout of the page,' Vijay panted, 'and what more do you know about him?'

Birender stopped chewing his biscuit and gaped at Vijay. 'You better calm down.'

Vijay closed his eyes and meditated for about five minutes. Birender ensured that nobody entered his cubicle and disturbed them. Vijay slowly opened his eyes. He smiled languidly.

'That is better.' Birender sounded relieved. 'By the way, Nasiri looks after his customers very well and replies promptly.' Birender retrieved the paper from the printer tray and handed it to Vijay.

'Any criminal record?' Vijay asked.

Birender laughed. 'You should know that.'

Vijay stood up. 'I need to leave urgently.' He turned back as soon as he reached the door. 'Birender, do you know his business partners?'

'He was involved in some project in South Africa. By the way, I read a tweet that he is quite close to Bharat Rao, the famous scientist.'

'Thanks.'

Vijay showed the photograph of Nasiri to Kalu.

Kalu rammed his finger on the face of the photograph. 'That is the man. He paid me ₹5,000 for milking the venom of Dharmendra. These foreign snakes have a lot of venom. I kept just a little and gave the rest to the man. I milked it again after three weeks.'

'Why did he need the venom?'

'I do not know, Sir, but he would be coming back to take Dharmendra away from me.'

Dr Gaikwad called to inform that Dr Vikram Joshi, a herpetologist, had already reached the lab. Vijay estimated that he would be reaching there in five minutes. He took out his mobile to ring Dalvi. He stopped. As a cop, he could not break the law by talking on the mobile while driving. He parked in a secluded corner.

Dalvi took it on the eleventh ring. He apologized for the late response.

Vijay made light of it. 'I am giving you an address and a couple of phone numbers.'

'Sir?'

'Tap the phones; have two men posted near his home, two men to tail him and report anything unusual.'

'Sir, I will give you an hourly update, and if anything unusual happens, an extra update will be given.'

'Fine. The man's name is Ali Nasiri; you have to get all details about him.'

'Sir.'

Vijay was back at the wheel and at the stroke of noon had reached the laboratory.

Padmini came running towards him, with outstretched arms. She was bursting with news.

Vijay waded into her arms and allowed her to grip him. Looking into her eyes, he said, 'I will hear you later. Just listen to me now.'

Padmini's face showed a range of emotions: Disappointed at being silenced, yet thrilled at seeing Vijay's excited face and an anticipation of things to come, she gave him a saucy grin. 'I think you have hit a jackpot.'

'Maybe the route to the treasure.' He winked.

Kalu followed, over-awed by the occasion.

Dr Gaikwad was talking to an unshaven, travel-weary, bespectacled man who had his hands deep in his pockets. Dr Gaikwad introduced the man to Vijay. 'This is Dr Vikram Joshi, one of the top herpetologists in India. He just returned from Zimbabwe.' Dr Joshi extended a limp handshake.

Vijay smiled warmly. But an anxious lump in his throat stopped him from speaking out loud. He was filled with a sense of inexplicable dread, and a fear of being ridiculed, of being castigated for wasting precious time gripped Vijay. He felt his muscles tighten and his breathing turn rapid and shallow. He looked around. Padmini stood, rock solid behind him. Dr Gaikwad's face was impassive; Dr Joshi's eager eyes were rooted to Kalu's bag. Vijay's nerves soothed.

Dr Joshi smiled wryly. 'I need to identify the snake.'

'Right.'

'Wait.' Dr Gaikwad showed a restraining hand. 'We will go to the shed behind.'

Everyone followed Dr Gaikwad unquestioningly. He led them through the parts of the laboratory that Vijay had never been before. They went through what seemed like a rear door into a shed. Dr Gaikwad latched the door behind him and put on the lights. The illumination was perfect.

'Now,' Dr Gaikwad said, taking charge, 'Let Kalu show the snake to Dr Joshi, and we will stay back and not disturb them.'

Vijay looked at Padmini. She showed a V sign.

'Be careful,' he warned Kalu, 'Or we could have a real problem.'

'Don't worry.' Kalu sounded confident. He removed the jar from the pouch and placed it on the ground.

'Do you want gloves?' Dr Gaikwad asked.

Kalu refused. 'I am comfortable.' He measured the distance between himself and the jar with his hands. He lowered his left hand to the lid of the jar and suddenly lifted it. In the blink of an eye, Kalu held the struggling snake by the head in his fist. The tail dangled, but Kalu's grip was vice-like.

The snake was nearly ten feet long and gunmetal grey in colour.

'Open the mouth.' Dr Joshi focused his eyes on the serpent's mouth. As Kalu pulled apart the jaws, Dr Joshi had a good look. Needle-like fangs, two of them, shone brightly.

'Okay,' Dr Joshi said, 'you can put it back.'

Kalu thrust Dharmendra back into the jar and kept it in its pouch.

Vijay handed a five hundred rupee note to Kalu. Kalu bowed and reverentially kissed the note.

Dr Gaikwad led them back to his chamber where water and coffee awaited them. Dr Joshi drank nearly half a glass in one gulp. 'That was a black mamba,' he announced, 'a highly venomous snake.' He waited and then went on. 'The snake gets its name from the colour of the inside of its mouth, which is obviously black. It is an African snake, very swift, and its venom is the fastest spreading venom. Even ten milligrams of venom can kill a human being.'

'What is this all about?' Dr Gaikwad demanded. 'Explain all this.'

Vijay smiled. 'It is a hypothesis. The orange potion used to kill Dr Mashelkar was black mamba poison.'

'Impossible,' Dr Gaikwad countered, 'This is venom, not poison.'

Padmini asked, 'What is the difference between the two?'

Dr Gaikwad turned to Dr Joshi. 'You explain.'

'Poison,' Dr Joshi lectured, 'can be toxic when inhaled, ingested, or injected directly into the bloodstream. Venom is toxic only when it goes directly into the bloodstream. When an animal bites, the venom goes directly into the bloodstream. Black mamba venom, if ingested, is not toxic.'

Dr Gaikwad nodded his head to every word that was said. He looked steadily at Vijay. 'Dr Mashelkar drank the potion. If it was black mamba venom, then nothing would have happened.'

'Wait a minute.' Vijay smiled and posed, 'What if the consumer of the venom has ulcers in his mouth, tongue and gastric lining?'

'In such an eventuality,' Dr Joshi responded almost

immediately, 'the venom would seep into the bloodstream and cause death.'

'Mashelkar,' Padmini cried out, 'visited a doctor for treatment of ulcers just the day before his death.'

Dr Gaikwad took off his spectacles and placed them on the table. He pondered and then wore the spectacles. 'Interesting, but I apprehend,' Dr Gaikwad said contemplatively, 'that it will be difficult to prove that black mamba venom caused the death because venom metabolizes into proteins.' He looked at Dr Joshi.

Dr Joshi seemed to agree. Then he proposed, 'Could you try an immunoassay?'

'What is that?' Vijay and Padmini queried together.

Dr Gaikwad answered, 'By analysing the antibodies produced in the blood, we can work backwards to determine the venom that caused the production of those antibodies.'

'So, what are we waiting for?' Vijay asked.

'I am afraid,' Dr Gaikwad said regretfully, 'I do not know how to do it, nor do I know anyone who knows it.'

Vijay slumped dejectedly.

Padmini, deep in thought until then, said brightly, 'We have a little bit leftover of the liquid that Mashelkar consumed. If we match that liquid with the venom of black mamba—'

Dr Gaikwad did not allow her to complete the sentence. 'Yes, we can surely do that.'

Feeling reassured, Vijay instructed Kalu to hand over the bottle with Dharmendra's venom to Dr Gaikwad.

Dr Gaikwad patted Vijay on the back. 'Great work,' he beamed. 'You know, the proteins in the blood are probably on account of that. I am sure you will be proved right.'

For Vijay, the tide had turned. The forensic results were awaited, but he was ready to count his chickens before they hatched and he had a strange feeling that he wouldn't regret it.

'This is one area,' Dr Joshi concluded, 'where medical science needs much improvement. For instance, we normally get complaints saying so-and-so was bitten by a snake, so we administer the antivenom, but to identify snake venom is otherwise a tall order.'

Kalu handed the bottle to an underling of Dr Gaikwad, who carefully transferred the contents to a bottle and labelled it.

'How did you reach this conclusion?' Dr Gaikwad asked.

Vijay narrated the events beginning from the jewellery mart burglary to Kalu's coming, to expressing gratitude for his spotting Dharmendra's venom in a small glass. Padmini was watching him with pride as though she owned him. Vijay did not need any other morale booster.

Another round of coffee followed.

Dr Gaikwad looked at Padmini and said, 'The lizard indeed died of cyanide poisoning.' He sipped coffee and continued. 'The washbasin nozzle had traces of cyanide.'

Vijay was standing near the window, talking on his mobile. This conversation had been lost on him.

'Padmini'—he tugged her arm—'we have to rush to Mumbai.'

She looked enquiringly at him.

'We have a flight in three hours' time. We would be meeting Srikanth Mahapatra.'

'Where?'

'At Hotel Trident, Bandra Kurla.'

It was half past one. The flight scheduled to depart at half past four would be landing at Mumbai around six, and Vijay had booked a return flight at half past ten.

'A hectic day awaits us.' Vijay sighed as he and Padmini took leave of Dr Gaikwad and Dr Joshi.

Chapter 31

Padmini followed Vijay into his beige Toyota Corolla. She squeezed his arms. 'Let us go to Hotel Heaven. I will demonstrate how David was poisoned.'

Vijay's initial reaction was one of disbelief. Then he squeezed her body to his own and kissed her softly, on the top of her head, on the brow. She shut her eyes. He kissed her eyelids.

'I love you,' he whispered.

She leaped into his arms, hind leg on the gearbox.

Abruptly, Vijay said, 'We are on the road.'

She smiled and slowly slithered back to her seat.

Dalvi was instructed to join them at Hotel Heaven.

'Hi Dalvi,' Vijay greeted him with breezy informality. 'What news?'

Dalvi answered, in a business-like tone, 'I have gone around, speaking to a dozen scientists, junior scientists and scientific assistants, and the general buzz is that—'

'Bharat Rao,' Vijay interrupted, 'intended to secretly smuggle endangered species of snakes, kill them and use them in his experiments.'

Dalvi moved in his chair. Then he nodded acquiescingly at Vijay.

Padmini, who was leaning backwards, jerked herself to a bolt upright position. The chain on her neck peeped out of her cleavage. 'How many laboratories did you cover?'

'Four,' he said mechanically. 'Two in Nagpur, one in Pune and one in Mumbai.'

Vijay was thoughtfully silent. Padmini turned to him. 'So, the fire has spread everywhere.'

'That clearly,' Vijay deduced, 'gives Bharat Rao a solid motive for murder. Those who disagree with his methods stand between him and a billion dollars. By the way, did you do it yourself?' Vijay asked.

'No, I got Bloodhound Detective Agency to do it.'

Padmini dug her fingers into her handbag and fished out a water tap. She placed it on the table. Seeing Vijay's puzzled look, she said, smiling, 'Follow me.'

Vijay and Dalvi followed her into the bathroom. She pointed to the washbasin. 'I saw a dead lizard there, then I had Dr Gaikwad comb the place. They found traces of the same poison at a couple of spots in the washbasin, but most of it was on the nozzle of the tap. The lizard too died of the same poison.'

A torrent of questions rained in Vijay's mind. He framed one. 'How did the poison get into David's body?'

She walked out of the bathroom. She picked the water tap laid on the table and thrust it into her mouth. Vijay gasped. She took the tap out of her mouth and laid it back on the table. 'Like that.'

Vijay bought time by raking his fingers through his hair. The thought of another million-dollar question being resolved in the day was a heavy load to bear. He had to temper his excitement. He had a wary tone. 'Why do you think David thrust his mouth into the nozzle?'

'That,' she replied, 'was because of the disease he suffered from. He felt relief from the symptoms of Meige's Syndrome, when he sucked either from a straw or nozzle of a tap, especially when he needed to moisten his mouth. I confirmed this with his wife and daughter.'

Vijay hugged her. 'When people talk for long periods, their mouth dries up. That is why lecturers sip water every now and then. David was talking on the mobile, and considering his disease, his mouth was bound to dry. He needed urgent moistening and sucking from the tap would have been the easiest option.'

'You mean,' she said, flinging her arms around his shoulders, 'the murderer deliberately made David talk a lot to force this action?'

Vijay nodded.

Dalvi's eyes were fixed like the twin barrels of a gun. 'What a day,' he exclaimed. 'Two murders solved by two geniuses. I am blinded by your dazzling brilliance.'

Vijay ordered three glasses of orange juice to be sent to Padmini's room. They locked room 701 and went back to Padmini's room.

Vijay absent-mindedly held open Padmini's purse. Resettling it, he shifted his focus to Dalvi. 'Organize a press conference.'

'A press conference?' Padmini echoed, with surprise in her voice.

'Yes, a press conference,' Vijay clarified.

'I will take care of that,' Padmini offered.

Dalvi was only too glad to allow her to do the job.

'It is not a big deal organizing a press conference,' Padmini declared, 'but why do you want to organize one?'

Vijay stretched his legs and placed his heels on a stool. He looked at Dalvi, who looked equally flummoxed. 'What do you guys think of the murderer?'

'A cool genius,' Dalvi reflected.

'Diabolical, intelligent, elaborate planning,' Padmini added. 'Flawless.'

Vijay motioned them to stop. 'See, our murderer,' Vijay propositioned, 'may be a genius, unflappable and flawless, but like Federer, he too will err when put under the hammer.'

'How do you—' Dalvi asked.

Padmini interrupted. 'Put him under pressure?'

'That is where the press conference comes in.' Vijay laughed.

'I get it,' Padmini screamed.

Dalvi looked nonplussed.

'See, Dalvi,' Padmini explained, 'the killer will get the shock of his life when all the secrets of his perfect murders are revealed.'

A wide toothy grin broke on Dalvi's face. 'That will hit him like a mace. He will probably do something silly to cover his tracks and we will nab him.'

'Yes, my lions.' Vijay laughed. 'That is the trap we lay for him. So, Mr Bharat Rao, the fun begins!' Vijay clenched his fists.

Chapter 32

Vijay and Padmini went through the motions of checking in and passing their luggage through the scanning machines. Vijay noticed that none of the security men checked the X-ray pictures diligently. They boarded the plane. The plane taxied along the runway. Up and above it soared with a typical roar.

The flight touched down on time. It took another fifteen minutes to disembark, with the front door getting jammed.

'A taxi will be there to receive us.' Vijay leaned towards Padmini.

There was a mad scramble to board the first bus. Vijay and Padmini stayed back and boarded the relatively emptier second bus.

Two policemen in uniform received Vijay as soon as he alighted from the bus. One offered to carry Vijay's bag and the other Padmini's. Both refused, smiling. Padmini was at ease talking shop with the constables. Vijay admired her ability to juggle roles with élan. No wonder people took to her easily.

The Bandra Sea Link had shortened distances to the airport from many parts of Mumbai. The traffic moved faster than expected. A giant billboard with a cut-out of Sachin Tendulkar advertising Boost as the secret of his energy could be seen.

Padmini winced as they passed the cut-out. 'I guess he should have retired after the World Cup win.'

'Everybody,' Vijay retorted, 'seems to be his consultant.'

The car stood at the traffic lights.

The driver joined the debate. 'I also agree with madam. He is making a fool of himself.'

Vijay shook his head sadly. 'Listen, each man is free to make his own decisions. I do not want anyone telling me when I should quit and the same goes for him.'

The car sped on the newly constructed sea-link bridge. The board for the Trident shone in neon.

Varsheney, the inspector who had arranged the meeting, walked towards them. 'This way, Sir.' He directed them to the bar.

A bald man, with an oval face and a French beard dyed orange, sat with a glass of red wine and a newspaper spread out in front of him.

Padmini giggled. 'Isn't he quaint?'

Vijay suppressed a laugh. He walked ahead of Padmini. 'Professor, I am Vijay and this is Padmini.'

The man smiled, showing his artificial teeth.

'Your autograph,' Padmini extended a scrapbook, 'is something that I will treasure.'

Professor Srikanth Mahapatra carefully placed the wine glass on the table, signed the scrapbook and looked eagerly at Padmini.

Vijay had a feeling that it could be smooth sailing.

'Tell us about your latest work.' She could be mistaken for

a student talking to her favourite teacher.

The scientist took a swig. 'I am working on a permanent cure for diabetes.'

Padmini jerked her head in his direction. 'Isn't that—'

The scientist arrested her speech with a wave of his hand. 'Everyone,' he said with contempt, 'thinks that Bharat Rao and Mashelkar have already achieved that.'

The conversation had become a dialogue. Vijay was a piece of furniture, but still things were moving.

'I worked with them,' he said acidly, 'for more than a decade. We had a breakthrough.'

'Then what happened?'

Srikanth paused and asked Padmini, 'What will you have?'

'Cafe mocha.'

He turned towards Vijay for the first time, 'You?'

'Green tea.'

He called a boy and instructed the beverages to be served.

'We noticed,' he continued, with a faraway look in his eyes, 'that the mixture we had prepared increased blood circulation into the pancreas and kidneys.' He coughed and his chin looked comical, with traces of red wine on an orange beard.

Padmini wiped it with a tissue. She had taken to him like a daughter. If she was acting, a great future awaited her at Bollywood.

'Where was I?' the scientist asked.

'About the increased blood circulation—' Padmini was again interrupted midway.

'The increased blood circulation is regenerative and curative.'

'Wow!'

'This would help cure not only diabetes, but even pancreatitis quickly, but...' He swirled the ice cubes in the glass, almost causing the liquid to spill. 'There remains a fair chance of patients developing fatty liver disease.'

'Can you explain it in common language?' Vijay requested.

The scientist polished off his glass of wine and put it away. He answered Vijay, but addressed Padmini. 'The increased blood circulation to the pancreas was at the cost of the liver. I noticed that blood circulation to the liver was getting compromised.'

Padmini took notes. Vijay looked surreptitiously at his watch. Srikanth wasn't going anywhere.

'I protested against submitting this formula for clinical trials and withdrew myself a few months back.'

'If I remember rightly,' Vijay pointed out, 'Mashelkar had also supported you.'

'True, but Bharat came back, saying that we could apply for a patent, and then use the money to rectify shortcomings. Mashelkar was sold to the idea.'

'You called him a traitor.'

'More out of anger,' Srikanth defended, 'that Mashelkar, such a great scientific brain, could be so naïve.' He poured more drink into his glass. 'Wrong and non-factual presentations were made to the Jaryyd Laboratories of Sweden, who almost bought the patent for a billion dollars.'

A buzz of excitement swept over Vijay. 'Almost?'

'Yes, contrary to popular perception, the all-important presentation has been withheld.'

'Why, then, did Mashelkar go along with Bharat Rao?'

'Not true!' Srikanth asserted and banged his right fist into the palm of his other hand. 'Mashelkar was fooled. Later, he decided to withdraw and finally even Bharat agreed. Unfortunately, Mashelkar died and Bharat nearly so.'

'I don't find your story believable,' said Vijay in a sceptical voice. 'In fact, it is defamatory to Bharat Rao.'

Srikanth's eyes became bloodshot, his body shrank, his face

contorted to a scowl, and his voice became harsh. 'You sceptic, you dare doubt me! Wait, wait!' He craned his neck and cried, 'Patankar! Patankar!'

A slim man of medium build appeared.

'Get me my laptop.'

Srikanth powered on his laptop. Uneasy silence prevailed. 'Look!' He directed the laptop to Vijay.

These were mails sent by Mashelkar to Srikanth over a period of time. Vijay took out his visiting card, scribbled a message and squeezed it into Padmini's palm.

Padmini said softly, 'Sir, will you please forward these messages to my ID? We are investigating Mashelkar's murder and these could be useful for us.'

Almost straightway, Srikanth complied. 'There.' He smiled at Padmini.

Vijay signalled to Padmini that their time was up.

Padmini told the scientist that she was confident that he would win the Nobel Prize one day. She sounded genuine and Srikanth glowed.

Chapter 33

Dalvi sat in his living room, twiddling his thumbs. A workaholic, he felt restless having nothing to do. The twin successes of the day had geared him up. He wanted to do his bit. He sat on his computer and opened a folder titled 'Checklist'.

The folder contained a list of items to be taken care of during a murder investigation. Item 26 had not been ticked. The unticked item read, 'Check laundry markings.'

Dalvi racked his brains. This item did not seem relevant since they had no suspect whatsoever. Still, they had the victim

Mashelkar's coat, as an item of evidence.

Dalvi, meticulous as ever, dressed up, packed his kit, wore his helmet and rode to the crime branch record room. The caretaker ushered him in. Dalvi wore his recently prescribed reading glasses and looked at Mashelkar's coat.

There were laundry markings. It had been to Dev Drycleaners. Dalvi knew the shop and its owner. He recorded an entry in the evidence register and carried the coat with him.

Kanhere was about to bring the shutter down on his shop when he saw Dalvi. He immediately stopped in his tracks.

'About to leave?' Dalvi said.

Kanhere smiled.

Dalvi looked at his watch. 'I would not be detaining you for long.' He took out the coat from his bag.

Even without touching it, Kanhere cried, 'That is Bharat Rao's coat.'

'Are you sure?'

Kanhere grimaced. He went back into his shop and stopped. He fished out a receipt book and turned the pages. 'There.' He pointed to a receipt. 'I had delivered the coat duly dry-cleaned on 22 October at around five thirty in the evening.'

Dalvi processed the information. 'Who took delivery?'

'The professor himself.'

Dalvi stared, as only a policeman can, at Kanhere.

'I swear,' Kanhere placed his right palm on his heart, 'by God. The professor came himself. He thrust something into the inner pocket and left.'

Dalvi continued to stare enquiringly at Kanhere.

Kanhere's discomfort was obvious. He motioned Dalvi to wait. He took a stool, stood on it and searched in the lofts. 'There.' He removed a paper bag. He handed it over, after dusting it.

Dalvi felt a CD under the cover. He realized it was the CCTV footage of the day. 'I will take a look.'

※

Back home, Dalvi inserted the CD into his computer and watched. He fast forwarded it to five in the evening. There wasn't much happening at the shop. A lady customer came and went after making an enquiry. A tea boy served tea in a thermocol cup. Dalvi watched patiently and intently.

A sedan pulled up. A man got down from the driver's seat. His face wasn't clear. The timer on the footage indicated 17:23. The customer placed his hands on the counter. Kanhere delivered a plastic bag. The customer peeped into the bag. He thrust his right hand and pulled out a coat. Now the face was discernible. It was Bharat Rao. He removed a bottle from his pouch and inserted it into the inner pocket. Dalvi remembered reading in Godbole's diary notes that Bharat Rao was so obsessed with the latest version of Gandhiv, that he carried it on his person. Dalvi rewound the sequence and zoomed in on the last bit. The coat was unmistakably the one he had as evidence. The bottle was roughly the size of the one from which the fatal drink was served. Riddles invaded Dalvi's mind. He needed answers! Vijay would provide them, but he had to wait for the morrow.

Day 3

The clanging sound, indicating the receipt of a WhatsApp message, woke Vijay.

Padmini informed that she had gone through the mails forwarded by Shrikanth Mahapatra and had marked only those with relevant information to him. Vijay clicked on the attachments sent with the mails.

Message 1

From: Bharat Rao
To: Mahapatra

You greatly exaggerate the possibility of fatty liver emerging as a side effect. We have not experienced that in our test trials. Out of the thirty-five volunteers, only one showed a fatty liver and that was probably due to his excessive intake of alcohol. I am pained that you accused me of misrepresenting to Jaryyd Labs.

Message 2

From: Mahapatra
To: Bharat Rao

I never claimed that fatty liver cases were observed during safety and clinical trials, but the plausible reaction of the compounds indicates such a side effect as a strong, even inevitable, possibility. I am independently working on the issue, and I strongly object to your going ahead with a presentation to Jaryyd Laboratories without resolving the problem.

Message 3

From: Mahapatra
To: David

I am appalled that you are a party to our endeavours of over two decades being sold to a dubious entity like Patterson's Laboratories.

Message 4

> From: David
> To: Mahapatra
>
> Sir,
>
> I am shocked at what you are saying. I have greatest regard for you. I will lay down my life rather than compromise any reputation that has been earned over a lifetime.
> Sorry to have brought agony to you.

Message 5

> From: David
> To: Mahapatra
>
> I will be going over to Nagpur in a few minutes. I will learn about the entire Patterson episode and update you.

॥

Vijay noticed that the last message had been sent by David a couple of hours before his death.

Chapter 34

The press conference was arranged at Hotel Heaven itself. After the conference was concluded, Vijay, Padmini and Dalvi congregated in Padmini's room.

Vijay and Padmini watched the video footage that Dalvi brought.

'It is difficult to say,' Vijay surmised, 'but I think that is the same bottle.'

'If that were so,' Dalvi concluded, 'then Bharat Rao is our

man. He also has a motive.'

Vijay picked up a pen stand and admired its carvings. 'There has been considerable bad blood between Bharat Rao and his partners. Srikanth cried off, but Mashelkar vacillated. Mashelkar's last e-mail indicated that he was about to quit. Bharat Rao may have got rid of David, Mashelkar and Anirudh so that there is no one to stop him from making non-factual presentations to Jaryyd Labs, and pocket the entire billion for himself.'

It suddenly struck Vijay that Padmini had not spoken a word. He caressed her arm and yelled into her ear, 'Wake up!'

She smiled absent-mindedly. 'Let us,' she said, standing up, 'visit the doctor whom Mashelkar consulted a couple of days before the ill-fated day.'

෴

Dr Nilesh was in Bangalore, but he was ready to talk.

'Did Mashelkar come alone?' Vijay asked.

'No,' he responded instantaneously. 'Bharat Rao came with him.'

'Are you sure?' Vijay asked.

'Hundred per cent sure. I saw them off to their car myself—the car that Mashelkar's driver almost banged into mine.'

'Thanks Doc, I will call you if need be.'

'My pleasure.'

෴

'So, all points to Bharat Rao,' Vijay declared.

'I am beginning,' Padmini said, 'to believe that we have a one-sided socialite version of things.'

Vijay jumped up as if he had received an electric shock. He looked at Padmini searchingly. 'I don't get you.'

Padmini straightened herself. 'We have heard,' she said, as she fixed her hair, 'from people about Anirudh visiting women or Bharat Rao wanting to smuggle banned species.' She looked around for effect. Two pairs of eager eyes were transfixed on her. 'But all these people were the ones referred to by Vasudha. We never talked to anyone who is close to Anirudh but not to Vasudha; ditto for Bharat Rao.'

Vijay tucked his chin into his chest and frowned thoughtfully.

Dalvi countered, 'But husband and wife are bound to have common friends.'

Before Padmini could reply, Vijay growled. 'Dalvi, check all the massage parlours with female therapists, and find out if Anirudh visited them. Ask if anyone actually saw Anirudh with women.'

Dalvi took his cap out and placed it back on his head.

Padmini smiled affably. 'He is carrying out these orders under protest. He believes we are throwing a monkey wrench into the machinery.'

'We have very little time,' Dalvi sounded cagey, 'and we might be wasting ourselves running around in circles.'

'You may have a point,' Padmini conceded, 'but what if we reach nowhere because we went the whole hog galloping on the wrong trail?'

A slow smile crept on Dalvi's face.

Vijay had closed his eyes and dropped himself on the chair.

'He is sending his queries to the universe,' Padmini said with a straight face.

Vijay blinked his eyes open. 'Dalvi, let the detective agency handle it for you. After all, we have an unlimited budget.'

Dalvi propped up his chin with his hand. 'The universe has given me a breather.'

Padmini joined in his laughter.

Chapter 35

'Sit back,' Vijay said, acting out his words, 'and wait for him to make the next move.'

Padmini was watching an episode of *Desperate Housewives* on the flat-screen television. Dalvi was praying yet again.

Vijay could not fathom his devotion. For all his faith, Dalvi had been an underachiever in his career; his personal life had hit a dead end. Despite meagre returns, this true man of God was relentless.

Dalvi half jumped, when his mobile rang. His face became sullen. 'Ali Nasiri's landline was contacted twice from a PCO.'

'Which PCO?'

'Outside the city'—He stood, head bowed down—'where our men were not positioned.'

'So,' Vijay said thoughtfully, 'we have the first reaction to the press conference.'

'How did he get to the outskirts of town without us knowing it?' Padmini wondered aloud.

'He did not do it,' Vijay said, 'but his accomplice was dispatched for the job.'

'Nobody met Bharat Rao today,' Dalvi informed, 'nor did he phone anyone.'

'He could have mailed,' Padmini interjected.

'That means his accomplice was the one doing the talking. We have been barking up the wrong tree,' Vijay said, in a dejected tone.

Vijay's mobile trilled. A constable was on line. 'Can I,' the constable enquired politely, 'give your personal mobile to Bharat Rao? He wants to talk to you.'

'Sure.' Vijay looked at the ceiling. Then he said, 'If Mohammed cannot go to the mountain, the mountain will come to him. Guess what?'

Padmini sighed and threw her hands up. Dalvi followed suit.

'Bharat Rao wants to contact me.'

'Probably to throw you off the track,' Padmini said.

Dalvi added, 'What nerve! What cheek!'

Vijay's mobile rang again.

It was Bharat Rao. 'I want to meet you.'

'Sure, we shall come over right now?'

Bharat Rao agreed.

※

Bharat Rao looked pale, almost ghostlike. To Padmini, it was the fear generated by revelations made during the press conference. His black trousers and light blue shirt gave him a formal appearance.

Vijay introduced Padmini and Dalvi to Bharat Rao.

'What will you have?' Bharat Rao asked.

Vijay shrugged his shoulders. 'Anything to drink?'

'Tea?'

'Fine.'

Bharat Rao stirred his tea briskly. Some of it spilled from the cup to the table cloth. Without a warning, he uttered, 'Your press conference has rattled me.'

Vijay leaned forward to show his eagerness.

'I had been to Mashelkar's home and gave him my coat and a bottle of Gandhiv. The Gandhiv had been prepared here at my home.'

'By whom?' Vijay asked.

Padmini was recording the conversation on her mobile. Dalvi was taking notes.

'By my manservant, Raju.'

'Then?'

Bharat Rao's elbow brushed against the holder of a lamp. The holder fell, and the glass bulb it held shattered to smithereens. Raju came with another servant, who carefully swept the smashed glass pieces, while Raju supervised. Bharat Rao suggested, 'Let us go and sit in the lawn.'

Vijay and Dalvi followed Bharat into the lawn, but Padmini stayed back inside.

She went up to Raju and asked, 'Is your master clumsy?'

'Very, he keeps dropping things. Hasn't changed in the last fourteen years that I know him.'

Bharat Rao moved his chair closer to Vijay. 'I cannot understand how we were made to consume black mamba venom?'

Padmini went closer and stared into his eyes. He barely noticed her. Vijay was the one who mattered to him. The fear and dread in Bharat Rao's eyes looked genuine. If it was an act, he deserved an Oscar for his performance. But, more importantly, Padmini got no bad vibes from him.

'I found the taste strange and unpalatable. The odour wasn't there. I actually regurgitated and maybe that's what saved me.'

Vijay recollected. 'I saw it in the video footage.'

'Oh, the video,' Bharat sobbed softly. 'That was David's idea.' He broke down. He staggered, coughed and stammered. He could not form words coherently. It was genuine grief.

Bharat Rao could not have killed his dear friend. Padmini's observation, corroborated by Raju, had highlighted his clumsiness, and clumsiness was the last thing to be associated with their adversary.

'I am sorry,' Bharat Rao said.

'You may have a superhuman brain,' Vijay smiled, 'but you are a human after all.'

'It just pains me,' Bharat Rao said in a distressed tone, 'that

Anirudh, Mashelkar and David are all gone. The very purpose of my life is over.' He covered his head in a towel and wept unabashedly. Raju came and slowly led him away.

Raju returned in five minutes. 'I am sorry, but the scientist is unwell.'

'So,' Dalvi spoke for the first time, 'you made the Gandhiv.'

'Yes, Sir,' he said. 'It is a concoction of hibiscus oil, aloe juice, orange peel and pumpkin seed extract in an orange juice base. We add bitter gourd juice to make it bitter.'

'You come with us,' Dalvi said.

'Why?' Raju demanded.

'Because he says so.' This was said by the constable who had accompanied them. The tone was constabulary, and Raju quickly surrendered. Padmini couldn't help admiring the voice and its impact.

Dalvi whispered to Vijay, 'I will take care, Sir.'

Vijay waved goodbye and beckoned to Padmini to follow him.

ಹು

The hotel room smelled mustier than usual. Padmini noticed that the bedding hadn't been changed. 'Am I overstaying my welcome?'

Vijay laughed. 'Occupational hazard,' he said. 'You are taken for granted after some time.'

Padmini contemplated complaining to the manager about the falling standards of housekeeping, but on second thought, the boys were sweet. Her thoughts were disrupted by the jingle of Vijay's mobile. It was Dalvi. Vijay put the mobile on loudspeaker again.

'Sir,' Dalvi's voice sounded urgent, 'Raju says that the bottle we have in the evidence kit is not the one he gave to Bharat Rao.'

'How can he be so sure?' Padmini shouted.

'Madam!' The politeness went up a notch, though the excitement remained. 'The bottle into which he poured the Gandhiv had a cork lid. This one has a proper metallic cap.'

'Okay, leave him,' Vijay instructed.

'What next?' Dalvi enquired politely.

'Interrogate the servants in Mashelkar's home. The bottle must have been changed there.'

'I will do it right now, Sir.'

'No, tomorrow morning. Now you join the patrol car outside Nasiri's villa.'

'Right, Sir.'

Padmini had her back to the door and was staring at the monitor. She typed 'Patterson Laboratory' in the Google Chrome bar. Vijay walked in, breathing heavily and clearing his throat. Distracted, she turned round. Vijay wore his impish smile. She pretended to be angry.

Vijay's mobile rang. Switching on to the loudspeaker mode, he placed it on the side table.

'Sir,' Dalvi's surcharged voice began, 'Nasiri has just spoken to Bharat Rao. The voice was muffled as though there were back-to-back phones.'

'Did you hear what they spoke?' Vijay shouted.

'They did not speak much,' Dalvi continued breathlessly, 'but Nasiri was warned that cops are tailing him.'

'You wait there,' Vijay said. 'I am coming.'

He turned towards Padmini and moved his eyes to one corner, indicating her to follow.

'You go.' She continued surfing the internet.

'Trying to prove,' Vijay uttered sarcastically, 'that it is not Bharat Rao, but Vasudha.'

Padmini clasped Vijay's hands tightly. 'Time will tell,' she said, sounding combative, 'that my intuition doesn't err.'

Chapter 36

Vijay was thankful to the Board of Control for Cricket in India. People were glued to their television sets watching an India–Pakistan T20 match. The streets were deserted, allowing Vijay to breeze through. The speedometer touched the three-figure mark as he deviated into a desolate stretch. The GPS wasn't of much use. He was relying entirely on Dalvi's instructions.

'Along the stream,' Dalvi had said. Vijay drove on the narrow road adjacent to the stream. At a distance, he noticed a car. It was Dalvi, with two more constables. Vijay drew alongside them. He saw that the earlier car had been wedged behind two massive tree trunks and wasn't visible except for close scrutiny. Vijay, however, did not take pains to conceal his vehicle.

He surveyed the scene. A manicured lawn surrounded the two-storied building—its backside opening to the hillside. On the far side was the lake, serene and picturesque.

'Looks like he is alone,' Dalvi observed.

Vijay found it unusual that there were no servants. Maybe they had been packed off for the day. He swirled to face his men. 'Dalvi, you come with me, and you two keep watch.'

Vijay strained his ears. He thought he heard a door creak open. He moved towards his left to get a better view. A louder sound, unmistakable this time. A motorbike had roared to life. Vijay darted into his car, followed by Dalvi. Their prey had a considerable head start.

'Doesn't matter,' Dalvi consoled him. 'Because this is a dead end. The road goes uphill and ends at the woods.'

In less than ten minutes, they were at the foothill. Vijay parked his car next to a motorbike. The engine was hot, the headlights still on; it had been used a few minutes back.

Dalvi spoke in a voice indicating that he was delighted.

'The forest is a dead end. There is no way for him to escape unless he has a boat ready.'

Vijay followed Dalvi from the clearing into the woods. His eyes blinked, adjusting to the dimmer light. Dalvi was a decade and half elder to Vijay, yet he was every bit as swift.

Dalvi removed a torch from his trousers' pocket and shone it ahead. The ground was wet and Vijay ran carefully, fearing that the soil would give away. A colony of bats flew and fluttered and flapped its wings against Dalvi's forehead. He fell at the base of a trunk of a tree—a species that Vijay, a botany graduate, could not identify. The torch fell out of his hand.

Vijay helped Dalvi to his feet. Both men were panting and perspiring. Vijay retrieved the torch, in the nick of time to scare a fox that had come perilously close. He said, 'Take out your gun,' and he did the same himself.

Moving the torch ahead in circles, Dalvi ran further uphill.

A sound, faint but steady, startled Vijay.

Dalvi listened carefully, with his cupped hand close to his right ear. His face brightened. 'It is the sound of running water. We are going towards the lake.'

Dalvi had slowed down since the fall. But Vijay was confident of the direction: he only needed to follow the sound of the water. He now walked in front, followed by Dalvi.

He blocked Dalvi's progress with his arm. 'I can feel something moving,' he whispered. More leaves rustled, indicating further movement. Vijay advanced towards the leaves. Now, he could hear someone panting. It was certainly a man.

'Surrender!' Dalvi ordered and then threatened, 'Or we shoot you like a dog!'

There was no response.

Dalvi warned again, 'I will count to ten, if you don't—' Dalvi was interrupted by a bright flashlight. He blinked.

Vijay stared at their adversary.

Ali Nasiri's scared eyes were studying him. Nasiri was pointing his knife downwards, an indication that he was a novice. There was no gun in his hand.

Vijay thought of diving at Nasiri and incapacitating him. He hadn't abandoned his gun 'as the last-resort policy', despite his bitter experience from two days back. Unexpectedly, Nasiri flung the flashlight at Vijay, who evaded it comfortably.

Vijay picked up the flashlight, which fell on a thick patch of grass. It wasn't damaged at all.

Nasiri swayed away from them. Still running, he turned his head backwards and threw his knife. The throw was wayward and landed way off the mark.

Dalvi smiled at Vijay. Vijay smiled back. Their opponent had squandered his only weapon, as well as his source of light. He was heading towards the dead end. He was one against two; the odds were loaded against him. No wonder the veteran cop was sensing victory.

Dalvi had by now recovered and matched Vijay, stride for stride. They were gaining on Nasiri.

'Stop!' a panic-stricken Dalvi yelled. 'It is a sheer drop!'

Nasiri, distracted by Dalvi's cry, tripped over a stone. He continued crawling forward on all fours and from a distance could be mistaken for an intermediate species between an ape and a human.

They were nearing the edge of the cliff. Dalvi slowed down, and Vijay followed suit. They were three metres behind him, but Nasiri stood on the brink. Vijay flashed the light towards him. He instructed Dalvi, 'Do not unnerve him by your voice.'

Nasiri moved forward from land to air. Feet first, his descent began. Dalvi's horror-stricken face turned to Vijay. Nasiri's heart-wrenching cry reverberated.

Vijay heard a splash, the kind of sound that is generated when an object falls into water. He stood at the edge and aimed his flashlight downwards. Dalvi was doing the same.

'He hit the rocky surface,' Dalvi speculated, 'and rolled over into the lake.'

Vijay agreed.

'The lake is pretty deep at this point.' Dalvi sighed.

Vijay looked for a sign of life. If Nasiri knew how to swim, he could still be saved. He waited, hoping against hope. Dalvi stood by him. Then he walked away. Vijay realized that it was all over.

Vijay and Dalvi walked back, without exchanging any words. Vijay felt creatures crawling and creeping over his ankles and skin. They itched.

Dalvi swatted a swarm of mosquitoes with his hands. The bright lights attracted more insects. 'We never noticed these obstacles earlier,' Dalvi observed.

Vijay nodded. Then he said, 'Let us search Nasiri's home.'

Dalvi was keen to finish off the search before nosy reporters with cameras and anchors swarmed the place. What kind of noses did these journalists have, that smelled news from miles away? Padmini would spill the beans someday, he hoped.

The gates were invitingly left wide open. A gravelly yard separated the gate from the garden. The flooring was marble.

The hall had a window with a good front view. Dalvi could see the patrol vehicle clearly. Maybe Nasiri had seen them from here before making his escape. Expensive chandeliers hung from ceilings of every room.

A notebook, with a pen jutting out from one of the pages, lay on the table near a telephone. Vijay picked it up. Nasiri had written directions to reach a destination. Since the notebook was placed near the phone, Vijay surmised that Nasiri had received instructions over the phone. The last words were, 'stairs leading to an ancient temple'. Dalvi, who was also peering at the notebook, commented, 'Maybe, Nasiri thought he was heading towards the staircase.'

Vijay underlined the telephone number—0712-2695069—and looked at Dalvi.

'That is Bharat Rao's number, the very number we intercepted,' Dalvi noted.

'So, Nasiri was led to believe that a boat awaited him at the lake,' Vijay said.

Dalvi opened the refrigerator. 'He had planned to stay or maybe return—fresh fruits and milk inside.' He slammed the drawers and cupboards in a bedroom leading to the kitchen. He peeped into the washing machine. Clothes for washing in the machine confirmed Dalvi's hunch that he had planned to stay on. From a closet, Dalvi retrieved an envelope, 'Sir, sir,' he cried. The envelope contained a photograph of Kalu and a set of directions to reach him.

They searched a file cabinet, but found nothing more of interest.

Vijay smiled wryly and remarked, 'The bird has flown from the nest.'

Dalvi caught sight of himself in an ornate-framed mirror. He was never an 'Adonis' by any stretch of imagination, but right now he looked haggard and dishevelled. Vijay, too, had aged years in the last three days.

Dalvi, not known for hyperbole, uttered, 'Wow, what a bathroom!' Glass shelves opened up the wooden storage. Towels, napkins and bathrobes were stacked in the cabinet. A counter organizer made of brass occupied another end. Shampoos, conditioners, moisturizers, aroma oils and other cosmetics were neatly arranged. Dalvi rotated the counter organizer.

The bathtub was sunken with a wooden cover. The tiles looked like quilts. Dalvi touched one to make sure that it was actually a tile. He then took off his clothes and stood under the shower. Water poured like a cascade. He felt all his stress melting away.

Vijay looked at him, head to toe. Then he grinned. 'Free spa treatment.'

A patrol policeman called Dalvi on the mobile. 'The media are hot on our heels,' he announced. Even before Dalvi could convey the message to Vijay, the first reporter was knocking at the door.

༄

The mood was one of despondency when Vijay drove back to Hotel Heaven. Dalvi also did not initiate any conversation.

Chapter 37

Two weary figures, with defeat oozing out of every bone, trooped in. Padmini poured coffee into two mugs and handed one over to both Vijay and Dalvi.

Vijay went to take a quick shower.

Dalvi began with, 'Nasiri scooted...and ended with...the body will be recovered by divers tomorrow.'

Vijay came out looking refreshed.

Padmini looked at him. 'Tough luck.'

'How was your day?'

'I haven't been growing grass under my feet either.'

Vijay and Dalvi smiled meaningfully at each other. Still smiling, Vijay ribbed her. 'Something to prove Vasudha's guilt?'

Her reply was matter-of-fact. 'It is now established that Nasiri rang Vasudha.'

Dalvi jerked himself to an erect position. Vijay cocked his head forward. 'I thought,' Dalvi said defensively, 'that he had called Bharat Rao's landline.'

'I went to Bharat Rao's house and enquired. They swore that the landline never rang.'

'Then?'

'I met your friend who traces telephone calls.'

'You mean Trevor—haven't seen him for months now.'

She looked at Vijay. 'Trevor, the teddy bear.' The nickname was apt. Both laughed. 'He was both sweet and efficient,' she reflected. 'He checked and then it turned out that there was a call divert request registered on that number.'

'Where to?' Vijay leaned forward.

'All incoming calls went to David's mobile. It was still active. The call was received at Buddha Gardens.'

'Where is the mobile now?'

'Thrown into the drain. The battery is not to be found nor the handset.'

Dalvi acknowledged, 'You have administered shock and awe on us.'

Vijay looked at her with a mixture of affection and pride. 'What made you smell rat?'

She said, with passion, 'I somehow got the feeling that Vasudha had used Bharat Rao as a smokescreen. So, with you two out of the way, I fried my own fish.'

Vijay picked up a fork and pretended to eat. 'The fish fry is delicious.'

Dalvi laughed. 'What next?'

'A showdown,' Padmini said, gritting her teeth, 'with that bitch.'

Dalvi walked with his chair, crossed Vijay and settled next to Padmini. 'I have crossed the floor,' he declared.

'Majority,' Vijay countered, 'is not always right.'

Day 4

Karun's neighbour had a spare key, and Vijay looked around the flat. It was a two-bedroom apartment. Vijay had once climbed down a manhole. This stench matched the one he had experienced then. Old torn blankets were lying around. The sofa cover had grease on it. The bed had not been made for weeks, probably never since Kumudini's death.

A large pile of unwashed clothes, including handkerchiefs, socks and undergarments lay in a far corner. Cockroaches crawled over broken eggshells in the kitchen sink.

Vijay found the drawer he was looking for in the bedroom. The printout that had incensed Karun to commit a murder was there, neatly kept in a transparent folder.

It was a morphed image, something that could have easily been done on a computer by someone with reasonable skills. It followed that Anirudh did not rape Kumudini.

Vijay knew at least a dozen people who were capable of doing that. He felt sad for Karun. If he'd had a friend in whom he could confide, then he would have never done what he did. Vijay nurtured hopes that Karun could still be let off with a light sentence.

He peeped into the other bedroom. The wardrobe contained women's clothes. *It must be Kumudini's room*, he reckoned. A photo frame with the caption: 'Roopali, my dearest friend' cried for his attention.

He wiped the dust off the photo frame and unscrewed it. The back of the frame was punctuated with dark, thick cobwebs. He blew them away, and then wiped the frame clean with a wet cloth.

He shuffled through the papers on the table. Beneath a stack lay a visiting card holder. He leafed through the cards. He found two cards of interest, one for Roopali Phadnis, Marketing Executive, Safer Insurance Limited and the other for Vasudha, Director, Amrit Laboratories.

Vijay sat down on his haunches and opened the lowest case in the book shelf. A neatly bound appointment diary stood erect, it's back supported by a massive dictionary. The last item read 'Dinner with Vasudha.' It was dated 14 September, the day she met with the fatal accident.

Chapter 38

'We are getting nowhere,' Dalvi said, his voice sounding ominous, 'because everyone who testified that Anirudh was a womanizer has never actually seen him with a woman. None of the employees of the massage parlours have seen him either.'

'But his wife thought so,' Vijay argued, 'and a wife's feeling may not necessarily be factually correct.'

Padmini looked thoughtful and sullen.

Vijay prodded, 'Any ideas?'

'Just as I suspected.' She flipped through her notes taken down on the reverse of tarot cards. 'It is most likely a paste-on.'

'Paste-on?' Vijay echoed.

She smiled. '"Paste-on" is a term coined by me and my friends. It is used for spreading false information about people by pasting stuff on their Facebook wallpaper. Meaning, a Facebook frequenter can easily spread word about someone and that is likely to stay if the counter party is shy of social media.'

'So, you reckon that Anirudh was not a womanizer.'

'He did not look like one to me,' she said rather emphatically, 'nor does he have any record of social media activity. The entire effort has been to discredit him.'

Vijay chewed his lip. 'Difficult to understand her action, because this turns the needle of suspicion towards her.'

'The attempt,' Dalvi pointed out, 'has been planned and systematic. So we need to find the motive.'

Vijay snapped his fingers in exasperation. 'Motives for murders,' he whined.

'Sub-motives for other actions,' Padmini added.

Dalvi made a clucking sound with the tongue on the roof of the mouth and shook his head.

Padmini cleared her throat noisily. 'I can decipher the motive. She made us presume that Anirudh did not come home from the post office, so that we would rule her out as a suspect.'

'If that be the case,' Vijay contested, 'then why did we observe lipstick marks on his cheeks and nail polish on his beard?'

'They could be hers as well,' Padmini countered.

'It is inconceivable,' Dalvi protested, 'but very much possible.'

Chapter 39

Day 5

Vijay joined Padmini for the buffet breakfast at Hotel Heaven. The hotel staff was no longer in awe of him, though respect was still forthcoming.

Padmini wiped her fork with a napkin. 'The endgame has begun. We have only two days left.'

'As long as I give my best shot,' Vijay philosophized, 'I do not regret.'

'All the same,' Padmini countered, 'defeat from now on will be a bitter pill.'

Vijay waited with an empty plate. A waiter came closer. 'Masala dosa.'

'Madam?'

'Uthappam for me,'

Vijay rotated a fork on an empty plate. 'If Bharat's accomplice applied the poison on the nozzle of the washbasin tap, then when could he have done it?'

'Well before David checked in.'

Vijay's eyes twinkled.

'When is that—well before?'

Padmini shrugged her shoulders and raised her eyebrows.

Vijay carried the tea cup to the reception desk. 'Can you give me,' he asked, taking another sip, 'the occupancy details of room 701 from a week before the murder?'

'Please be seated, Sir.' The woman smiled. Vijay sat on the sofa, leafing through the morning's newspapers. He finished his tea and placed the cup on a side table.

Padmini joined him.

The receptionist handed him a printout. Vijay put his thumb on the third line. 'The previous guest, Mr Rohan Labra, vacated at twelve noon the previous day.'

'I will be back in a minute,' the receptionist promised. She opened a drawer and took out a register. She placed it on her counter and flipped a few pages. She then walked over towards Vijay and Padmini, register in hand.

'David's booking had been confirmed from 2:00 p.m. on the day that Labra vacated, but he arrived a day later. In fact, we had even received advance payment for the same, and were told to reserve that very room.'

'Thanks. Please send the CCTV footage of the previous day to our room.'

※

The tapes arrived. Vijay flicked on the recorder. The scenes were repetitive.

'I can't bear to watch this stuff.' Padmini yawned.

Vijay ignored her and concentrated hard. The quality of the recording was poor. The images were at times blurred. Ghost images appeared, making it difficult to discern what was going on.

Padmini got up. 'Enough is enough.'

Vijay continued unabated. Suddenly, he pushed the pause button. He rewound the tape. He went near the screen and watched intently. 'There!' he cried.

Padmini stood next to him. 'I cannot,' she grumbled, 'make head or tail of it.'

Vijay said excitedly, 'Someone has been caught pilfering cash from the counter.' He sent for the manager.

The manager tried to remember. 'Yes, one temporary cleaner was caught.'

'Bring him here right away,' Vijay demanded.

The manager spoke, in a frightened voice, 'We fired him, but we have his address.'

Few minutes later, a tall man with a bushy moustache extended his hand to Vijay. 'I am Rakesh, the housekeeping head. The housekeeping staff,' he mentioned, 'went on a flash strike, so we employed casual labour.'

Vijay stood up. 'For how many days?'

'Just two days,' Rakesh replied. 'They returned after we raised their wages.'

'This means,' Padmini said, 'that we have not interviewed this man.'

'I am afraid so,' Rakesh admitted, 'but the man stole nothing, so we did not report the matter.'

'Anything you remember about the incident?'

Rakesh looked around. The manager had left. He went and closed the door. 'Please keep it confidential,' he whispered.

Vijay put a comforting hand. 'Nobody comes to trouble when he helps me.'

The colour returned to Rakesh's cheeks. 'This man who had been nabbed stealing cash from the drawer wanted to get caught,' he said.

'Why?'

'No idea, Sir.'

'Then,' Padmini inquired, 'How did you reach this conclusion?'

'He made no attempt to hide or escape. He was slow and brazen. Then, once caught, he only pleaded to be sent.'

'Anything else?'

'Not with this man,' Rakesh said, 'but something queer happened.'

Vijay saw Padmini's eyes shining.

'I received a phone call, within minutes of the incident,' he halted and then fear gripped his face. 'Sir, do not arrest me.'

Padmini stood between Vijay and Rakesh. 'I give you my word,' she said, placing her hand on her heart, 'that you will not come to grief unless you have murdered.'

'No, no,' he screamed. 'The caller offered me twenty thousand rupees. In fact, it was credited to my account straightaway. I got a mobile alert for the same.'

'What did he pay you for?'

'He told me,' Rakesh confided, 'not to give out room 701

any further till it was occupied by David.'

Padmini moved forward in her chair. 'You obeyed?'

'Yes,' Rakesh confessed. 'The room had been done up by then, and we were having staff problems, so this was a godsend.'

'Who did up room 701?'

'The guy who was caught stealing.'

Padmini held Rakesh's hand. 'Never take bribes in the future,' she warned, 'but this time your information to us is invaluable.'

Vijay advised, 'Do not mention the fact that you received any money to anyone else.'

'By the way,' Padmini asked, 'how did you get the money?'

'Through cash deposit at an ATM.'

'Thanks, you may go, but just give us the photograph, name and address of that man.'

'Sure, Sir.'

Rakesh went off.

Vijay turned to Padmini. 'Diabolical,' he uttered, with admiration in his voice.

'Meticulous,' Padmini added, 'to the extent that it was ensured that we did not interview the cleaner, who actually applied the poison.'

A polite knock disturbed their conversation. It was Dalvi.

Vijay filled Dalvi in with the morning's events.

Dalvi expressed a doubt. 'How could the killer be so sure that the cleaner who dabbed the poison on the tap would be left scot-free?'

Padmini sprang up. 'Even if he were reported to the police, he would have been in jail and below our radar.'

'Superb,' Dalvi muttered under his breath. Then he added, 'Anyhow, the cleaner would have escaped with ₹10,000. I am sure he was paid much more.'

'Dalvi,' Vijay said, 'your turn.'

Dalvi gulped a glass of water. Then he said, 'Where to begin?'

'Just recall the day,' Padmini suggested.

'We went with Bharat Rao's servant Raju,' Dalvi began, 'to Mashelkar's house. There, he identified the bottle that was given to Bharat Rao.'

'Did it have a cork lid?'

Dalvi nodded.

'I am certain,' Vijay explained, 'that one servant would be missing from the Mashelkar household. That missing servant would have exchanged the real Gandhiv with black mamba venom.'

'You are suggesting,' Dalvi said, 'that the missing servant joined Hotel Heaven as a cleaner, dabbed poison and scooted.'

'Exactly.'

Dalvi did not respond immediately. A lot was on his mind. He uttered a monosyllable, 'Unlikely.'

Vijay pinned an intense gaze on him. Dalvi slipped off his dark glasses and kneaded his temples. He got up and walked a few steps. Vijay saw him reflected in the mirror.

Dalvi's face twisted into a grimace rather than a smile. 'Yadav stood guarding the gate; Naman guarded Mashelkar's room. Both of them frisked every entrant, insider or outsider. Even Vasudha and David were not spared. They are our best men, who do not flag.'

Vijay went into the washroom. When he returned, he drolly remarked, 'Still, someone got past both of them with a bottle of black mamba venom.'

Dalvi fell abruptly silent, as if a tape had been switched off. Then he added laconically, 'Mystery within mystery.'

Vijay looked at Dalvi levelly. He handed over the photograph and the other details of the missing cleaner.

'I will,' Dalvi said, 'first confirm from Mashelkar's servants whether he is the same man, and then search him.'

'Dalvi, get me the man and you get a bravery medal.'

'Dead or alive,' Dalvi promised, 'He will be at your knees by tomorrow.'

'No, only alive,' Padmini corrected, 'because he is the murderer's footprint and that footprint will lead us to the ultimate prize.'

After Dalvi left, Vijay received a call. It was from the mobile service provider. Rakesh had received the call from a public telephone, as feared. Again, no electronic lead.

Vijay looked at his watch. 'Nearly one,' he said. 'I will grab a quick lunch and go to the court. Karun's case is up for hearing at two-thirty.'

Chapter 40

Roopali lived in a paying guest accommodation in Gokulpeth. She had just shampooed her hair and was drying it with a blow-dryer. She half opened the door.

Padmini said firmly, 'Police.'

Roopali let her in. Roopali was tiny, but cute-looking. Her eyes were fearful.

Padmini turned on her charm. 'I hope I am not inconveniencing you in any way.'

'No, I am on leave today.'

Padmini smiled warmly. She patted Roopali's wrist and held her arm lovingly. 'Do not worry,' she said.

Roopali forced a half smile.

'Was Kumudini your best friend?'

Roopali answered even before Padmini finished her question. 'Yes!'

'If you cooperate,' Padmini postulated, 'I can bring her murderer to justice.'

'I never knew,' Roopali confessed, 'that Kumudini was murdered. I heard that it was an accident.'

'I am not so sure,' Padmini said.

'Kumudini loved, adored and worshipped her brother Karun. She would never tire of telling me how much she owed him.'

Padmini asked, 'Did she have any complaints against him?'

'Oh yes, she did,' Roopali emphasized. 'Kumudini lamented that he imposed his puritanical values on her. Kumudini desired money, parties, boyfriends, jewellery, cars. She despised her brother's over-honest approach.'

'Over-honest?'

'That is how Kumudini described her brother,' Roopali clarified, 'but she was beginning to break free, albeit on the sly.'

'Like?'

'She partied, she drank and she watched porn.'

Padmini stared at Roopali, her eyes goring into Roopali's face. 'Are you sure?'

'Of course,' Roopali said. 'Her big break came when the director scientist of Amrit Laboratories offered her a plum post with a salary of eighty thousand per month. She was given an advance of two months to join.' Roopali broke down. The last few words were spoken while weeping. 'What a stroke of luck! Alas, she did not live to enjoy it.'

Padmini offered her a tissue. Then she put a supportive arm over Roopali's shoulder.

'Kumudini was told that she could retain her job at Safer Life and also work at Amrit Labs,' Roopali said.

'Did she join?'

'Yes.'

Padmini placed Vasudha's photograph before Roopali.

'She is the one whom Kumudini referred to as her godmother,' Roopali said, looking at the photo.

'What did the two talk about?'

'That was the only thing,' Roopali said in a melancholic voice, 'that Kumudini never came clean about. She did not confide in me.'

'Anything else you remember about that ill-fated day?'

'Kumudini was thrilled. She kept looking at her appointment letter. I called her mobile at least seven times after ten in the night but she did not respond.'

'Was that unusual for her?'

'Very.'

Padmini fiddled with her mobile and a voice recording played.

'That is Kumudini!!' Roopali shrieked.

'You have been invaluable,' Padmini hugged Roopali, 'and I assure you that her murderer will not escape.'

※

Padmini, accompanied by Dalvi, went towards Wardhaman Nagar Police Station in a car driven by a constable. The car was parked in a paid slot. Dalvi called Inspector Wagle, the station house officer of the police station on his mobile but got no response. He turned to Padmini, mobile still glued to his ears. 'You please wait here until I call you.'

Padmini stood leaning on the car.

Dalvi went into the police station. Seven minutes later, he called, 'Please come.'

People moved in and out of the police station in groups. A guard wielded a baton in the air to push away the queue-breakers. Two constables rushed out to escort Padmini. A constabulary yell and a constabulary push, and everyone made way for her. The noisy police station abruptly fell to pin-drop silence. Cops, commoners, complainants and inmates all behaved as though a film star had stepped in.

Padmini walked in slowly. The station house officer offered his chair to her. Activities resumed in the room—complaints were made, inquiries conducted and First Information Reports registered.

Inspector Wagle handed her a file. 'I have made a copy of the file. It is for you, Madam.'

Padmini held the file. 'Tell me what you remember.'

'She was totally drunk and she drove without headlights and collided with an approaching truck. Died on the spot.'

The walls of the police station were crying for a replaster. The windowpanes had cracks, and the floors, although neatly scrubbed, needed to be retiled.

Padmini asked. 'Did you find anything else?'

Wagle tried to remember. 'She had a prepaid card of Reliance Digital. It had been activated just the previous day. It was cancelled the following day, even though we had the card with us.'

Wagle yelled at a constable who was hogging aloo bonda from a plate resting atop a Remington typewriter. Wagle, who was dignity personified while talking to Padmini, was nasty with his subordinates. His ability to move in and out was admirable.

'In whose name was the card?'

Wagle scratched his head.

Padmini leafed through the file. 'It was in Vasudha's name,' she read from the file.

Wagle smiled.

Padmini stiffened at the sight of a prisoner in chains,

struggling like a dog on a leash. Wagle offered her water.

Dalvi stopped him. 'Get mineral water.'

A bottle of Kinley was thrust before her. She drank two huge gulps, emptying half the bottle. She leaned back on the chair and smiled.

'We went to the address,' Wagle went on, 'from where Kumudini had made the last phone call. It was a service apartment rented for a day by Mohinder Singh, a diminutive effeminate Sikh. He vacated the next day. In between, the room boys working in the apartment saw two women partying. One of them was Kumudini.'

Dalvi tugged at Wagle's elbow—'I had asked you to bring those room boys here.'

Wagle grinned, 'Can I afford to disobey Dalvi?'

Wagle shouted orders over the intercom. A constable held a boy with broken front teeth by his elbow and dragged him into Wagle's cabin.

'He saw the women.' Wagle informed.

Padmini tapped a few times on her mobile. Vasudha's face popped out. She showed it to boy.

'It is her, I am sure,' the boy said.

Chapter 41

Dalvi suddenly remembered the conversation he had with Madan awhile back, regarding the black Nano car. Madan had revealed that it had been driven by a lady. At that point, Dalvi had dismissed the lead as a false one, because he hadn't factored a woman as the culprit. *Could that woman be Vasudha?*—the thought reverberated in his mind. He met Madan again and showed him Vasudha's photograph.

'That is her,' Madan confirmed.

Dalvi patted Madan on the shoulder and said, 'This is the second time you have helped the police. I will get you an appreciation letter from the department.'

'You are a great soul,' Madan said.

Dalvi wasn't listening to Madan anymore. His focus had drifted elsewhere. It was the same car that Vijay had seen making surreptitious moves. Dalvi had verified that the vehicle belonged to Bharat Rao, but now it was proven that Vasudha was at the wheel. Dalvi proceeded to the site of Anirudh's murder, Laxmi Road. He surveyed the area. There were four restaurants, all of them similar, offering snacks as well as thali meals.

He went to the restaurants, talked to the managers, showed them Anirudh's photographs and enquired if they knew him. At Aryan Restaurant, they recognized him. According to the hotel staff, he was a regular customer.

'Very sad...' the assistant manager remarked. 'He had reserved a table and wanted a South Indian thali to be served. Unfortunately, he never lived to see it.'

'Why did he need to reserve a table?' Dalvi asked. He had guessed the reason, but wanted confirmation.

'He was a diabetic, so if he took insulin,' the manager spoke like an expert physician, 'he needed to have food within half an hour.'

Dalvi thanked him for his cooperation. He sat down and ordered a cup of coffee.

ॐ

When Dalvi entered room 701 in Hotel Heaven, Vijay was simultaneously on two phones, his mobile and the hotel intercom. He smiled and motioned to Dalvi to sit. He first hung up the hotel telephone and then disconnected his mobile.

Dalvi blurted out before anyone could speak. 'Sir, Vasudha is the culprit.'

Padmini coughed, cleared her throat and smiled teasingly.

'Your evidence first,' Vijay snapped. 'Conclusions later.'

'Vasudha,' Dalvi said, 'had parked her car right opposite Anirudh when he was shot.'

'Why on earth,' Padmini asked, 'did she do that?'

Vijay said, 'I believe, she had given up hope that Karun would act. She expected Anirudh to fall due to the ricin shot. She had parked her car, near about where she expected him to fall. As soon as he fell, she would have announced that she was his wife and whisked him away in her car. It would not have been a police case at all in that eventuality, because he would have fallen dead in front of a hundred witnesses.'

Dalvi concurred. 'Getting a death certificate and arranging his funeral would have been child's play for her. If you had not been there at that moment and spotted the vehicle, it would have never occurred to anyone.'

Chapter 42

Vijay drove himself to Lucy's home, accompanied by Dalvi.

Dalvi hummed a soft tune, while Vijay remained immersed in thought; neither spoke a word. As they neared her home, Dalvi pointed to a corner, 'Let us park the car and walk. That will warm us up.'

Vijay obeyed without a murmur.

They traced their steps slowly towards Lucy's home. Although both were seasoned investigators, nervousness was apparent in their bearing.

Lucy ushered them in cordially. Her daughter, Nancy,

brought a jug and two glasses of water in a tray and placed them on a table.

'There are a couple more things,' Vijay began cautiously, 'that we need to know about David.'

The expression on Nancy's face changed. She was looking like a dam ready to burst. Vijay was eyeing her surreptitiously. She did what Vijay expected her to do, explode into tears. After around five minutes, she smiled sheepishly, 'Suddenly, I cracked up.'

'Doesn't matter,' Vijay said with empathy. Dalvi offered her water. She took a sip or two, after which she looked much better. Vijay asked politely, 'Can I have a look at David's room?'

Lucy led Vijay and Dalvi into David's study. Once they were alone, Dalvi asked, 'What are we aiming at?'

Vijay peered through the pages of a book that seemed to have been purchased recently. He slammed the book shut.

'Lucy told Padmini that David had recently acquired the unusual habit of thrusting his mouth into the tap. We have to find out, why?'

Dalvi removed his cap and put it on again. 'You are an incurable optimist.' They combed the bookshelf, trying to speed read through the books to see if any clue would emerge. Dalvi's eyes caught a sheaf of paper below the study table. He squatted on the floor and tenaciously leafed through them. He held out a paper, dusted it and then read it aloud. 'Sucking water from a tap relieves Meige's Syndrome.'

Vijay took the paper. It was an article published in a medical journal. There were images of various exercises that a sufferer from the disease was advised to perform to seek relief. Ball juggling was one, and thrusting one's mouth into a tap and sucking was also one of them.

Vijay whistled delightfully. He folded his index finger and

rammed it against the upper end of the article.

Dalvi leaned over. It was an e-mail sent by Vasudha two months back. No wonder, she was confident that he would do it without fail when reminded over the phone.'

Vijay drummed his fingers on the table. They thanked Lucy and Nancy. As they left, Nancy remarked, 'I am a Reiki master. I can see halos around both your heads. Failure can never touch you.'

Vijay knew this wasn't true. Both Dalvi and he had their share of reverses.

He managed a smile.

Chapter 43

Vasudha had an appointment with Dr Garg, a dentist, for root canal treatment. Padmini waited at the entrance to the clinic, ready to accost her. Vijay stood next to her.

Padmini stiffened as she saw Vasudha's car approaching. Vasudha wore dark glasses. She stood near her car and brushed her hair. From where she stood, she must surely have seen them. She walked, pretending as though they didn't exist. As she neared them, Padmini blocked her way. Vasudha smiled, 'Hi.'

Padmini replied, 'Hi.'

'So,' Vasudha said sardonically, 'are you looking for my dental records?'

Padmini replied in a matter-of-fact tone, 'Not really. We just wanted to enquire about David's mobile.'

'David's mobile?'

Vasudha pretended to be surprised.

'Yeah, the mobile number, to which all incoming calls from Bharat Rao's landline were diverted. The mobile from which

Nasiri was warned, and which was dismantled and destroyed and thrown into the drain in Buddha Gardens.'

For the first time, worry lines creased Vasudha's forehead. Vijay could see fear in her eyes, behind the dark glasses.

'What are you talking about?'

She was sounding less confident than before.

Padmini asked in an earnest voice. She seemed in greater control of herself, 'Any idea who could have done it?'

Vasudha's voice had traces of hysteria. 'How am I to know?'

'I wonder'—Padmini paused and enunciated every word—'whether you did it?'

Vasudha paused for an eternity. She did not have a ready answer. Vijay thought of parroting Padmini's question. Vasudha spoke just then, 'It could be Bharat Rao. After all, it was his landline.'

Padmini took a step closer and stared at Vasudha combatively. Vasudha did not flinch either.

'You had easy access to his house.'

'So did Bharat in his own house.' She laughed.

'But,' Padmini raised her eyebrows, 'only you could have had David's mobile.'

Vasudha shook her head and laughed, so much that she coughed.

'David often forgot his mobile, and he could have forgotten it in Bharat's house.'

Padmini stood transfixed. Vasudha flashed a V sign with the fingers of her right hand and chuckled. 'Excuse me'—she brushed past Padmini—'I am getting late for my appointment.'

Vijay tucked his arm into Padmini's and whisked her away. 'You were great,' he remarked in an appreciative voice.

'But she won.'

'No, I could see that she was rattled. Under stress, people

say and do what they don't normally.'

'Like?'

'She countered your argument by pointing fingers at Bharat Rao.'

'But wasn't she logical?'

'Yes, but that also proves your point that she has been using others as a smokescreen. The first hint of trouble and she pushes someone else into the firing line. That is her style. We have established that.'

'Really?'

'She was prepared for your questions, so she knows you suspect her and was ready with counters and alibis—all the more reason to believe that she is guilty.'

'I feel so much better.'

Chapter 44

Vasudha sat at the edge of the sofa in the lobby of Dr Garg's dental clinic. From that point, she got a good view of the road through the glass doors.

Vijay's police jeep pulled away. Vasudha trespassed into the chamber where Dr Garg was examining another patient.

Seeing Vasudha, he spoke through the green face mask. 'Five minutes, tops.'

'I need to go,' she said. 'I have some urgent work.'

Dr Garg lowered his mask, 'The receptionist will schedule your next appointment.'

'Thanks.'

Vasudha steeled herself against a creepy train of thought. She had spent many years disciplining her mind, and now she was granite hard. She drove—her mind almost blank. She parked her car in the basement car park of a popular mall. She sauntered to Starbucks Coffee and occupied a single table in a dark corner.

Another carefully crafted deception had been blown apart. These guys were a formidable lot. Two more days remained, and the fearful shadow of defeat that seemed unthinkable less than two days back now loomed on the horizon.

They had discovered her cover-up trick and knew that it was she and not Bharat Rao who had contacted Ali Nasiri. Vijay most certainly only had her now in his cross hairs and that thought sent a chill down her spine. Padmini's fiery determination, Vijay's incisive analysis and Dalvi's organizational abilities represented a redoubtable combination; they were relentlessly chipping away at her.

'Think positive.' She repeated the mantra over and over again. Coffee, along with two chocolate cookies on a large tray, nearly covered the table, edge to edge.

Sipping her coffee, she regrouped. They had zeroed in on her and would be breathing down her neck. They had a little over two days. These would be the longest three days in her life.

She crushed the cookie to powder with her fingers. That unexpected action suddenly released her bottled-up stress. She felt her head grow lighter, her breathing more even, and soon enough, her thinking became clearer.

Very few people could give evidence connecting her to the crimes. The most lethal one—Nasiri—had been accounted for. Kumudini was no more. Everyone else saw and interacted with a Sikh. And there was no way anyone could prove that, it was her disguised as a Sikh!

Yet, a thought bothered her. She had overlooked someone— someone who had interacted with her and who could identify her as Vasudha, and who could therefore connect her to the crimes. No name came to her mind. She brushed aside the thought.

She paid in cash, slammed the door shut and walked confidently to the car. She circled the trunk and took her position behind the wheel. Again, the thought burnt her, acid-like, that some loose end remained to be tied. Damn it, the all-important fact was not springing to her mind.

Half an hour later, she was at home. The bedcovers needed to be washed. She heaped them in a corner. She sat on the bare bed and recoiled as if she had been handed a physical blow.

Chakravak!

If they got to him, her goose was cooked. Her heart raced faster than an express train. She picked herself up and felt for the car keys in her pocket. Hair spilled in front of her eyes, momentarily blinding her.

She stopped. If they had tracked Chakravak, then they would be waiting for her to contact him. She would walk into a trap. Her only bet lay in them not getting that far.

Two days back, she had been in an unassailable position. Now, it was anybody's game, and considering the momentum they had built up, they were favourites.

Vasudha's brain was now very much in the thinking groove, and in such situations she could be diabolical.

She had laid her finger on the problem. She had been in front, when she took the initiative. Now, she had surrendered the whip and was merely reacting.

A bold aggressive step—or rather a string of such steps—would be required. She sized up her constraints and jotted down two points:

- » *She could not use her favourite disguise. The cops would pounce on the effeminate Sikh.*
- » *She could not use any pay phone. Even neighbouring towns would be guarded this time round.*

A television news channel informed that the State Home Minister Suryavanshi was in town. He was lying low after an aborted attempt at toppling the chief minister.

Vasudha picked her landline and dialled. 'I am Vasudha, Director of Amrit Laboratories. Connect me to the minister.'

'What is it regarding?' the voice inquired.

'Something of extreme importance for him.' Her voice had sounded urgent. It did the trick. She heard a click.

Suryavanshi spoke. 'I am sorry to hear about the murders of Mashelkar, your husband and—'

'David,' she finished for him. 'If you can spare some time, I can help you in your mission.'

The tone from Suryavanshi was harsher. 'What do you know about my mission?'

'I can help,' she paused, 'to smear egg on the chief minister's face and also project you as a knight in shining armour.'

There was a lengthy pause. Then Suryavanshi relented.

Vasudha now dialled Godbole. 'Who gives you sleepless nights?'

Pat came the reply: 'Vijay.'

'Do you know my sworn enemy?' There was a silence at the other end. Vasudha continued. 'It is Padmini.'

Godbole breathed heavily. 'Our enemies have joined hands. It is time we did the same too.'

Vasudha caught her own face brighten up in the mirror. 'Come over to Hotel Radhika and wait at the lobby. At the opportune time, I will call you. We will meet the state home minister.'

꽃

Vasudha underplayed her sense of fashion. She dressed as a traditional Indian housewife would. Suryavanshi greeted her with folded hands. She reciprocated. They sat at respectable distances from each other.

'You know,' Vasudha said softly, 'I am going through a bad patch in my personal as well as professional life.'

'I know, I know,' he nodded. 'You are widowed. The great Mashelkar is murdered. I mean, you might be feeling insecure.'

'Yes, Sir.' She lowered her voice to a whisper. 'An officer called Vijay harasses me to no end.'

'Vijay,' Suryavanshi remarked affectionately, 'is a brave boy. I had awarded him with a bravery medal last year.'

Vasudha buried her head in her hands. She pretended to pull back her tears. She spoke in a voice that trembled. 'I have no place to go.' She got up.

Surya beckoned her to stay. Then he asked gently, 'Why is he harassing you like this?'

'He is punch-drunk since the chief minister backs him to the hilt.' She waited for effect. It was instantaneous.

'So, the bastard works for the chief minister! The traitor. I thought he was *my* jewel.'

'If you do not believe me,' she squealed, 'there are some senior police officers waiting in the lobby to complain about him to you. I bumped into them just before entering.'

Surya leaned and instructed someone to show the police officers in.

Godbole, accompanied by Rathore, walked in. Lemon juice was served. Godbole spoke in a soft, unobtrusive voice that convinced Surya that Vijay had to be reined in.

Provoked, Surya picked up the phone. 'Get me Commissioner Patel!'

Godbole loped across the room and stood close to the minister. 'Sir, let us not,' he pleaded, 'do anything that affects your image adversely.' Rathore nodded. Godbole continued.

'Vijay is supposedly battling for a natural cause. We should not take any action that attracts negative publicity.'

The minister seemed to agree. Vasudha's enthusiasm dampened a touch, but then Godbole was speaking sense.

'We will take Dalvi off their team,' Godbole suggested. 'That will not attract much attention, but it will cripple their team. We will also work to keep Vijay disoriented.'

'Good work.' Suryavanshi looked pleased. 'Gentlemen and lady.'

'Commissioner Patel on line.' Vasudha heard the minister's personal assistant call out on the phone.

As they trooped out of the hotel, Vasudha told Rathore, 'Keep me informed of their movements.'

'Done.'

Chapter 45

Day 6

The day dawned bright with blue skies. A cool breeze blew, making the day pleasurable. Late October in Nagpur was pleasant. Not hot, not chilly, just a nip in the air but with plenty of sun. Diwali was just a week away. The mood was, understandably, already festive. From Janamashtami in late August to Diwali in early November, Hindus celebrated a number of festivals. The hangover of one festival left a residue that would enliven as the next one approached.

Shoppers were out in the traditional markets of Sitabuldi, with women leading the way. Although schools were still in session, children accompanied their mothers, adding gaiety to the atmosphere. Vendors of traditional sweets made a killing, as did ice cream shops. Even dogs and squirrels had a ball licking the melted ice creams on the roads. As winters set in, coffee would replace ice cream as the favourite among shoppers.

Vasudha had gone to her office as early as seven in the morning. She was now driving back. Her son Manish was waving at her through the window of his school bus. She waved back, but felt little love for him. Maybe she would pack him off to a boarding school next summer.

Vasudha was close to achieving her immediate goals. Mahapatra had severed ties, Mashelkar was no more and Bharat Rao's health worsened by the day. David and Anirudh had been accounted for. Amrit Laboratories had now become her pocket borough. She had already gone, inking a deal with Patterson Laboratories. A presentation was to be made the following week in Monte Carlo and she would be sitting on a billion-dollar bank balance.

Rathore had rung up to convey glad tidings. Dalvi had been severed from Vijay's team and placed directly under Godbole. Patel was likely to hold Vijay at bay for at least half a day. Buoyed by the success of her counteroffensive, she drove faster.

※

Vijay received an early morning call from Commissioner Patel. This would cost him at least two hours, something he could ill afford, with the clock ticking away. However, he had to comply. He was confident that Padmini and Dalvi would be covering for him effortlessly.

Patel had his spectacles resting on his nose, an indication that he was tense and angry. Vijay took long deep breaths and told himself to relax. Patel motioned to Vijay to sit. He was writing orders on a file. A few minutes later, he looked at Vijay, his countenance stern and the spectacles sliding down further.

'Now, what is going on?' he demanded.

Vijay realized that he had made the mistake of not updating Patel every evening as required, and in that respect, he had exceeded his brief. He said slowly, 'I got so engrossed that I forgot to update you. In fact, I am racing against time.' He looked at his watch.

Patel glared. 'Now you have gone too far. Why on earth did you,' he thundered, 'not oppose Karun's bail?'

'We need his help to solve the current case.' Vijay looked Patel straight in the eye. 'Also, he is unlikely to murder anyone else or tamper with any evidence, so what is the harm in granting him bail?'

Patel looked hurt.

'Sorry for raising my voice.'

Patel swatted the apology. 'Never mind. I am under the hammer.'

'From whom?'

'The well-wishers of Rathore and Godbole,' Patel said sadly. 'They are baying for your blood and also accusing me of partisanship.' He rubbed his thumb against the little finger to indicate the number one. 'First, you insisted on having that girl; second, the press conference; third, allowing Karun to go scot-free; fourth, keeping the entire police force in the dark.' Patel paused, 'You are also spending lavishly on that girl's hotel bill.'

Rage spread through Vijay, almost blinding him. His words slurred. 'I was given complete autonomy by no less a man than the chief minister himself, and I refuse to accept it as a lapse.' He paused. Then his voice became combative. 'As for the rest—'

Patel signalled Vijay to calm down. 'See,' he said, as if placating, 'people are blaming me, and if'—he now sounded like he was warning—'you fail to deliver the goods, as seems likely, I cannot save you.'

In Vijay's heart, old anger flared up again. His body shook so badly that he could hardly speak clearly. 'What do you mean, as seems likely? We have two full days left before the deadline.'

'Vijay,' Patel offered a truce, 'if you call off the project, I will somehow save you.'

'What do you mean call off?' Vijay demanded. 'Do you not want the culprits to be nabbed?'

'Vijay, see reason,' he pleaded. 'I have been your age. I have done many more cases than you have. I know that you cannot meet the deadline. In your own interest,' he said, looking away, 'I advise you to quit.'

'A winner never quits.' Vijay thumped his chest proudly. 'And a quitter never wins.'

'That is all right in movies, but life is different.'

'If I do not quit, and also fail?'

'We will have to slap some charges on you and initiate disciplinary proceedings, even suspend you,' Patel replied nonchalantly. 'If you quit, I will adjust you somewhere.'

'I would rather die by the sword,' Vijay declared, 'than surrender.'

Patel poured water from a jug into a glass. He pushed it towards Vijay. 'Drink and cool down.' He smiled.

Vijay sipped water and spoke nothing. His heart raged. Instead of supporting a national cause, the department's officers were busy settling petty personal scores.

'I can understand your anger,' Patel said, 'but ideals and reality seldom converge. The chief minister,' he continued, 'is busy keeping his flock together. He faces a rebellion in the ranks. His chair is shaky.'

'What about the Union home minister?' Vijay asked sardonically.

Patel laughed. 'He is more concerned about the helicopter scam. Why, even the media and the common men have moved away from these murders!'

'I do not know,' Vijay sneered, 'whether to laugh or to cry.'

'Neither,' Patel advised. 'Do not wear your heart on your sleeve, more so a passionate, patriotic heart.'

'So passion and patriotism are crimes?'

'No, but be pragmatic. Cover your bases, and a smooth career will follow. Why work your butt off for something that nobody cares about?'

'Thanks, but I go my way.'

'Remember,' Patel said, 'I have to give something to the other side. You do not know how much pressure I have resisted.'

Vijay now got the wind. Both Rathore and Godbole were highly connected, and they must have been piling pressure on poor upright Patel. Anger retreated from his heart. 'I regret,' Vijay said, feeling genuinely sorry, 'about not keeping you updated.'

'Your choice, but you won't have Dalvi with you.'

The statement went through Vijay like a low-voltage shock. 'You take him the day after tomorrow,' Vijay pleaded.

Patel shook his head. 'His transfer orders have been issued. He would have already reported to Godbole.'

Vijay turned his back to Patel. He heard Patel cry out. 'Surrender and I will take care.'

Vijay paid no heed and marched out of the office. He looked at his mobile, which he had kept on silent mode. Dalvi had reported to Godbole as ordered. He was idling, the WhatsApp said. With less than two days to go, his sword arm had been snatched away. He was surprised that Padmini hadn't called him even once.

Maybe she is up to something, he mused and smiled.

Chapter 46

When Vijay reached Hotel Heaven, he was greeted by the manager. 'Can I have a word with you?'

'Sure.'

'There is something,' he whispered, 'that I remembered about the strike.'

'Shoot.'

'First of all, the union leader, Shinde'—he paused thoughtfully—'called a flash strike and climbed down for a pittance. Unusual for a hard bargainer.'

'Why did not you tell me before?'

'I thought'—he swallowed—'that it had nothing to do with the ongoing investigation. Only when the connection to the casual labour was established, I remembered this observation of mine. I have been trying to convey this to madam since morning, but she is not replying.'

'She may have gone out.'

'No, she is in the room.'

Vijay took the elevator. A huge rock was ramming into his heart. Padmini stood groggily at the door. When Vijay held her, she willingly collapsed into his arms. Vijay bent his right knee and lifted her as though cradling her. He placed her gently on the bed. He felt her forehead.

'You are running a fever,' he cried worriedly.

She nodded weakly.

Vijay called for a doctor and also ordered for a plate of idlis to be served in the room.

A silver-haired matron-like woman came carrying a bag. 'Dr Kusum.' She held Vijay's outstretched hand. She placed a stethoscope on Padmini's chest. 'Take a deep breath. Turn back.' She moved the stethoscope away and felt the pulse. A digital thermometer was thrust into Padmini's mouth. Vijay's mind flashed back by two decades, when he had bitten into a mercury thermometer. A commotion had followed at home.

'102,' she said aloud, and recorded it on a pad. She wrote a few prescriptions. 'It is a viral flu,' she declared. 'It will pass in two or three days.'

Idlis were brought into the room and placed on the table.

'Idli,' the doctor observed, 'is ideal, because it is light on the tummy.'

Vijay sent a constable with the prescription slip.

'Complete bed rest,' the doctor advised. 'Watch television if you are bored.'

Vijay thanked the doctor.

Padmini chewed the food more than usual. She took a long time to eat. Then Vijay handed her the medicines. She swallowed them.

'Antipyretics, antibiotics and an antacid,' she reeled out.

Vijay gave a wry smile.

Padmini placed a pillow under her head and wrapped a blanket over her body. She lay down and smiled. 'Vijay, you look pensive.'

'Just when we need to be at our best, we are at our worst.'

'Explain.'

'My department colleagues,' he lamented, 'are conspiring to ensure my failure. Dalvi has been withdrawn and put under Godbole. Now you are indisposed.'

'Vijay,' Padmini called out like a mother, 'the biggest obstacle lies just before the pot of gold.' She halted. 'He who is resolute will not wilt and he will leap over the biggest hurdle.'

Vijay saw radiance in her face. 'When the going gets tough—'

Vijay completed the sentence. 'The tough get going.'

'Vijay, all is not lost. I may be indisposed, but I can think.'
'Sure,' Vijay smiled brightly.
'Dalvi,' Padmini asserted, 'is dedicated, both to you and his duty. He will,' she asserted, 'find a way out.'

Vijay felt uplifted. 'You are a motivational speaker. I am recharged.'

'Let us not waste time.'

Vijay pecked her on the cheek and left. He sat in the hotel lobby sipping tea. He thought of the three tasks that had to be completed. He wrote them down on a piece of paper:

» *Interview Bharat Rao*
» *Trace the casual labourer*
» *Talk to Shinde, the union leader of Hotel Heaven*

He weighed the three tasks. He felt that he should be taking on the first one. The other two would best be handled by Dalvi. Padmini seldom erred, and if she was so sure of Dalvi clawing his way back, then it would happen.

Vijay drove at a speed slower than normal. He parked his car outside the gate. By now, he was well recognized at Bharat Rao's residence. The watchman executed a clumsy salute that had Vijay try hard at concealing his laughter. The gardener was clipping the grass, and the driver was washing the car with a hose. Although the servants were carrying on with their usual routine, something was wrong. It almost felt like attending a funeral. Vijay walked to the visitors' lobby. Raju folded his hands and ushered him in. Another servant brought a glass of water that Raju placed on the table opposite Vijay.

'Will you have tea?' Raju asked.

'No, but I want to talk to your master.'

The other servant was sent off by a glance from Raju.

'Sir'—he burst into tears—'something horrible has happened

to our master.' Huge teardrops rolled down Raju's cheeks. He made no attempt to wipe them off. 'Sir,' he urged, 'please do something. Master has been blabbering for the last hour or so.'

Vijay tiptoed towards Bharat Rao's room. The scientist was lying on his bed. The light was on, but the scientist did not see Vijay. He kept muttering to himself. The words were incoherent. Vijay listened hard. Certain words were being repeated. Vijay wrote them down.

'She has double-crossed us. Sold to Patterson.'

Vijay called his family doctor, Dr Srivastava, and described what he saw.

'I will be there in fifteen minutes,' the doctor replied.

Vijay told Raju that Dr Srivastava was to be ushered in. Bharat Rao kept muttering incoherently. Dr Srivastava came, accompanied by another doctor.

'Dr Jha, a neurologist,' he introduced.

Dr Jha asked Bharat if he could sit. Bharat Rao sat on his bed, but fell back.

'What is your name?'

'Bharat.'

'What are you?'

'A scientist.'

Bharat seemed to speaking explosively.

Dr Srivastava checked his blood pressure and counted his pulse. The two doctors whispered to each other.

'It is a neurological stroke,' Dr Jha declared. 'I have called the ambulance.'

Dr Srivastava explained, 'Some shock has triggered the stroke. He will be in the hospital for two weeks.'

'Not life threatening?' Vijay hoped.

'Depends,' the doctor replied, 'on how the stroke progresses.'

'Are we too late?' Vijay enquired.

'Not necessarily,' Dr Srivastava opined, 'but unlike a cardiac stroke, not many interventions are possible in a neurological stroke.'

The ambulance's hooter disturbed the conversation. Two paramedics came with a stretcher and carried Bharat Rao out. The doctors followed. Vijay instructed Raju to go to the hospital as an attendant.

Once the ambulance was underway, Vijay left the place. He drove towards Birender's travel agency.

'He started it all. Maybe he will help end it.'

He handed his car, along with the keys, to a parking attendant. He walked into the travel agency's office, only to be told that Birender was away for the day.

Vijay kicked the air in disgust. Nothing was working for him.

Then, he repeated his favourite quote: 'A winner never quits; a quitter never wins' and 'When the going gets tough, the tough get going.' He felt rejuvenated. He decided to put himself in Anirudh Babu's shoes. That had been tried before, but no harm in trying once again.

He walked towards the site where Anirudh had been shot. Barring the massage parlour, there was no place where he could have spent time or where someone could have injected ricin into him.

Vijay came back to the post office. He walked away from the murder site (Laxmi Nagar), in the reverse direction from the post office. He walked, or rather sauntered, for about twelve minutes, when he halted. A missed call, but it was from a credit card salesperson. Vijay politely disconnected the call. His rhythm had been broken. He looked up. He was right outside Anirudh's flat.

An autorickshaw driver hailed him. Vijay declined. The autorickshaw purred away, but suddenly turned back. The driver halted his vehicle and came out. He pleaded, 'Sir, can we have a picture together?'

Vijay was nonplussed.

'Sir,' he explained, 'we saw you on television the other day and my eleven-year-old son idolizes you.'

Vijay laughed. The press conference had many spin-offs.

Vijay stood with his arm around the autorickshaw driver's shoulder while a passer-by clicked. Vijay had to then pose with the passer-by while the autorickshaw driver clicked. The passer-by left after saluting Vijay.

'Sir,' the autorickshaw driver predicted, 'you will be nabbing the culprit tomorrow.'

'May your words come true!'

'Sir,' he said, 'I may be uneducated, but I am gifted with clairvoyance.'

'Is it?'

The autorickshaw driver sensed that Vijay did not believe him. 'Sir, I only took Anirudh from here on that ill-fated day, and somehow, I had a premonition that he was going to die.'

Vijay's antennae suddenly fired up. 'Tell me,' he demanded, 'every detail!'

'Sir,' the autorickshaw driver said, trying to remember, 'Madam told me.'

'Which madam?'

'His wife. They stay there,' he pointed to Anirudh's home.

Vijay gesticulated, asking him to continue.

'She even paid me five hundred in advance for waiting. He came walking from there.' He extended his finger in the direction of the road that led to the post office. 'He went home, came after nearly an hour, and then I took him to Lakshmi Road.'

Vijay stepped into the vehicle. 'Drive me,' he ordered, 'just as you took Anirudh.'

The driver brought the vehicle to life with a turn in the ignition key. He drove straight. Vijay observed that there were no traffic signals to slow the progress. The stop clock ticked noisily.

'This is where I dropped him. Beyond that is a one-way road, so I could not go further.'

Vijay tipped him generously. He looked at the stop clock. It had taken them seven minutes flat.

He got off the auto and walked down the road, right to the spot where Anirudh was shot. It took Vijay three minutes. An older, slower man would take six. Vijay looked around. He now summed the position. Anirudh came back from the post office to his own home. He took a shot purportedly to be his insulin dosage, but it was actually ricin. He spent the in-between, unaccounted time at home. He went in an autorickshaw, so seven to eight minutes. Five more minutes to reach the restaurant. The pre-ordered lunch would be served in another two or three minutes, so Anirudh would be having his meal well within a half hour of receiving insulin (as he thought).

So, the ricin had been injected at home. That missing part of the puzzle had now been sorted.

Chapter 47

Padmini slept for two hours. When she woke up, she felt better. The fever had subsided. A cup of tea refreshed her. She changed into jeans and a top. She sat thinking about Vijay. *How was his day going? He hasn't rung up, so maybe nothing exciting, or maybe he has stumbled on something very extraordinary.* She started thinking about the murders.

She took a pencil and a pad and began writing questions.

» How was the bottle containing the energy drink (Gandhiv) replaced with the one containing black mamba venom.
» Where was ricin injected, if not at Sneha Massage Parlor?
» Anirudh had left the post office at 12:10 p.m. but reached the murder spot at 02:00 p.m. It would take only 20 minutes even for a slow walker. Where did Anirudh spend the intervening time?

Little did she know that Vijay had unearthed answers to the second and third questions. These couldn't be answered by sitting in the hotel. Still she had to make herself useful. She rubbed her hands vigorously and indulged in a mini-Reiki kind of procedure.

Another question came to her mind.

» Why did the murderer choose room 701?

Padmini was excited. This bit of riddle could be unravelled at the hotel itself!

The room was similar to most deluxe rooms. The cyanide had to be smeared on a washbasin nozzle, and that could be done in any room—so what was special about this one? She racked her brains no end, but a satisfactory answer eluded her. Not knowing how to proceed, she instructed the manager to provide her with the list of occupants of room 701 for the last two months.

The manager brought a printout. He handed it over to her and smiled. 'You cannot stop working even when you are ill.'

'We are racing against time,' she said. 'We have only until tomorrow evening.'

He nodded his head. 'I have no doubt about your success. You guys have been doing your job in an assured manner and with a smile.' He paused, and then added, 'Such people always emerge triumphant.'

Padmini thanked him. She began to scan the list, last day first. The first month before the murder day provided no clue or pattern. People from different walks of life, from different parts of the world, had checked in. She put the first sheet away.

The second sheet consisted of details of occupants two months back. The seventh name made her sit up. Vasudha had occupied the room!

Had Vasudha occupied the room as a reconnaissance exercise? Room 701 had been chosen because the murderer had to choose a room and what better room than one that the murderer had occupied earlier?

Padmini called for the identity papers of the occupant. Her eyes lit up when she saw them.

※

Vijay had reached Hotel Heaven. He kept thinking about the incoherent mutterings of Bharat Rao. He rang Srikanth Mahapatra. His call was disconnected. He rang again, only to be meted out the same treatment. His mobile squeaked, indicating a new message. It was from Srikanth.

In a conference. Call me at 7 p.m.—it read.

Vijay couldn't wait to meet Padmini. The elevator took him non-stop. He felt her forehead. Padmini's fever had subsided.

'Why don't you have something light but energizing like khichdi?'

She agreed. Vijay ordered a thali for himself.

Padmini finished her lunch and wiped her mouth. Vijay had sunk into the chair and was snoring.

※

Vijay opened his eyes. He realized that he had slept for nearly half an hour. Padmini too had draped a blanket over her body and fallen asleep. Vijay stretched his limbs. Padmini half opened her eyes and then opened it wide. She too got up.

Tea was served. Vijay looked at his watch.

Padmini did not react. Suddenly, she sprang up. 'Vasudha accused her husband of infidelity. Is it not a motive?'

'Not strong enough, because she was reconciled to it. She herself was dabbling with David. Anyway, how do you connect it to the other murders?'

Padmini retreated glumly.

A familiar knock sounded on the door.

Vijay exclaimed, 'It can't be!'

Padmini had a promising smile. Indeed, Dalvi stood at the door.

Vijay heard some pushing and jostling, and he looked beyond Dalvi. Dalvi stood aside for Vijay to get a clear view. Two policemen held a frail man. His arms were tied with strong ropes. Vijay recognized him as the casual labourer who had helped in the murder of Mashelkar and David.

Dalvi pushed the securely bound prisoner in front. 'Anything that you want to ask him?'

'First, tell me,' Vijay said, 'how come you are here?'

Dalvi chuckled. 'Godbole left for Mumbai because his prospective son-in-law is arriving from New York.'

'So,' Vijay said, laughing, 'no work going on in the department.'

'I am attached to him personally, so in his absence, I have no work,' Dalvi said.

'The moment he sees you with me,' Vijay said in a worried tone, 'he will make mincemeat of you.'

'The hell I care,' Dalvi responded, nonchalantly, 'I cannot

abandon the two persons dedicated to their duty, nor do I shirk my responsibility.'

Padmini intervened. 'What has the guy'—she said pointing to the prisoner—'told you so far?'

'He was in dire need of money,' Dalvi began, 'because his son needed an operation.'

'Then?'

'A Sikh gentleman,' continued Dalvi, 'offered him money for the task. He confesses to smearing the poison on the washbasin nozzle.'

Padmini quipped, 'It is very easy to disguise as a Sikh.'

'Yeah, the head,' Dalvi added, 'is covered by the turban, the face by the beard. He even wore dark glasses. The communication was through a PCO.'

Vijay grimaced out of frustration.

Padmini turned to Dalvi. 'Call him in.'

The constables held him even more tightly as they walked in.

'Show me,' Padmini said softly, 'how did you apply the poison?'

'Madam,' he swallowed fearfully, 'I did not know it was poison. I had been given a small bottle with a liquid in it. I was instructed to dab the liquid on the nozzle of the washbasin tap as well as the handle of the tap with a brush. I did first that.'

'How were you paid the money?'

'In cash.'

'Where is it?'

'It paid for my son's surgery.'

'Take him away,' Vijay ordered.

Three cups of tea were on the table. Dalvi toyed with the tea bag. It floated around like an island in a brown sea. 'I have spoken to Dr Nilesh. He confirms that Vasudha spoke to him on the very day that the two scientists visited him.'

Before Vijay could question, Padmini spoke. 'When?'

'Immediately after they left. She enquired about Mashelkar's ulcers, and he told her all about it. He says he revealed the information because she was a close confidante of Mashelkar.'

Everything was adding up. They only needed incriminating evidence.

Dalvi called it a day.

※

'Okay,' Padmini said, smiling. 'Actually, Bharat Rao was livid that Vasudha had entered into a huge deal with Patterson Laboratories. Patterson Laboratories,' she explained, 'is a laboratory with a shady reputation.'

'What do you mean?'

'They have been accused of killing endangered species, organ trading and unethical practices. Even catering to corrupt dictators, drug runners and terrorists.'

'Why has no action been initiated?'

'They are highly connected. A few arrests here and there, some inquiries, maybe not enough proof, but good clean scientists do not have truck with them.'

Vijay pulled a wry face. 'How do you know this?'

'I surfed the Net,' she said, with a sly smile, 'while you were trying to ping Srikanth. How do you account for Vasudha's contract?'

Vijay sat down thoughtfully. 'We can deduce,' he said, 'a motive for Vasudha. Quick money connects all four people. Getting rid of all of them was her passport to a billion dollars, because they had shelved their plans for applying for a patent.'

Padmini pushed a lock of hair from his forehead backwards. 'So, if we establish that Vasudha had a contract with Patterson, then we have proof.'

'Not so easy.' Vijay sighed. 'It provides a motive, but not proof.'

'What constitutes proof?'

'Something that proves that Vasudha did something connected with the murder.'

'How about the testimony of the casual labourer?'

'He saw a Sikh.'

Padmini gritted her teeth in anger. 'I hate that witch.' A nasty look came on her face. 'It was hate at first sight. That smirk is the worst spectacle on earth.'

'Do not work yourself up,' Vijay advised. 'We will probably truss her like a turkey this time tomorrow.'

Dalvi calling, Vijay's mobile announced.

'Same old story,' Dalvi informed tonelessly. 'Shinde was paid handsomely by a Sikh in cash, and he was contacted through a public phone booth.'

'Tomorrow is another day,' Vijay said, and disconnected.

'I am done for the day,' Padmini said.

'I will also take a break.'

Chapter 48

Vasudha had put her phone on silent mode and gone off to sleep. The tension was taking a toll on her. She popped Valium regularly. Rathore had called in three or four times, so it must be something urgent.

Rathore's voice sounded as much. 'Vijay has procured a search warrant for your computer centre.'

Vasudha was still groggy—the after-effect of the tranquilizer. She yawned. 'Excuse me?'

'Never mind.'

'What would that imply?'

'You have to part with any computer hard disk or document demanded by him. He is authorized to whisk any equipment from your office to send to the Police Cyber Centre.'

'How to stop him?'

'You cannot.' He paused. 'It is better to cooperate.'

Vasudha hung up the receiver. Despite having two of his wings clipped, Vijay had forged ahead.

She washed her face, dabbed on some make-up and snatched her car keys from the holder. She had to reach the computer centre before Vijay did.

She opened the front door, but instead of stepping out, she stopped at the door. *Would anything be gained by being present at the premises when it was being searched? That would, in fact, betray my anxiety. Cool nonchalance was a better option. Even if I went there, I would have to cooperate with the law.*

She slammed the door shut and picked up the magazine section of the newspaper. She tried solving the cryptic crossword puzzle. A few minutes later, she tried listening to her favourite music, but relaxation evaded her.

Chapter 49

'Hi, Supercop. I have news for you.' Neeraj's cheerful voice rang out. 'The origin of the mail has been traced to Amrit Research Labs.'

'How about meeting me outside the lab gate in an hour?'

'I do not know,' Neeraj joked, 'if that is a proposal or an order.'

'Cut the crap, rascal!'

Padmini had heard everything. Vijay gently caressed her

forehead. 'I would love to have taken you, but you better rest.'

'I am really going to miss the fun, but I guess rest will recharge me.'

A constable drove Vijay. The finger of suspicion was rapidly and repeatedly moving towards Vasudha, but they did not have evidence that could stand testimony in a court.

Vijay only knew too well how the slow-grinding wheels of justice got stuck when clever defence lawyers latched on to incompleteness of evidences produced. Garnering foolproof evidence requires time, and in this case, time was not an ally.

Neeraj was leaning on the boot of his car, wearing black jeans and a white shirt. He had spare tyres around his midriff.

Vijay pinched his abdomen. 'Sign of prosperity.'

'Let me see your belly in three years,' Neeraj challenged.

'It will remain a washboard, but business first.'

'I have no doubt,' Neeraj asserted, 'about the veracity of my report. We have identified the server that shook hands with the Google server as belonging to Amrit Labs. I have all the necessary documents to nail them if they deny.' Neeraj retrieved a file from his briefcase and showed Vijay. Vijay nodded.

The receptionist looked shell-shocked when Vijay introduced himself. 'I need to consult my superior,' she said incoherently.

'Connect him to me,' Vijay replied coldly.

'Our technology head will see you.' She gestured towards the elevator. 'Third floor, second office.'

If ever there was a disproportionate head on a body, then it belonged to Ram Kumar, the technology head at Amrit Laboratories. He was a small man, probably less than 160 centimetres and weighing around fifty-five kilograms. His head was large and round, the size accentuated by a broad forehead. 'What can I do for you?' he asked in a business-like voice. His voice was surprisingly deep.

'We—' Vijay began.

Neeraj spoke over him. 'We have back-traced an e-mail as originating from your server. We would now need to zero in on the terminal, then on the sender.'

Ram pressed his right nostril with his left pointer. 'This would mean adverse publicity for us,' he commented.

Vijay and Neeraj looked at each other.

'I cannot permit you,' Ram went on, 'to proceed.'

Vijay stood up to his full height. Then he glared down at Ram's eyes, which were way below his.

'We have a search warrant,' Vijay warned. 'If you do not cooperate, we will load all your equipment in a truck and keep it for as long as we please.'

Fright, great fright and deep concern, showed on Ram's face. He was weighing the options. He didn't fully believe Vijay's threat. 'I will consult my legal adviser.' He lifted the receiver of the intercom.

Vijay put his left hand on the phone and stopped him. 'Do as you please,' Vijay said, 'but do not blame me if the media swoops on you.'

'Media can be,' Neeraj added, 'irritating and intrusive.'

Ram closed his eyes and pondered. He poured water in a glass, took a gulp, and coughed.

Vijay waited patiently.

'Show me the mail,' Ram said, 'I have access to our central server, which is housed in Mumbai.'

Neeraj followed Ram through a maze of workstation cubicles.

Vijay wondered how he could connect the mail sent by Kumudini to Karun with Vasudha even if it were established that the mail originated from Amrit Laboratories.

Ram's intercom rang. Vijay hesitated, and then lifted the

receiver. Neeraj asked him to come to the fourth floor by the staircase.

Neeraj and Ram were waiting at the landing. Ram looked as if he had seen a ghost. Neeraj was seething with rage. 'You better clarify,' he roared, 'or we take you into custody.' On seeing Vijay, Neeraj explained, 'We have identified the terminal. That is the one.' He walked over and placed his palm on the monitor screen. 'This was used by an intern, Kumudini, who had joined them then.' He paused. Then he said harshly, 'The logs indicate that the password of that corporate mail identification address was altered at 6:42 a.m., *after her death.*'

'I...I...' Ram mumbled. He talked in truncated sentences. These were signs of a fragmented, stressed mind.

Vijay toyed with a change of tack. He sat next to Ram and offered him water. He said softly, 'Take a deep breath, relax and think.'

'I will be back in a minute,' he said and walked slowly towards the restroom. Vijay noticed that he had destressed himself by splashing water on his face. His breathing had become deeper and his body language eased. 'Do you want to be left alone?'

Ram smiled. 'Thank you.' The articulation was clearer now. Ram went to the next work station. He sat and pondered. Then he walked over to the coffee dispenser machine and refreshed himself with a cuppa.

Vijay smiled at him. He smiled back reflexively. Then the smile broadened. Soon, his face had a hundred flash bulbs. 'Can I,' he asked enthusiastically, 'go to the server room again?'

Vijay nodded.

Ram swung to Neeraj. 'Sir, please follow me.'

Vijay called Padmini.

She snatched the words from his mouth. 'I have hit a gold mine.'

He laughed. She was becoming normal.

Seeing Neeraj and Ram return, he disconnected. Ram and Neeraj were talking in friendly overtones. They seemed pleased with themselves.

'So, share the spoils.'

Neeraj looked at Ram. 'You speak.'

'Actually, our unit was subjected to its first information system audit. We were advised that every user should change his or her password on a monthly basis, but none followed it. So I, on the advice of the chief director, Vasudha Madam, changed the passwords globally from the central server itself. Everyone was allotted a common password. I sent a mail requesting everyone to reset their password using the newly given password to log in. This intern had not complied with my instructions, probably because she did not understand its gravity.' He took a break. He was not used to talking so much.

Neeraj took over. 'Somebody logged in to Kumudini's mail using her identity and the common password to send the mail to Karun. The same person presumably altered the password the next morning from the same terminal.'

'So,' Vijay concluded, 'we need to find out who came in at 6:42 a.m. that day.'

'Sir,' Ram said, 'we have a morning shift. Our access log can give you the details of those present.'

'Can you provide it now?' Vijay asked.

'Give me ten minutes.'

It took around fifteen minutes for Ram to arrive with the list. There were seven people, including Vasudha, who had come in the morning shift.

'Did everybody come to the fifth floor?' Vijay asked.

'In fact,' Ram replied 'none of them would have come to the fifth floor in the normal course.'

'But somebody did come,' Vijay said, 'and how do we find that?'

Ram motioned Vijay to wait, and he talked on his mobile. 'I have called Captain Rajendran, our security chief. There he is.'

Rajendran may have become heavier in the middle, but he could easily be identified as an army man. On hearing Vijay's query, Captain Rajendran said, 'Normally, the guard opens the fifth floor doors only at 8:30 a.m., just before the cleaners arrive, but definitely not at 6:42 a.m.'

Vijay digested his information, but said nothing.

'Shall I summon the guard?' Rajendran offered.

Vijay agreed.

The guard said, 'The door was locked, but I thought someone had entered.'

Rajendran extended his arm and held the guard's collar. 'Why didn't you tell me?' he demanded.

'That can wait,' Vijay interjected and pushed Rajendran's arm away.

Turning to the guard, Vijay asked, 'How did you reach that conclusion?'

'Sir, the washbasin tap in the ladies' washroom leaks. I always make it a point to close it tightly. In fact, many women have complained that I close it so tightly that they cannot open it. So I normally loosen it the next morning.'

'So?'

'I distinctly remember having closed the tap the night before. But when I went to loosen the tap in the morning, as per my normal routine, I found it dripping. Someone had opened it.'

'Who else has the key?' Vijay asked.

Rajendran answered, 'Only Chief Director Madam.'

'You mean Vasudha?'

'Yes.'

Vijay profusely thanked Rajendran, Ram and the guard.

As they descended the elevator, Neeraj enquired, 'Any headway?'

'Lots. We know that the mail was false and we know that only one person could have possibly accessed that terminal at that time.'

'True,' Neeraj said.

By now, they had come out of the building. Vijay asked, 'Neeraj, why did Vasudha need to go to the fifth floor to reset the password?'

'The fifth floor is not a part of the LAN,' Neeraj said. 'It forms a separate LAN, although it's connected to the central server. So you have to go to the fifth floor. Also,' he added, 'the password could not have been reset using any other terminal, because Kumudini had access rights restricted only to that terminal.' He looked at his watch. 'Good luck,' he said. 'Do not forget me in your credits when you get the next award.'

Vijay laughed. Finally, they had something concrete to grill Vasudha on. In this case, circumstantial evidence was against Vasudha, even if it was not proof beyond doubt.

Proof beyond doubt was what Vijay aimed for, and for that there was still some ground to be covered.

Chapter 50

Vasudha had drifted into another bout of heavy but fitful sleep, with a series of vivid, unconnected dreams jerking her to consciousness every now and then.

The shrill ring of her mobile jolted her to total alertness. First Ram and then Captain Rajendran gave her complete accounts. She listened patiently and intently.

'Thanks.' She ended the call and looked out of the window. Vijay hadn't achieved anything frightful. True, it was a significant breakthrough, but probably a case of too little and too late.

Rathore was calling. 'He came back empty-handed.'

Although she could not smell him over the phone, she was certain that he had been drinking. Vocal chords rub smoothly on a moist throat. His throat was dehydrated, and it showed in his voice.

'What else did you expect?' She caught herself in the mirror with a lopsided sneer.

'The guy is, however, going ahead with guns blazing. He has applied for a search warrant, this time of your residence.'

Vasudha found her grip loosening on the phone. She tightened her fingers around it.

'He probably wants to make a show of having made some progress,' Rathore continued, 'but actually it is zilch.' Vasudha wasn't as sure.

When she hung up the phone, she wasn't laughing. Vijay was not a showman. He was most certainly moving according to a well-laid-out plan. Despite igniting her brain into an overdrive, she could not fathom the reason for Vijay itching to search her apartment.

In her estimate, only one real weak link remained, and that was Chakravak. Surely, Vijay couldn't hope to find him at her residence. Then, there was the 'winding sound' that she had heard, but Anirudh hadn't. She wasn't sure whether the sound actually emanated. So it was incomprehensible that Vijay could decipher it.

She then walked into her bedroom. Maybe the change in venue would do the trick. It was stuffy in this room. She leaned to switch on the air conditioner. Her elbow brushed against the computer printer.

Her heart leapt out of its place, and instant darkness clouded her brain. She stumbled, rather than walked, to the bed. She popped a Rika pill and sat quietly. Soon, the drug began to take effect. Her nerves soothed.

She rang Rathore. 'When do you expect Vijay to raid my home?'

There was silence over the phone. Rathore was thinking. 'Tomorrow afternoon or evening,' he finally said.

'Sure?' Relief was palpable in her voice.

'Definite,' he emphasized. 'He is yet to pick up the warrant. He will get the warrant tomorrow morning only. He needs a lady officer with him, and he can storm your home before dusk only.'

A huge load had lifted off Vasudha's shoulders. Confidence resurged through her.

She carried a stool and placed it below the loft. Holding a torch in one hand, she stood on the stool and peeped into the loft. She yanked an electric mini saw and placed it gently on the ground. She stood tall on the stool, slid her right arm into the loft, and groped. Her fingers grazed against a cord. She slid her fingers under the cord and gently pulled. She got an armful of the cord. She pulled hard and lost her balance, almost slipping off the stool. The electric mini hammer had been retrieved.

Vasudha dismantled the printer part by part. She separated the colour cartridge from the rest. Starting with the paper tray, she set the electric saw on the machine part. The machine had been cut into many sheets. The electric hammer pounded on the sawed parts, smashing them to bits. The smashed bits were huddled into a bag; the cartridge, along with scissors, was packed in another bag.

She carried both the bags and thrust them in the front passenger seat of her car. She drove assuredly. She stopped near a gigantic dustbin. She poured a part of the contents of the bag on to the heap. The action was repeated in three other garbage heaps. The printer was now a part of four different garbage bins.

She drove towards the west end of the Ambajari Lake. The cartridge was sheared into several pieces. A few pieces were immersed into the lake. She walked back to the car and drove to the south end of the lake. A few more sheared pieces were dropped.

The printer had now ceased to be a threat. Chakravak remained, but nothing could be done about him. It was a long shot for Vijay to find him. The 'winding sound' nibbled at her peace of mind. She brushed it aside. Now was the time to chill.

※

Vijay rang the chief librarian of Nagpur Public Library. He felt sheepish, almost silly, making a request at ten o'clock at night.

'Kaul here,' a warm voice answered.

Air hissed out of Vijay's mouth. He cleared his throat. 'Sorry to disturb you at this hour,' he began, 'but I need to urgently look up the local newspapers for the last fifteen days.'

If Kaul was annoyed, his voice did not give it away. In a matter-of-fact professional tone, he conveyed his assent. 'Saklecha, a junior librarian, will help you.' Kaul had hung up before Vijay could mouth his profuse thanks.

Vijay rang Padmini to find out if she was game to accompany him to the library. She declined, citing fatigue. He drove alone.

He parked his car outside the massive colonial structure. An Irishman, Richard Belfast, had imported finely wrought white limestone for constructing this historical library. It had a stately appearance and looked better in daylight. He followed Saklecha through archways leading to massive rooms with steep ceilings.

Saklecha, a man with many chins and rimmed glasses, hardly spoke, but went about his job efficiently. Different dailies were stacked neatly in separate heaps.

Vijay took a deep breath and chose the first lot. It was *The Hitavada*. He separated the local supplement from the main paper. The local supplement was his focus. He went through each news item with great care.

A familiar voice rang out. 'Has the murderer left his fingerprint?'

Vijay whirled around.

Dalvi and Padmini were standing with devilish smiles.

Padmini chuckled. 'We were checking on you, but what have you found?'

Vijay raised his hands in a gesture of helplessness. 'Nothing so far.'

Padmini's arrival electrified Saklecha. He beamed. He prepared tea, using his tea bags and electric kettle and served everyone.

Vijay finished his tea and set about scrutinizing the remaining newspapers.

Padmini sat next to him. 'What are you looking for?'

'Some unusual, interesting happening.'

She tickled his armpit and induced laughter. Vijay said firmly, 'You are disturbing me.'

'That is my favourite hobby,' she retorted. 'Anyway, I do not have the patience to go through boring stuff.'

Dalvi told Vijay that he would drop Padmini at the hotel and be back.

※

Vijay timed himself. It took him nearly an hour to finish one heap. There were three more. He contemplated calling off the wild goose chase. But on second thought, he went ahead. With the fourth paper, he drew blood.

He stabbed Dalvi's number on his mobile. 'Dalvi, get me this man. Get him to me right now at my home. I am awake the whole night.'

'Done, Sir.'

※

Vasudha was washing away her stress in Joy Nagpur, the best-known restobar in the city. For a night out, this was the only place in the town.

A DJ was performing on one end of the stage. Neon lights flickered, adding drama. Other members of the band danced as though possessed by animal spirits. A huge banner with the words 'Radio Chilli' was the most prominent feature of the ballroom. Tables were lined on both sides. Older men, with women half their age, formed the bulk of the crowd.

With a vodka glass in hand, Vasudha felt her tensions melting away. Occasionally, she would go up to the dance floor and shake a leg. Men offering to partner were rebuffed.

The meal was delicious. Tomorrow night would be a bigger celebration. Amidst the clutter of ladles, she heard her mobile ring.

It was Rathore. 'Vijay is in the public library.'

Vasudha froze. This was a most unusual place for him to be. If he was hunting for Chakravak, it made sense, but at the library in the eleventh hour?

Her peace shattered, she spat the partly chewed food on her plate. She signalled to the waiter that she wanted to pay up and leave.

'Did you like the food?'

She nodded. 'I have urgent business to attend to.'

He handed her the bill. She did not check. She paid in cash, tipping him generously.

'Come again.' His voice hardly registered, although he was just a metre away.

Another Valium tablet—but no tranquilizer was going to help now.

Chapter 51

Day 7

Padmini's eyes were a bit sunken, but the glow was back on her face, and so was her irresistible smile. Vijay considered it to be an auspicious sign. Dalvi joined them.

'Let us go out in the sunshine,' Padmini suggested, 'I feel dreadful, locked up here.'

'We will sit on the lawn,' Dalvi said.

The elevator boy smiled at them as did the doorman. Vijay turned to Dalvi. 'You have a lot of work to do.'

'At your service.'

'Go to the post office,' Vijay replied blandly. 'See if she has withdrawn money near about the dates on which she has paid to her associates.'

※

Padmini strolled round the lawn. She admired the flower beds. Vijay was about to follow her when his mobile trilled. It was Srikanth.

Srikanth confirmed everything that Padmini had deciphered. 'Stop this somehow,' he cried. 'It is an insult to humanity.'

'Her travel records indicate that she leaves for Monte Carlo in three days.'

'She must be making a presentation to Patterson. Stop her,' he implored.

※

'Padmini,' Vijay said, patting her shoulder, 'you go with Dalvi to the post office.'

'What about you?' she asked.

'I want to look around Vasudha's house.' Without another word, he drove off himself.

※

Padmini and Dalvi settled in the passenger seats of the police vehicle. Padmini frowned.

'I felt Vijay was being economical with the truth.'

'You are on the ball.' Dalvi smiled. 'He likes to work alone towards the business end of a case.'

'That is mean of him,' she remarked, 'to suddenly distance from us.'

'No,' Dalvi clarified, 'he needs laser focus and another person's presence will diminish the strength of the concentration. Sages meditate alone; champion athletes train alone.'

Padmini let out an exasperated sigh. 'You are more loyal than the king.'

'Than the queen also,' he added.

They had reached the post office. Men, women and young adults went in and out of the post office. Long but fast-moving queues tailed behind cash counters. Mouses clicked away, keyboards twanged, papers slithered under photocopier machines like hissing snakes, printed paper emerged from trays to rhythmic beats. It was a busy day. People held parcels in their arms as they stood in serpentine queues waiting for their turn at the speed post counter.

Padmini put on her dark glasses while entering the premises. A black nameplate with golden-yellow words inscribed on it—Gopal Meena, Post Master—hung precariously outside the office. A uniformed peon stood outside. Gopal Meena had a ready smile, looked poised and seemed to be in general control of things. He was appropriate for such a vital post. When Dalvi introduced himself, he smiled affably. 'Privileged to be of help to you.'

Padmini showed the photographs of Kumudini and Vasudha.

'She,' he said, holding Vasudha's photograph, 'is a long-standing and valued client. Rarely do people of such wealth patronize the post office anymore. I do not know about the other.' His fingers punched a few commands. The printer wailed before springing into action.

'Sounded mighty like a police siren,' Dalvi said.

Gopal laughed politely. 'There.' He handed over the account statements of both Kumudini and Vasudha to Padmini. 'You can see that the other lady has not transacted since 17 September.'

'That is extraordinary,' Dalvi commented, 'that transactions have taken place in her account after her death.'

Padmini circled some entries in the statement and showed them to Gopal.

Gopal's countenance drifted from poise to extreme nervousness. He fidgeted. 'We have no information to that effect! Believe me,' Gopal beseeched, 'I have done no wrong.'

'Relax, Mr Gopal,' Dalvi advised. 'We are here to gather facts, not arrest you.'

Gopal excused himself to have a smoke. Dalvi permitted him. Gopal took the smoke deep into his lungs and exhaled with a sigh of pleasure. He came back, relieved.

Padmini gently moved the papers towards Gopal. 'Explain these transactions to us.' She pointed to the encircled ones.

Gopal chewed his lip while studying the transactions. Then he sent for Usha, the cashier.

Usha was a middle-aged woman, in her late forties, short and stocky. Her face was cute. Padmini reckoned, even hazarded a guess, that she must have been a draw in her younger days. Usha sat next to Padmini and studied the transactions.

'Only this woman,' she said, pointing to Vasudha, 'came to the branch on 13 September. I remember very well, because we had an argument.'

Padmini leaned in anticipation.

'She had a different hairstyle on that day,' Usha continued.

Dalvi stopped her with an upraised hand. 'Are you sure it was her?'

Padmini demolished his doubts. 'Women seldom err on such counts.'

Laughter all round.

Usha went on. 'I pointed it to her that she had encashed a National Savings Certificate of ₹1,10,000 a couple of hours back, and now she wanted to deposit the same amount in another account. This is kind of suspicious because she was trying to conceal the linkage between the two transactions.'

Dalvi took notes in shorthand. He signalled Usha to carry on.

'Nine times out of ten, this trick would pull through. I attend to payment and Dinesh to receipts. So the first transaction was from my counter, and the second would have been from Dinesh's. Dinesh needed to go somewhere urgently, so I manned both counters for an hour when Dinesh was away.'

'That is why,' Padmini said, 'you caught her.'

Usha nodded. 'I brought it to the notice of my manager, who instructed me to accept the transaction. She made a strange request.'

Dalvi jerked himself to a ramrod straight posture.

'She wanted me,' Usha paused, 'to write the deposit receipt. She claimed to have sprained her wrist.'

'What did you do?' Padmini asked.

Usha answered evenly, 'I complied with her request, but I informed my manager.'

A peon came and handed a bunch of vouchers and checks stitched together. A yellow label with the date 13 September 2012 had been pasted on the top. Gopal leafed through the bunch and folded one credit receipt slip. He showed it to Padmini and Dalvi.

'That Vasudha,' he stressed, 'was our valued customer, so I pandered to her requests, but I recorded the unusual behaviour on her part on the reverse of the slip under my signature seal and date.'

Gopal overturned the receipt slip. His notings were crisp and unambiguous. Padmini took a copy of this voucher.

Dalvi got up. Padmini followed him. Then she ran back.

Dalvi, who instinctively felt her absence, turned around. He followed her.

'Who was the beneficiary of the debits to Kumudini's account on 17 September?'

Gopal's fingers rested lightly on the keyboard, his eyes rooted to the monitor. 'The credits,' he replied, looking at Padmini, 'were to the account of Vasudha. This was an internal transfer transaction.'

'How did they reach you,' Dalvi wanted to know, 'when Kumudini was no more?'

Gopal contemplated. Then he said, 'Someone must have gotten Kumudini's signatures on the two checks when she was alive. Those checks with a credit slip would have been dropped into the pickup box at the entrance.'

'So you wouldn't know,' Padmini said, 'and you had no reason to suspect, since you had no information regarding Kumudini's death.'

'Exactly.'

Padmini shook hands and said, 'Thanks for your lucid explanations.' She gave Usha a hug on her way out.

Padmini saw a Barista Coffee outlet opposite the post office. 'Let us take a coffee break,' she suggested, 'and discuss our findings.'

They crossed the road. The outlet was deserted at eleven in the morning on a working day. Padmini asked, 'What do you make of our position?'

Dalvi sipped on the mango milkshake. He licked his lips, savouring the taste. 'We have evidence to arrest her on suspicion, but not hold her for long.'

The smile on Padmini's face faded. 'After all this, we have barely moved forward.'

Dalvi sipped again. He rolled his tongue around his mouth. 'We have established that she indulged in some shady financial transactions. We have proof that she reset Kumudini's password after her death, which meant that she had access to her mail identity. Nothing more.'

Padmini's eyes glinted with disappointment. 'By the way,' she wondered, 'where is Vijay?'

'Gathering evidence,' he said, with a smile, 'to make our case ironclad.'

'But how?' Padmini sounded perplexed. 'Can he do it? Where is he? What is he doing?'

'Have faith,' Dalvi exhorted, 'in me and Vijay.' He stood, resting his left palm on the right shoulder. He jolted to a stop. 'I have to collect the search warrant from the magistrate.'

He looked uncertainly at her, not knowing whether to take

her with him or drop her at the hotel.

Padmini ended his dilemma. 'Drop me at the hotel.'

Dalvi backed away from her and walked briskly. He kneeled before a Sivalinga in a makeshift temple. He came back with a mixture of vermilion and sandalwood paste and ash on his forehead. He carried some in his hand and applied it to Padmini's forehead and the remaining on the driver's forehead.

Padmini asked, 'What did you pray for?'

Dalvi's voice trembled. 'I prayed for peace of mind.' He looked out of the window while talking, and some of the words were incomprehensible.

Chapter 52

Vijay parked his car on the opposite side of the road and walked over to Vasudha's flat. He rang the doorbell politely. Vasudha opened even before the ring was through. Her eyes met Vijay's and she smiled. 'Come in,' she said warmly.

Vijay bent down to take off his shoes.

'No need.'

Vijay, however, removed his shoes and entered in his socks.

'Water?'

Vijay nodded. He moved closer to the mantelpiece, where medals, trophies and shields were packed tightly together. He looked intently, as though searching for something,

'You are so talented,' Vijay gushed.

She blushed.

'I have come to apologize for Padmini's behaviour,' he said, unable to meet her in the eye. He continued. 'She has no business talking to you like that. I have admonished her, and I promise against a recurrence.'

Vasudha's face glowed. She smiled endearingly at Vijay. 'You are too nice to be a cop,' she said and held his hand.

'I need to go,' Vijay said defensively.

'You are a charmer,' she said and waved.

※

Rathore sounded buoyant on the phone. 'They are in the post office branch where you hold an account.'

Vasudha laughed, almost in a reflex. 'What do they expect to find there?'

Rathore laughed. 'A drowning man clutches at a straw.'

'By the way,' Vasudha said, 'Vijay came and apologized for his gal's behaviour.'

'So, he has already forfeited—'

Godbole's voice suddenly came through. He had snatched the phone from Rathore. 'Do not underestimate the rat,' he cautioned. 'He has come with a purpose. He is not one to down the shutters easily.'

Rathore spoke again. 'Vijay went home from the library.'

Vasudha hung up with a warning. She heaved a huge sigh of relief. She stood near the door, hands on her heart.

'Saved,' she said to herself.

Chapter 53

Vijay headed towards his car. He drove for half an hour and stood at the entrance of Vidyadevi School, after parking his car in the visitors' parking lot. He watched a group of boys, probably in class twelve, playing football. It pleased him that they were athletic. Vijay felt a hint of nostalgia on remembering his days as a school kid.

A lady's voice said, 'Excuse me.'

Vijay was jolted back to the present. He walked to the reception counter and showed his identity card. The receptionist guided him through a long corridor into the principal's office. A silver-haired woman, who could have been Vijay's teacher, sat on a chair with an ergonomic backrest. The receptionist seated Vijay on the visitors' sofa. The principal walked over to Vijay and said cordially, 'What can I do for you?'

'I need your help in an investigation.'

'I understand,' she said, smiling, 'that the reputation of Nagpur police hinges on you.'

Vijay felt tongue-tied. Then he recovered. 'I want to talk about Manish, the son of the late Anirudh Babu.'

'Manish,' she said, her eyes displaying a mixture of pride and sadness, 'is one of our best students. He won the Mathematics Olympiad last year.' She paused and then offered, 'Nirupama, his class teacher, can help you.'

Nirupama was a petite woman with a baby face and a ready smile. 'Manish is brilliant,' she remarked, 'but his focus is not restricted to securing high marks in examinations. He loves tennis and writes great poetry.'

'What kind of poetry?'

'Deep, emotion-filled poetry. He dwells on what has been denied to him—the need for a happy family, where husband, wife and child love each other.' Nirupama seemed so immersed in talking that she didn't notice Vijay's eagerness to ask a follow-up question. 'Let me,' she volunteered, 'read out his latest poem—'

'Please,' Vijay said, 'explain the essence, since I am not into poetry.'

'I hold the symbol of my mother's love for my father,' she recited, with her eyes closed, 'with me all the time, another treasure lies safely with Chitnis aunty.'

Vijay asked in a voice loud enough to attract Nirupama's attention, as Nirupama still had her eyes closed. 'Who is Chitnis aunty?'

'She is a kind of godmother. She nurses him when he is ill, organizes his birthday parties and occasionally even attends parent–teacher meetings.'

'Can you give me her contact details?'

'Sure.'

'Would you like to meet Manish?' she enquired.

'No, I want to see him and observe him from a distance.'

She looked at her watch. 'Now is the time. It is sports period.' She led Vijay to the sports field. 'In most of his poems, his mother is the vamp.'

The school bell sounded like a fire engine. Children came streaming out on to the school ground, almost pushing each other. The field was lush, green and well maintained.

A boy was clicking photographs on his mobile. 'That is Manish,' Nirupama pointed. 'He takes photos, then describes them in his poems.'

Vijay watched the boy click a few more times.

'We have,' she informed, 'allowed him only to use mobile in school as an exception. As a rule, children can't bring mobiles to school.'

Vijay thanked Nirupama and took leave.

'Do you not want to talk to him?'

'No, I have got what I wanted.'

Chapter 54

It was well past Vasudha's normal lunchtime. This day had to be seen off. Amrit Laboratories was floundering due to lack of direction. She had to take charge of that in a big way. A good endgame and she would be leading the life of her dreams.

Her phone rang. She looked expectantly at the caller identification number.

It was Rathore. 'They should be at your residence any time between four and five in the evening.'

'I have laid a red carpet.' She laughed at her own joke. 'What should I serve them?'

'I like your nerve.' He roared with laughter. 'I have never seen anyone like you.'

'You never will.' Her confidence in her invincibility was returning. She could feel it in her nerves, in her blood.

'You will be glad to hear,' Rathore's voice sounded jubilant, 'that the suspension letters for both Vijay and Dalvi have been typed out. They await Patel's signature. He will sign at the stroke of midnight. A constable will deliver them by hand thereafter, and from tomorrow, they will be out of circulation.'

'Great,' she exclaimed. 'You are great, but I want one more favour from you.'

'Shoot.'

'Can't you get that vixen raped?'

'I will do it myself.'

'Wow, I would give anything to watch that live.' Vasudha hung off. Everything was in place. She awaited her foes.

Chapter 55

Vijay retraced his steps into Hotel Heaven. Two new chairs had been placed in the room—ergonomic and trapezium-shaped, with the top wider than the bottom. The legs of the chair formed an inverted semicircle. Vijay sat glumly.

Padmini, who was meditating with her eyes closed, sensed his presence. He was faking pessimism. She was annoyed at his sudden reticence after being large-hearted for so long. She ignored him. He ran his fingers through her hair. She still ignored him. He kneaded her temples. She opened her eyes.

'You think I am hiding things from you.' He raked his fingers through her hair. 'I thought raising expectations that may not be fulfilled is a bad idea. Better to underplay and create a sensational result.' Vijay's eyes shone with sincerity. There was a mixture of sadness and anger in his voice. 'I will reveal everything.'

Padmini's anger had melted. She placed her middle finger on his lips and sealed it. Then she planted a kiss. She now felt guilty. 'Sorry to have suspected you.' Tears seeped out of her eyes.

Vijay lifted a crumpled napkin and wiped her eyes. 'What have you visualized?'

'Victory, nothing else.' She covered her mouth and coughed. 'Once you visualize triumph, the supreme power of the subconscious mind will manifest it.'

Vijay smiled approvingly. 'Anyway, I cannot think of anything, apart from searching for clues in Vasudha's house.'

'Any hunches?'

Vijay took a deep breath. 'We have a search warrant, so why not use it?' He glanced at his watch. 'Why is Dalvi taking so long?'

'He is a gem,' Padmini mused, 'always giving his heart and soul, never complaining, never looking for a reward.'

'That is his way,' Vijay philosophized, 'of running away from reality.'

Padmini moved in her chair, leaning forward. 'What reality?'

'Many years ago, probably a decade and a half back,' Vijay recounted, with his eyes looking upwards, 'Dalvi busted a child prostitution racket. He single-handedly stormed into the hideout and overpowered half a dozen men.'

'How typical,' Padmini responded, with a tinge of affection and admiration.

Vijay's tone turned cynical. 'What followed was also typical.'

'Wait.' Padmini waved her hand. 'The kingpin,' she said with a know-it-all air, 'was a guy with a long reach. He used his clout and went scot-free.'

'Sad, but true.'

'Then?'

Vijay's face turned sad, almost mournful. 'The guy swore revenge, but Dalvi was not one to flinch.' Vijay coughed and continued. 'That son of a bitch had Dalvi's only son kidnapped and murdered. The body,' Vijay recounted, 'was chopped into pieces, put in a sack, and delivered to his home.'

Tears escaped Vijay's eyes.

'How horrible!' Padmini could not stop tears from escaping her eyes.

'What is going on?' A perplexed Dalvi stood at the door with the search warrant, almost feeling guilty for intruding.

'How can God be so cruel?' Padmini sobbed.

Dalvi's eyes shifted to Vijay.

'I told her,' he informed, 'about the Wadala case and its aftermath.'

Dalvi flinched at the utterance. A wave of sadness swept over his face, but he mastered it instantaneously. He sat beside Padmini. 'Do not open old wounds,' he begged.

Padmini took his hands in hers. 'I am sorry,' she said, wiping her tears, 'but I am sure something better is in store for you.'

'I live,' he said, 'in this very hope. At least I can immerse myself in police work. I have people like Vijay Sir to look up to. My wife is the real sufferer.'

Padmini was at a loss for words. She stared blankly. She noticed that Vijay was equally confused.

'Sir,' Dalvi said slowly and deliberately, almost like a wake-up call, 'there is one trivial piece unticked in my checklist.'

'Nothing is ever trivial.' Vijay and Padmini rebutted in unison.

Dalvi opened his briefcase. He picked a folder, carefully removed a paper, and held it for all to see.

Padmini recognized it instantly. She cried out excitedly, 'Dalvi, you nailed it!'

Vijay was amused.

'I remember,' Padmini panted.

Vijay motioned her to calm down.

She took a few long, deep breaths. Presently, she explained, 'I saw a colour printer in Anirudh's home when I talked to her first. I am certain that this must have been printed on that printer.'

Both Vijay and Dalvi looked at each other.

Dalvi explained, 'Sir, this is the printout that was sent to Karun. It indicates that Anirudh raped Karun's sister. It is clear that this was a morphed printout.'

Vijay smiled. 'I always thought that if evidence is available, it would be at Anirudh's home.'

Padmini moved forward in her chair and leaned towards Vijay. 'You have been parroting this logic but what is the basis?'

'This is the only murder,' Vijay asserted, 'where a mid-course correction took place. The other murders were smooth as butter.'

Dalvi did not seem to grasp what Vijay said. Padmini turned to him. 'Initially, the plan was to get Anirudh shot by Karun. The poisoning was a sudden afterthought.'

'Despite all that,' Vijay said meditatively, 'no real evidence has been found.'

'But all that is history,' Padmini said brightly. 'Now on to our final frontiers.'

'Not so fast,' Vijay cautioned. 'A few loose ends have to be tied up.'

Dalvi had a sly smile on his face. He went to the door and announced, 'Let me present Lakshmi and Shantha.'

Two lady constables walked in shyly.

'Dalvi, you fiend,' Vijay remarked, 'You managed to read my mind!'

'Sir'—Dalvi's tone suddenly became serious—'we need lady constables when we are searching a lady's home.'

※

They were off. Dalvi took the wheel and Vijay sat alongside him while the three women sat behind. As they neared their destination, Vijay spoke. 'Padmini, you do the talking. Dalvi will coordinate the search, Lakshmi will search, and Shantha,' he said, looking back and directly meeting her in the eye, 'you must keep a watch on Vasudha.'

Padmini was amused to see the two women saluting Vijay as he uttered their names. Looking at Vijay, she asked, 'What are you up to?'

'I will snoop around,' he said heavily, 'and chat her kid up.'

'Always the softer option.' Padmini chuckled.

'I lead from the rear.'

They had reached the gates of the apartment.

'Let us park the car outside,' Vijay suggested.

The three women and Vijay got out. Dalvi parked the Wagon R close to a tree and joined them. He checked the papers in his pouch. 'The warrant is here.' He beamed. He closed his eyes and prayed.

Chapter 56

Vasudha opened the door with a smile as though welcoming a guest.

Padmini had never conducted a search. She looked at Dalvi.

Dalvi flashed the warrant. 'Madam.' He was professionalism personified. 'We need to search your home.'

Padmini watched her intently. Vasudha looked unflustered. She spread her arms. 'Barge right in.'

They went into a bedroom. 'We will put everything back,' Padmini assured, 'in its proper place.' She smiled. It was a cocky smile. Padmini looked around.

Shantha stood ramrod straight, her eyes transfixed on Vasudha. She was ready to pounce at the first provocation.

Lakshmi carefully removed every item from the cupboard, looked intently at one or two items. She showed an item to Dalvi. He waved her off and asked her to continue.

Padmini was puzzled by the goings-on. A printer could never be hidden in that wardrobe. What on earth was Dalvi doing?

She walked surreptitiously towards him.

The cupboard done, Lakshmi stood on a stool and scanned the loft. 'There is a bag,' she told Dalvi, 'but I cannot reach it.' She got down from the stool.

Dalvi stood on the stool, easily reached the bag and pulled it down. It contained old stockings. The loft over the box bed was the next target. Woollens were packed neatly. The strong smell of naphthalene spread in the room. Lakshmi sat on her haunches and tenaciously looked through and felt every sweater, jacket and shawl. They were neatly replaced.

Padmini looked at her watch. A fruitless hour had passed. She glanced at Vasudha.

She smiled nonchalantly at Padmini. 'It must be difficult,'

she chimed, 'for nice people like you to be rude to others.' The tone was sweet, but Padmini could decipher the biting sarcasm underneath it.

Dalvi led Lakshmi to the other bedroom. They started the search by looking into the flush tank in the toilet. Padmini thought it was a weird place to look for a printer. The printer could never get into that tank.

'They think—'

Padmini turned round. It was Vasudha in her soft voice, 'They fancy that the parts of the colour printer have been separated. They are hoping to find small parts here, there.'

Padmini felt as it was a kick on the solar plexus. Lakshmi nearly dropped dead. Shantha, however, looked inscrutable. Vasudha smiled coyly at her. She glared back. 'All muscle and no brain,' she whispered in Padmini's ear.

Dalvi signalled Lakshmi to get on with the search. He stood before a steel almirah and looked at Vasudha. She handed him the keys. As Dalvi opened the almirah, Vasudha turned to Padmini. 'You are not doing your bit,' she chided.

Padmini replied with a fiery stare.

That only amused Vasudha more. 'You are supposed to chat to me, aren't you?' She laughed a cackle. 'Your boyfriend,' she continued in her sarcastic vein, 'is hunting for clues outside, this constable is keeping a watch on me, the other two are searching, but you are not engaging me in a conversation as planned.'

Padmini wanted to run away from this witch. She looked at Shantha. Barely a ripple came on her stern face. Lakshmi carried on unflustered. Dalvi whistled nonchalantly.

Padmini admonished herself for being so timid. *How professional the others are.*

Lakshmi requested, 'May I open the locker?'

Vasudha nodded and smiled teasingly at Padmini. She held out a piece of paper that read: 'I do not know love, so I have no weakness.'

Angry words came to Padmini's tongue, but she swallowed them.

'If you do not love,' Vasudha commented, 'you do not lose your cool, then you make no mistakes.'

Dalvi found nothing in this room. He kept knocking at the wall, hoping against hope to discover a secret panel. He got down from the stool, disappointed.

'Why do you not,' Vasudha's shrill sarcastic voice rang out, 'check for a false ceiling on the roof?'

Padmini crossed her arms and frowned threateningly at Vasudha.

Vasudha giggled.

Dalvi took no notice of the jibe. 'Let us go,' he said evenly, 'to the third bedroom.'

'Aren't you,' Vasudha asked Padmini, 'wasting your time searching for a non-existent printer when your deadline ends a few hours from now?'

Padmini eked out a wry smile.

Vasudha laughed derisively, pointing a finger towards the main door. 'If you do fail, you will cause more harm to your handsome boyfriend.' The last two words were stressed.

Padmini walked away towards Dalvi. She heard the wicked laughter behind her.

'No luck,' Dalvi whispered.

'Do not lose heart,' Padmini advised, 'we always come up trumps at the eleventh hour.'

'If,' Lakshmi oozed venom in her voice, 'we do not get anything, I will shoot that bitch.'

Padmini felt vindicated. She was not the one only one in

whose heart was raging a tempest. Dalvi spoke in his calm, confident manner. 'Vijay will find a way out. If he doesn't,' he pointed to Padmini, 'she will.'

Lakshmi's face brightened. Padmini was touched by Dalvi's faith, but she did not trust herself to deliver. It was over to Vijay.

The third bedroom, followed by the kitchen was combed. The effort was fruitless.

'There is a garage outside,' Vasudha reminded them, the sly smile playing merrily.

Dalvi and Lakshmi walked out through the back door leading to the garage. Padmini stared at Vasudha more involuntarily than deliberate. The woman winked.

The wink brought pleasant memories in Padmini's mind. She smiled happily. She looked at Vasudha. Shantha was breathing down her neck. Vasudha was unable to decipher the change in Padmini's mood.

Padmini explained, 'Six years ago,' she said with shining eyes, 'in a tennis tournament final, an opponent whom I loathed bitterly was leading one set to love and five love in the second set.'

'I am dying to hear the rest.'

'She was serving for the match. She winked derisively, but that fired me up. I won.'

'Interesting,' she remarked, 'but I am not like that dumb tennis player. I have,' she pointed to her forehead, 'plenty of this.'

Padmini walked towards the garage. Vasudha tapped her shoulder and pointed to the east.

Vijay was waving his arms and demonstrating a cross court volley to Vasudha's eleven-year-old son. His crisp voice could be heard, 'Tennis is a cross-bat game, unlike cricket, which is a straight bat game.'

'Your man,' Vasudha teased, 'is quite charming. He seems

to have thrown in the towel.'

Rage knotted Padmini's chest. Had Vijay's senses taken leave of him?

Vasudha threw a key ring at Dalvi, who deftly caught it. Lakshmi pulled open the rear door of the car. She peered into the car. After five minutes, she gesticulated to Dalvi that it was all clear.

The garage door shut, everyone trooped towards the front door. The living room remained to be searched, but except for the shoe rack, there was no possible place to hide a printer. Padmini noticed that her own shoulders were drooping. The forlorn sensation of defeat and dejection loomed large. Dalvi's gait was quick and one of anticipation as was Lakshmi's. Shantha's watch on Vasudha was relentless.

Padmini felt small. She pulled herself up. 'Victory will be snatched from the jaws of defeat,' she told herself.

As they entered the hall, Vijay was there, smiling and seated on a sofa, with one arm resting on the armrest. He was messaging on his mobile.

He looked at Vasudha. 'Can I have water?'

'Sure, how about some tea and biscuits?' She laughed. 'You guys have been working hard.'

'No, just water,' Vijay insisted.

Padmini heard her mobile click. Someone had sent a WhatsApp message. It could wait, so she didn't look at it.

Dalvi too received a message. He browsed his mobile. He grinned. 'From my wife,' he announced, as Vasudha walked in with a glass of water.

Padmini noticed that Vijay and Dalvi had spoken in codes. Dalvi had conveyed something through his grin and the 'from my wife' comment.

A sense of anticipation began pushing the feeling of

foreboding and gloom. Vijay had a twinkle in his eye. She was beginning to get excited.

Looking at Vasudha, Vijay said, 'There is an African proverb, which says that your best bet against a venomous snake is getting so close to the reptile that it gets cramped to even strike a boxing bout—if your opponent gets *right under your nose*, you are done for.'

'Really?'

Vijay nodded.

'I am sorry,' she said, with an artificially induced tone of regret, 'that your search yielded nothing.'

'Do not be so sure.' Dalvi sounded like a warning.

Vasudha's face maintained its benign equanimity. Not the slightest hint of nerve could be seen.

'I was there with you all the time,' she said blandly.

'This search,' Dalvi grinned, 'was a false search meant to distract you. The real thing,' he emphasized with his eyes, 'was happening outside with Vijay Sir.'

For a fleeting moment, Vasudha's face was contorted with worry. She recovered her poise instantaneously. 'I have an appointment,' she said, looking at her watch, 'in an hour from now, so please excuse me.'

'You better cancel that appointment,' Vijay said politely but firmly, 'because your appointment is fixed with a jailer.'

'Mr Vijay,' she admonished, 'do you dare threaten me?'

Vijay smiled. Padmini knew that it was the smile of a winner, of a champion who had spun a web over his opponent. Dalvi was readying for the kill. She was thrilled at the prospect of victory but disappointed that she did not understand a word of what was going on.

'Now,' Vasudha demanded, 'either you furnish evidence or get lost.'

Shantha moved closer to Vasudha, poised to grab her.

Vijay said, 'Padmini, look at your mobile.'

She obeyed him instantaneously. The message she had received a few minutes ago, which she had ignored, was from Vijay. It contained an image of a woman in a yellow sari and a man with his sleeves rolled up. The woman was injecting him. On closer scrutiny, it became clear that the woman was Vasudha, and Anirudh Babu was the man. Good heavens, the crime had been photographed! The date and time of the photograph was displayed. A tidal wave of thrill swept her mind.

Vijay spoke again. 'Padmini, show her your message.'

Padmini turned the mobile towards Vasudha. 'You really look good,' she said in mock appreciation, 'in that yellow sari.'

It took a minute for Vasudha to grasp the enormity of the photograph. She made a desperate lunge for the mobile, but found herself in the iron grip of the alert Shantha. Lakshmi also held Vasudha from one side.

Vasudha forced a smile, but this one was a lid over deep despair. The élan about her came down a notch.

Vijay was holding a small thermos box in his hand. He walked up and stood near Padmini.

'Hold her tight,' he instructed Lakshmi and Shantha. Dalvi also now moved adjacent to Vasudha.

'In the earlier instance,' Vijay said, 'we had three more copies of the evidence, so even if you had broken Padmini's mobile, it would not have mattered, but not with this evidence.'

A tsunami of suspense sluiced through Padmini. She could barely stand.

Vijay addressed Vasudha. 'In this thermos,' he said, opening the box, 'we found a syringe with remnants of a liquid and a cotton swab with dried blood.'

Padmini craned to see the box. Vasudha wriggled, but the

two women cops tightened their grips. They were way too strong for her.

'The liquid,' Vijay said, slowly and clearly, 'in my opinion is ricin and the blood that of Anirudh.' He halted. 'This is my hunch: the forensic tests will establish the truth or otherwise.'

Vasudha's facial expressions showed a subtle shift. Her poise wavered, but soon, she recovered to fight. 'How do I know that these are not forged?'

Padmini gave Vasudha full marks for her fighting spirit, but in this instance, she was on the ropes.

Vasudha's son, Manish, was standing beside Vijay. Vijay put a supportive hand over the boy's shoulder.

'Manish, tell everyone about this photograph.'

'I always longed,' Manish said, oozing innocence and purity, 'for a happy family where Mom and Dad would love each other and me, but somehow I never got it.'

Padmini felt sad.

'One day,' Manish continued, 'Mom was unbelievable. She ironed his clothes, spoke kindly to him and even gave him his insulin shot.' Manish's eyes welled up with tears. 'It was too good to be true, so I photographed everything. Mother heard the winding sound and asked Dad about it. I winked at Dad and he denied having heard any sound. Mother couldn't turn her neck, so she never saw me. That was the last time I saw Dad.'

Vasudha had turned comatose.

Manish wept. 'I show this photograph to my friends and fool them that I too lived in a happy family.'

Padmini cried along with Manish. Dalvi offered water to both.

'The insulin injection,' Manish wept bitterly, 'is a symbol of a happy family for me and Dad's blood, his memory, so I preserved it. I hid it away from Mom.'

Manish coughed. Dalvi offered him water. Vijay gently patted his back.

'Mom,' Manish narrated, 'threw the syringe and cotton swab into the trash box. I retrieved both and gave them to Chitnis aunty for safekeeping. I replaced another syringe and a cotton swab with my blood.'

Dalvi looked thunderstruck. Padmini's own feelings were the same. Vijay smiled quietly.

'Immediately,' Manish continued with his story, 'after giving Dad his insulin, Mom drove in a black Nano that did not belong to us. Mom had brought the car the previous night. I never saw it again. Dad left afterwards in an auto. That is when I replaced the syringe and cotton swab.'

'Then?' Dalvi asked affectionately.

'Mom came back in half an hour. She smashed the syringe with a hammer, picked the fragments as well as the cotton swab and flushed them.'

Vijay explained that Manish had taken his neighbour, the Chitnis family, into confidence and they took care of this thermos box. He also told them about his visit to Manish's school. Vijay had retrieved it from the Chitnis home while the search was on.

'Why did it happen to me?' Manish, who had held his composure so admirably, broke down. Padmini hugged the boy tightly. She felt a unique kinship with him.

Vijay walked to the door and signalled to someone. A man wearing a magician's costume and headgear entered, almost as if he was making a stage appearance.

Vasudha could not bear to see him. Her world turned topsy-turvy.

Vasudha's mask had fallen off. Dread and anger replaced confidence and poise on her face. Defeat was slowly sinking in. Streams of tears washed down the cheeks on to her neck. She sobbed and muttered something incoherently. The tears kept coming.

Padmini reckoned that years of suppressed emotions were escaping. Someone else's tears had never given Padmini any pleasure, but this time the relish was ghoulish. Totally deflated and demoralized, Vasudha fainted. Lakshmi and Shantha carried her into the bedroom.

'Lakshmi is trained in first aid,' Dalvi informed.

Everyone's attention shifted to the stranger.

'I am Chakravak, a stage magician,' he introduced himself. 'I was called to perform for school children in Mashelkar's bungalow. I was asked by this lady to substitute a bottle in a coat pocket with the one given by her.'

Padmini perched on the edge of the chair. 'You obeyed her unquestioningly!'

'She told me,' he stammered, his eyes defensive, 'it was a practical joke. She offered me ₹10,000 for this minor act and that is a big amount'—he trembled—'for a struggling magician…'

Dalvi hauled a bag over his shoulder. He removed a diary and placed it on the table.

'Can you,' he challenged, 'get past me and put the diary on the computer table in the bedroom?'

Chakravak's nervousness vanished. He said jauntily, 'I will do it right now. It is all distraction and sleight of hand, no magic as such. The presentation varies from artist to artist.'

Chakravak stopped his rambling.

Dalvi gave him a thorough pat down. He repeated the procedure. He nodded approvingly.

Chakravak had a sappy smile. 'Check the computer table in the bedroom.'

Dalvi went and returned like a survivor of a shipwreck.

Chakravak grinned from ear to ear. 'I cannot reveal my trade secret.'

Vijay went to the bedroom and came out clutching the diary. He told Chakravak, 'You can go now, but testify in court when I tell you.'

Chakravak left.

'That is how,' Vijay chuckled, 'the bottle containing black mamba venom was replaced. Last night, I read through the newspapers of the previous month, hunting for interesting local events. I chanced upon this in the local supplement of *The Hitavada*. It struck me that a magician can always dribble past the best of policemen.'

'So,' Padmini concluded, 'that was the "chakra" that Karun had heard Vasudha speak on the phone.'

Vasudha walked, held by Lakshmi and Shantha on either side, looking like a boxer who had just been delivered a knockout punch.

Vijay turned to Vasudha. 'When I visited you this morning, I was astonished to see no photograph of a child, and that too of a son like Manish. He can walk on cat's feet, take a picture unnoticed and has inherited your intelligence.'

Vasudha did not reply.

Dalvi carefully placed the thermos box in his pouch. 'I will get it examined by Dr Gaikwad,' he said.

Vijay nodded.

'Sir,' Dalvi suggested, 'Shantha, Lakshmi and I will take her into judicial custody. You and madam should probably update the commissioner and the chief minister.'

Vijay shook hands with Dalvi, Shantha and Lakshmi. 'I congratulate all of you for fulfilling the task within the deadline.' Shantha smiled for the first time in two hours.

Lakshmi and Shantha marched Vasudha out. Dalvi informed

Vijay that a car had been requisitioned for Vijay. He saluted Vijay and Padmini and left.

Chapter 57

Vijay rang Commissioner Patel to inform him that the job had been done. Patel almost spoke nothing; he just asked for a couple of clarifications and then disconnected.

Vijay drove towards Hotel Heaven. Padmini looked weary, and so was he. They did not exchange any words between them. Vijay turned into a by-lane, a shortcut to the hotel. He squeezed his car to an extreme to allow a minibus to get past him. At this point, his mobile trilled.

It was Patel. 'The chief minister,' Patel said in an excited voice, 'wants to talk to you and Padmini. Come straight to my office.'

'Yes, Sir.'

Padmini looked questioningly at Vijay.

'The commissioner,' he said in an officious voice, 'wants us both in his office to hear the chief minister.'

'I am not coming,' Padmini shot back.

'You have to.'

'Thanks, but no thanks,' she rebelled. 'I do not want to be insulted.'

'When the commissioner or the chief minister calls,' Vijay reasoned, 'we have to obey.'

'You are the cop, not me.'

'Wrong,' Vijay countered. 'You are also a cop until tonight.' He stopped driving and stared at her.

'I do not buy your logic,' she countered, 'but I do not want to make trouble for you.'

Vijay pecked her cheek and drove on. When they reached the commissioner's office, the gatekeeper saluted them, but did not let them through the gate. Vijay waited impatiently as the gatekeeper talked on his walkie-talkie.

'What is going on?' Padmini asked.

Vijay, in reply, threw his hands up.

Patel himself walked out, accompanied by his deputy, Sarkar.

Vijay alighted from his car, followed by Padmini.

Seeing Vijay, Patel rushed with outstretched arms. He hugged Vijay. Vijay suddenly realized that Patel was taller than he was. He looked deceptively short.

'Forgive me,' Patel pleaded.

Vijay knew that it was a heartfelt gesture. He choked with emotion. 'Sir, you are my guru.'

Patel walked to Padmini and held her palm. 'I won't blame you if you do not forgive me,' he said, bowing his head as though in shame. 'I spoke ill of you so often.'

Padmini was touched by his genuine remorse.

Vijay then said, 'Sir, let bygones be bygones.'

Sarkar quipped, 'This is a time for celebration, not regret.'

The tension had vanished. All rushed in to Patel's chamber.

'It is a miracle,' Patel admitted, 'what you have achieved.'

Vijay was about to downplay the event when a youngster peeped, 'The chief minister is on the video.'

Patel led the way.

The chief minister was smiling broadly. 'Congratulations!' he declared. 'You,' he looked at a paper, he held in his hand, 'Padmini, are a role model for young women.' He halted, then announced, 'I will recommend both your names for bravery awards.'

'A request, Sir,' Vijay interjected.

'Speak.'

'The man who contributed most,' Vijay said, slowly and deliberately, 'should be honoured, not us.'

'Whom are you referring to?'

'Inspector Dalvi,' Vijay turned to Patel for support.

Patel said, 'All three deserve it.'

The chief minister nodded, smiling.

Vijay said, 'I thank both of you, Sir and the commissioner, for standing by us.'

Patel seemed relieved by the compliment. 'I can face the legislators with confidence.'

The chief minister signed off.

After some more backslapping, Vijay drove out with Padmini. Vijay informed the hotel manager that the case had been solved, and Padmini would be vacating the next day. Vijay requested for a room for himself. The manager duly obliged.

Chapter 58

As Vijay and Padmini checked out, a minor argument broke out. The manager, under orders from his owner, refused to raise a bill. Vijay insisted, but gave in.

'It is our token contribution,' the owner argued. The manager offered to get Padmini's things packed and delivered to her home.

'Dalvi is calling me repeatedly,' Vijay said, as he left with Padmini in tow.

'What is Dalvi reporting?'

'The forensic report,' Vijay gave a deep sigh, 'has established that the syringe contained ricin, the blood on the cotton swab was Anirudh's, and wonder of wonders—' Vijay halted.

'Cut the suspense,' Padmini said, irritated.

Vijay smiled. 'They even found Vasudha's fingerprints on the syringe.'

Vijay's car indicator blinked, crying for fuel. He knew that the petrol bunk was a couple of minutes away. He drove on.

While the boy at the petrol station fitted the hose into the fuel tank, Padmini asked, 'How did you hit upon the photo on Manish's mobile and the thermos box?'

'I expected to,' Vijay explained and then stopped to pay for the fuel. 'As I said,' Vijay continued, 'the first murder was bound to be her most vulnerable point.'

'Why?'

'She had initially planned to get Anirudh murdered, not murder him herself. The remaining three murders were entirely her doing.'

'Agreed, but you have not answered my question.'

Vijay drew the car into a parking lot. 'Let us have coffee,' he suggested.

They ordered finger chips and coffee. The coffee mugs were placed as was a plate of French fries.

'I reckoned that Manish was the only possible witness to the crime.'

Padmini stopped eating midway and raised her eyebrows in admiration.

Ignoring her, Vijay went on, 'After hearing his poems, I was sure. I noticed that Manish was an avid photographer and he had the knack for snapping people without their being aware of it.'

Padmini dipped a potato stick into tomato sauce and munched.

'I was apprehensive,' Vijay said, holding a fry, 'that he may have deleted any such picture, but as you say, the power of love can work wonders right under your nose.'

'Hats off!'

Vijay sipped the coffee. 'It is lukewarm,' he complained.

'What else do you expect if you keep it for ten minutes?'

Vijay ordered another coffee.

'I must confess that I was mad at you when you were demonstrating a cross court volley. When you asked for water, I was relieved. I knew we were past the post.'

Vijay smiled wistfully.

'That woman'—Padmini clenched her fist—'needled us so much that Lakshmi and I wanted to strangle her!'

Vijay was amused.

'Dalvi was, however, calm and confidently predicted that you would get the breakthrough.'

Vijay sipped coffee and then paid the bill, tipping the waiter generously.

'Back in the car,' Vijay said, with a finger on his chin.

Padmini immediately asked him to use both hands for driving. Huge droplets smacked into the windscreen. She gazed intently on the change of shapes they went through, before dissipating and sliding down the window. She looked through the rain-spattered windscreen.

They passed a temple. Padmini folded her hands devotedly. 'Dalvi's devotion has rubbed off on me.'

Vijay swivelled his head towards her. 'Fat lot of good it has done for him. His life is a wreck. Both man and wife pine for a son who will never return.' Vijay rotated the ignition. The car roared to life. Vijay's foot rammed on the accelerator, his eyes fixed on the road.

She cringed. 'It has given him inner peace, and you do not know how divine law works.'

Vijay drove straight ahead. The sun had come out nice and bright. Vijay was still preparing his reply. A minute later he was ready. 'If a law hasn't worked for a decade'—he laughed scornfully—'it is not worth knowing.'

Stumped, Padmini looked out of the window and watched the roadside flash by. She bowed before another shrine and prayed aloud, 'God, please knock some sense into Vijay's foolish head.'

A naughty smile developed on Vijay's face. 'If He existed, He could and He would.'

They had reached Dalvi's home.

Chapter 59

Dalvi came out with his wife to receive both of them.

His wife was dressed in a traditional, auspicious nine-yard sari and decked with ornaments. A priest was chanting hymns and performing rituals.

Both Dalvi and his wife were glistening with joy. Manish was also there, dressed in traditional dhoti and sporting the sacred thread.

Dalvi announced, 'We have decided to adopt him.'

'How lovely,' Padmini exclaimed. 'You cannot get a better son, and you,' she said, fondling Manish's cheeks, 'have found wonderful parents who will shower you with love.'

Manish hugged her tightly. Then he said, 'Congratulations to both of you.'

'Thanks.'

Padmini turned to Vijay with a triumphant grin. 'Take that, non-believer! Right under your nose, god has registered his presence.'

Vijay turned comatose. Then he folded his hands and bowed low before the Sivalinga, 'Om Namo Sivaya.'

Happy eyes belonging to Dalvi and Padmini watched avidly.

Vijay said, his hands still folded, 'The proof of God lies right under your nose and we do not believe it.'

Acknowledgements

I would like to express my special thanks of gratitude to Mr S.L. Manegaonkar from Reserve Bank of India (RBI) Pune for patiently and efficiently typing and retyping several drafts of the manuscript. I would like to express my very great appreciation to Dr Anjali Goel, the medical consultant of RBI New Delhi, for her painstaking research on snake venom and for helping me iron out the details of the murders, medical facts and hospital scenes.

Many thanks to Koral Dasgupta for her suggestions and to Suhail Mathur of Book Bakers for his contributions in taking the whole thing forward.

To the Rupa team, I am at a loss for words.

Made in the USA
Monee, IL
03 May 2026